THE RUNE STONE

JULIA IBBOTSON

ARCHBURY BOOKS

CONTENTS

PROLOGUE

Winter 1919 Derbyshire

he chilly January wind stung the church warden's rough raw cheeks as he offered back the spade to his companion. The grave digger, Ray, finished blowing his running nose with one final loud rumbling trumpet and shoved his sodden handkerchief back into his pocket. He reached out to grasp the steel handle, and the church warden recoiled as he touched the freezing flesh of the other man's hand.

Old Mr Bone thought of his forty years' service as church warden to the tiny country parish of St Michael's, as had his father before him, but he knew that he had never had such a sad task in all that time. Never before had he been obliged to see to the burial of their own rector. And at such an early age too, and the Reverend Aldridge having no family, no wife, no children to mourn him.

1

Ray leaned on the spade, pausing a moment, and staring at the poor beginnings of the hole before him.

"Reet, thanks. Let's be gittin' on wi' it. Ey, but it be a do, ain' it?" He shook his head and blew cold misty breath on his hands. "Ah'm well mizzen on. An' the ground's nowt but ice 'ere. D'you reckon we shoulda cut further back there?"

"Mmm, maybe. Just try a bit more, Ray. This is exactly where he wanted it, right in front of the south west buttress, as near to the altar as he could get." He looked up at the edifice of greying stone and wondered again how this church had stood here for hundreds of years, surviving wars and famine, plague and pestilence, watching over folks of the village being christened, married, dying, bringing some kind of peace to the ever dwindling congregation.

He could remember when every single one of the villagers came to Sunday communion, and most to Wednesday service too. When people thought of it as a social meeting point, to see and be seen in their Sunday finery. And of course, his grandfather had told him the tales of when the Squire, Sir Derwent-Thornberry, demanded attendance on pain of a reprimand and an uncertain chance of employment on the estate. They didn't argue then, didn't even grumble. It was just part of life. Now there were not so many faithful. The war had seen to that. And the testimony was engraved on the plaque inside the nave. He shrugged.

"Ey up. What the blitherin'? This ain' reet." Ray straightened his back and shook his head at his spade, stuck half out of the soil. "This ain' ice."

Mr Bone frowned and cast his eyes down from the

belfry tower to his companion. He'd often marvelled at how Ray managed his job, slight of frame as he was, looking as though a sigh would fell him. "What?"

"It ain' ice," Ray repeated slowly as though he was trying to convince himself. "It be stone."

"No, it can't be, Ray. There's no stonework here." He looked at the buttress, reassuring himself that the footings could not stretch that far. "And Joseph Crichton's just there." He pointed at the adjacent grave with its huge Victorian headstone carved with winging angels and cherubs with bugles aloft.

But Ray was on his knees, using the sharp blade of his spade to scrape away at the soil in front of him.

"Gad's alive!" He looked up at Mr Bone and the church warden immediately fell awkwardly to his knees beside him.

Revealing itself there in the cold earth was the top of a lying stone with strange markings carved into it. It was nothing like either of them had ever seen before.

"What's that? It doesn't look like proper gravestone writing to me." Mr Bone bent to scrape and scrabble at the soil covering the stone. "Is it an old headstone, perhaps? Fallen over and got covered over and forgotten?"

"Nay." Ray shook his head fervently. "There's never been anythin' in this spot, no grave or anythin', 'as they?"

"Not that I know of. But maybe long, long ago?"

It took them more than two hours to painstakingly scrape the soil from the stone. The winter's afternoon was darkening rapidly but they laboured on together as the stone slowly emerged into the shadowy gloaming light once again. The two men stared, and their eyes drank in the strange cross at the top of the stone enfolded in a carved circle, the peculiar symbols and the raised form of a figure.

"'E looks like a soldier," murmured Ray.

"Yes. A warrior, I think. Look at the raised arm ... looks like he's holding a shield, it looks like, in his left hand and a long sword or an axe or something like in his right." He indicated the worn features. "And his strange tunic and belt. Is that a knife across his middle?" Mr Bone peered more closely. "I don't really know much about history, but this looks like an ancient cross shaft to me. Some kind of memorial to someone like as not. And it looks like it's supposed to be someone important, maybe a king. But what's it doing here in this little country churchyard?"

"What's all this then?" Ray's finger cautiously traced the symbols above and below the figure and shuddered. "Ey up, looks like witches' writin' scratched into the stone."

His companion swivelled round to look at the grave digger's puzzled face, but he knew his own was drained of blood.

"Lord save us," he croaked. "Those are the letters of ancient writing, Ray. From many hundreds of years ago. They are called runes." He pulled his notebook and pen from his jacket and scribbled a copy of the letters as best he could, tearing the page out and stuffing it – as he thought – into his pocket.

CHAPTER 1

VIV

Derbyshire. Present day

Dr Viv DuLac pulled the heavy door of St Michael's closed behind her and jiggled the large old key in the lock, careful not to swing the baby papoose out of equilibrium. This lock wouldn't hold if someone was determined to break in, but at least there was the more substantial one to the main door of the church the other end of the porch. There frankly wasn't anything to steal in the porch itself, unless you wanted the old, dried flowers that had been left there, some dusty grotty paperbacks that nobody else loved, a forgotten umbrella and, strangely, a pair of rotting wellington boots.

A slight breath of air blew a crumpled scrap of paper across her feet as she struggled with the key, and wedged it into the corner of the porch step in front of her, damp-looking, muddy, and yellowing with age. It fluttered weakly. Viv sighed. They'd only had the village litter pick at the weekend! She bent to pick it up gingerly between thumb and forefinger and noticed the scribbles on it, ink spreading the letters together so that they looked for all the world like runes. A whisper of distant voices, ancient tongues, a rustling of robes, made her shiver and hesitate. She frowned. Not again, surely? No, no ... someone's hasty shopping list, no doubt. She dropped it into the bin beside the porch.

She supposed she ought to clean up inside the porch sometime. At least poor old Ivy Nettles hadn't been in since the last time she'd fumigated the place. Poor old woman, but, oh dear, so strange and difficult. And filthy. Nobody, not social services nor the health services, nor anyone in the village could get her to clean herself up – or her rat-infested cottage, much as they'd all tried to help her. She didn't want help, she wouldn't have it, she was adamant about that. She seemed to be happy as she was, although probably 'happy' wasn't the right word.

Maybe those wellingtons were poor Ivy's old boots. Oh well, she'd shut the door on it all. She didn't have time to deal with it now; she wanted to write a paper for the next annual university conference on the early medieval world.

It wasn't so easy with the baby papoose on her chest and as she fiddled to extract the key, a huge rusty old thing that she dropped into her bag at her feet, a little grunting noise issued from the precious bundle in front of her. She bent to kiss the top of the little pink beanie hat and stroked Ellie's back until the snuffling sounds turned to the deep sighs of sleep again.

"Right, come on, little Miss Trouble, let's get back to the rectory and see if daddy's home from his morning run." Viv picked up the tote bag that contained her church flower arranging equipment and the plastic bin bag that held the remains of the wilted blooms she had replaced. She tipped the dead flowers out of the plastic and into the composting bin on top of the ancient scrap of paper and crumpled the bag into her tote along with the key. She didn't hear the sigh of the air around her, because at that moment Ellie gurgled a low soft snore.

Planting another kiss onto the pink hat, Viv whispered, "Now we've done our bit, haven't we, shown willing. Can't have daddy's parishioners complaining now, can we? Can't have those tongues a-wagging yet again, hey? Not after that last time." Not that Rory's 'flock' really knew about her strange visions and slips back in time. That would really make them whisper about her weird abilities.

Viv turned to the right, avoiding the left-hand side of the churchyard and the spreading cherry tree by the wall. Not yet. Not with Ellie. She would introduce her to her sister at some point but for now she only went there on her own, or very occasionally with Rory.

She took a deep breath to still her thoughts and

drank in the pretty country churchyard. Even the ancient headstones looked solid and really quite beautiful in the sunshine and warmth of late summer. Folks had come out to lay new bouquets and wreaths in readiness for the Sunday service and the gardener had mown the grass between the graves only yesterday.

She bent to point out a particularly eye-catching rose arrangement set in a shallow brass vase on one of the ornate Victorian graves by the south west buttress, the one she always thought was completely over the top, with a mass of intertwined angels and cherubs.

"A bit weird, isn't it? But just look at these Old English roses, Ellie, aren't they pretty, such a lovely vibrant pink? Gertrude Jekyll, I think. Hmm, well, maybe. Still blooming in September. I can smell them even from here. Gorgeous. And look, here's the …"

"And here are my two favourite people!"

Viv, startled, swivelled round to see Rory standing over them. She pushed herself up a little awkwardly, one hand on the sleeping child. "Oh God, Rory, I didn't hear you coming."

He kissed the top of Ellie's head and then bent to kiss Viv's cheek then her lips and gave her his gorgeous lop-sided smile that still made her heart quiver.

"No, well, you were engrossed in talking away to someone who won't understand a word you're saying!"

Viv pulled a face. "As you know only too well, my lovely husband, I'm a great believer in talking to her even though she can't engage in a conversation with me!"

Rory pulled his sweaty running top away from his broad chest and flapped it to let a little air in. "I know, darling, but she's asleep."

Viv smiled and shook her head. "It makes no difference." She wrinkled her nose as he began to jog on the spot. "But goodness you're disgusting. Nearly as bad as our poor old Ivy. Go on home and get a shower."

He winked at her. "I thought I'd walk back with you ... if you can put up with another couple of minutes of my sexy masculine odour."

"Mmm, well, I'm not sure about that!" Viv looked over at the old rectory next to the churchyard, its tall medieval chimneys rising up towards the sky, its solid stone walls so dear to her now that they had returned from that eventful year on secondment in Madeira just in time for their precious daughter to be born safely here at home. So different from the last pregnancy and thank God for the vastly different result.

Rory took her hand in his usual firm grip and stroked it with his thumb. She felt good as a wave of contentment swept through her body.

"Something to point out to Ellie," he said with a teasing grin. "Our Saxon cross." He paused at the stone shaft with the broken Celtic head-cross at its peak. A shaft of sunlight swept across it and intensified the pits and mounds of the carving and enhanced the deep green of the moss that swathed it. "You could tell her all about its history and teach her to speak Anglo-Saxon, then she could read Beowulf with you in the original – as a bedtime story!"

"You're teasing me."

"Hmm, not entirely. I'm at least half serious. I mean, I was thinking that we have such a wealth of history right here on our doorstep," he looked over at the rectory gate, "quite literally. And what a great place to bring up our daughter and teach her all kinds of things. You're the medieval expert, history, language ... and I've watched you lecturing your students at the university. You're good."

"Well, thank you, kind sir. Not sure how much *use* it is though!"

"Never mind *use*, it's about knowledge, and understanding what went before and how it could reflect on what comes ahead. Isn't that what we're both about really, in our different professions?"

"Yes, of course. You're right."

Rory frowned at the stone cross. "You know, Arthur Bone, our church warden, was telling me that it was his father, or was it his grandfather? ... who discovered the cross nearly a hundred years ago. They were digging the rector's grave ..."

"Oh God, Rory, that sends shivers down my spine!" She clutched his hand more tightly and he stretched his arm around her, holding her shoulder, and pulling her closer to him. "What if —?"

"It's OK, I've no intention of following suit for a few decades more. I don't think God will strike me down in my thirties. But the story goes that the spade struck the stone and there it was lying buried beneath the earth, right here. They were apparently quite scared seeing the warrior figure and the runes. They thought it was something magic or evil in some way."

Viv shuddered. She peered more closely at the stone cross, a cold chill rising through her body as she looked properly at the warrior figure carved into the ancient, weathered stone beneath the scratched uneven runes. There was something strange about it, something unnerving. No wonder it had struck fear into their hearts.

"Not surprising. I guess in those days there would be a great deal of superstition about it. They must have wondered whose grave it marked and why such a stone cross was raised. It does look a bit spooky."

"Of course, later, after it was raised and set on the plinth, experts investigated it and declared that there was no evidence of a grave beneath. It probably wasn't a headstone but that it was possibly early Anglo-Saxon because of the Celtic cross at the top. Some kind of memorial to someone. But of course, investigators in the early 1920s didn't have the knowledge we have now from archaeological data."

"Hmm, yes, I would agree with early Anglo-Saxon. You know, Rory, it's strange but I've never really taken it in, the cross. It's something we pass by almost every day ... we can even see it from our bedroom window. And I suppose familiarity makes something retreat into the background. I don't know why on earth I didn't really see it properly before."

"It's your research era, so maybe it's something you ... and Ellie," he smiled, "could investigate? And actually, come to think of it, it would be good to have a historic feature we could put in the church leaflets. And maybe use it in some kind of logo? What do you think?"

"Mmm, yes, I'm warming to the idea." She grinned up at Rory, pushing away the tremor she felt inside. A wisp of air drifted around her and she shivered. "OK. I'll look into it. Now let's get you back to the rectory for a shower."

VIV LOOKED DOWN AT ELLIE SNUGGLED AT HER BREAST and smiled at the little mewling noises she was making as she suckled. One tiny hand was pawing at Viv's flesh and she caught it, little fingers immediately wrapping strongly around hers and holding on for dear life. She would never tire of watching her daughter and marvelling at every sound, every movement, every sign of life. Yes, of course, all parents were like that, wondrous at the new person they had created. But to her, to them, Ellie was extra special after the awful late miscarriage of baby Ana a couple of years before.

She let her mind wander to the secondment Rory had taken last year following Ana's death and the strange events they had stumbled upon surrounding Holy Trinity church in Funchal. But it had brought them closer together in the end and it was satisfying that they had found some kind of resolution to the mystery of the fourteenth century Lady Ana d'Arafet and the nun Anja-Filipa two hundred years later.

Viv smiled to herself. "Honestly, Ellie. You wouldn't believe the adventures your mummy and daddy have had since we met. And, goodness, poppet, we even met through a weird time-slip. You remember I told you about Lady Vivianne and Sir Roland in the so-called 'dark ages'?" When Ellie was a bit older, she'd tell her the story about how she first met Rory and his theories about the connections through time and space.

She lifted the baby up to her shoulder and gently rubbed her back until she heard the required burp. "Well, it's a good thing I still have maternity leave from teaching at the university for a while. Attending to all your needs takes up a lot of the day, little madam. Just enough time left for my own research and the odd paper. Right. Let's just wander round the house for a few minutes. Today it's looking at the pictures on the wall and discussing Bruegel's use of landscapes. Then you can go down in your cot for as long as poss while mummy does some clever work. What d'you say?"

The gentle snort behind her made her look around to see Rory leaning against the door jamb, grinning indulgently, his tall muscular frame in his black clerical shirt and white dog collar stirring her heart.

"Actually, I do love it when you do that," he said.

"What?"

"Chatting away to a little baby. Our little baby. I know I tease but it's rather ... cute."

Cute? He never said 'cute'. She laughed.

"So ... I have to go to see Simon and Michael. Are you going to put her down and do some computer work?"

He was so supportive. Of course, his profession meant that he was around more than many husbands. Like her he could do quite a bit from home. And it warmed her heart that he kept checking she was still spending time on herself, her research, and that he took his share of responsibility with Ellie. Obviously, the breast feeding was beyond his capabilities, but he was getting to be amazingly proficient at nappy changing and using the washing machine, better than her in fact, and he clearly loved taking his daughter out for walks in the fresh country air. Viv suspected that he also chatted to the baby as he carried her in the papoose or pushed the pram along the country lanes. She knew that it also gave him the opportunity to do his pastoral duties around the parish at the same time, so many were only too eager to peer into the pram and coo at the baby. The older ladies were delighted that their young rector had started a family at last, after all the problems. And the younger women … well, they perhaps had a slightly different agenda.

"Yes, I am, and when you get back I'm going to take a better look at the figure on the Saxon cross in the churchyard. I want to investigate it on the internet. I've taken a photo on my mobile and I can enlarge it, see if I can get some clues. I have an idea, but I want to check it out on a couple of websites first."

"Well, when I've finished with the church warden and my curate, I'll take Ellie out for a walk before lunch, then you can go over to investigate the real thing again if you want."

VIV RAN HER FINGERS ACROSS THE ROUGH STONE OF THE Saxon cross. It felt so cold and damp. She frowned. There was something about this carving, something that was bothering her. She held up her mobile to the side of the figure carved in relief on its face and compared the two images. She'd spent an hour on her computer while Rory was out, searching websites for the likeness, which she thought she recognised, and finally found a photo of the ancient Repton Stone that was now safely in the city museum. Holding it up against their own Saxon cross it was obvious that the images were so similar that it could hardly be a coincidence.

The other Derbyshire cross, the stone found in a

pit outside the eastern window of the crypt of the Anglo-Saxon church of St Wyaston's at Repton, was said to bear the image of Aethelbold, the eighth century Mercian king. She guessed it made sense that Aethelbold would have his image in other churches around this part of the county as a mark of his power, a sign of obeisance to him, a tribute. And, after all, Repton was not that far away, even in Anglo-Saxon times. Mercia, and particularly Repton as its capital, was such an important centre of the eighth century world in terms of religion and therefore also politics, that its influence would have been felt across the region. Yes, it all made perfect sense when you thought about it.

Viv traced the contours of the warrior king with the shield held aloft in his left hand and what looked like the broad seax in his right, ready to fight. He wore the same short, pleated tunic that Aethelbold wore, and there was something else, something across his torso, in front of his belt. A sword, maybe, or another seax? She reached for her reading glasses in her bag and peered more closely, running her fingers over the figure set in relief on the stone shaft, and over the runes above and below the carving.

What did the symbols mean? What were they saying to her? As she stroked them and quested gently with her fingertips, she imagined that they were calling out to her. As she listened to those ancient voices echoing in her head, she felt as though something was guiding her hand, and she touched something unexpected.

She paused, hesitating, then ran her fingers over the figure again, disbelieving. Tiny flakes of colour splintered off onto her hand. There was something painted beneath the image that looked so like Aethelbold.

It was another figure, hidden beneath.

CHAPTER 2

VIV

Derbyshire. Present day

"*I* can't see anything at all." Rory was squatting beside her, a little hampered by Ellie in the papoose at his chest but reaching out and running his hands over the carving on the Saxon cross shaft. He frowned and looked up at Viv. He'd been chatting to one of the old ladies in her garden on the far side of the village, having been proudly walking Ellie through his parish, when his mobile had rung out with the urgent message from Viv. "What am I supposed to be seeing?"

"It's feeling rather than seeing," said Viv. "Flakes of paint. They chipped off onto my fingers. Here." She bent to point at the side of the figure's torso. "Here, just at the right side of the face and here beside the shield in his left hand."

"Can't see or feel anything at all, Viv." Rory shook his head.

Viv knelt down beside him and ran her fingers along the edge of the raised stone head. The carving depicted a strangely shaped face, almost heart shaped, with a rounded crown and pointed chin, like a child's drawing. But the eyes were deeply gouged into the stone, and as she peered closely she could feel them boring into her. She shuddered. Her fingertips felt a defiance, an anger, a challenge, a plea ... She pulled her hand away.

"Are you OK?" She was aware that Rory was staring at her with a look of concern. She struggled to stand, feeling dizzy, and he pushed himself up from the ground and took her arm to steady her.

She could not seem to tear her eyes away from the stone figure, and as she looked the world juddered around her, the earth beneath her feet trembled and she thought she would faint. She grabbed Rory's arm and held on tight.

Her head was echoing with a roaring sound that was increasing in volume. Was she getting another migraine? She hadn't been plagued with them recently, in fact she thought the last time was last year in Madeira when she was engrossed with Ana d'Arafet back seven centuries. But now, her brain was spinning as though it had come loose from its moorings inside her head. Her GP had once told her that there were a lot of 'rubbish bits', tiny fragments of dead cells Viv supposed, inside our heads that sometimes displaced themselves during the night and jangled when we got up in the mornings. She had made an appointment with him because she was experiencing dizziness when she woke up. She could never quite get to grips with his theory, after all it seemed quite worrying that there was anything loose inside her head, but she knew nothing about medical stuff and maybe he was right.

The roaring in her head began to focus itself into distinguishable sounds. Was that the striking of steel against steel, the howls of fury, the clamour of men? She could hear yells of agony, roars of anger, the anguished neighing of horses. The clash of battle.

"Are you OK?" Rory's voice was insistent, emerging and focusing itself above the echoes of war in her mind.

She shook her head to try to clear her foggy brain, and the Saxon stone cross shaft, the graveyard and Rory pulled themselves back into focus again.

"Oh my God, Rory," she croaked. "Here we go. It's all happening again."

VIV SQUINTED AT THE LAPTOP SCREEN BEFORE HER, THEN she took off her reading glasses and rubbed her tired eyes, smearing eyeliner onto her fingers. She reached for the face wipes in the top drawer of her desk and removed the marks from her hands.

Turning back to the screen she tapped a few keys to find the website she had been looking at that had suddenly disappeared from view. She felt Rory's hand on her shoulder and swivelled round to take the glass of red wine from him.

"Here, this usually seems to be the panacea at times like this. Sudden shock."

She took a gulp and smiled up at him. "Thanks. But it makes me sound like an alcoholic."

Rory grinned. "Not at all. You hardly drink anything. Certainly haven't since well before Ellie was born."

That was true. She had been so careful throughout this pregnancy, everything in moderation and almost no wine or G and Ts. She was so scared of the same thing happening as the previous time, with baby Ana, but smiled as she remembered the way she'd been somehow prompted to name her after some distant predecessor on her mother's side, and how that had linked her to Ana d'Arafet in Madeira.

Ellie was named for Viv's mother Dr Elaine DuLac who was always called Ellie, and also of course for Viv's best friend from university, Eleanor, also nicknamed Ellie. So there seemed to be a very strong precedent for the name, and soon baby Ellie was to be christened Eleanor Netherbridge DuLac: a recognition of Viv's maternal family line and their secret gift that echoed across the centuries and meant that Viv could never change her birth name. Just as her mother had not when she found out the truth – a secret that she only managed to tell Viv after her death.

They'd chosen the Eleanor version of the name rather than Elaine because they liked the traditional sound of it but of course they also were aware that both were versions of the same: Eleanor, Elaine, Vivianne, Ninianne, Nymue and her own name Viv from Vivienne. All linked to the medieval stories of the Lady of the Lake and the women of Viv's own family line. All linked somehow to the Middle English text *Le Morte D'Arthur* written by Malory, and the traditional tales that predated it by centuries.

"What are you thinking about?" Rory's deep voice cut into her musings. "There's a strange look on your face."

"Oh, I was just thinking about our naming of Ellie and all the family names that precede her."

"Ah," he nodded, gently stroking her shoulder. "The Lady of the Lake."

"Yes, and the passing of those other-worldly powers from mother to daughter through the generations of the ancestral line." She frowned and bit her lip. Something she hadn't done for ages. "I was remembering when this happened before. When I time-slipped into 499 AD into Lady Vivianne. Do you remember we talked at the time about the idea that the

Malory tales were based on much, much earlier stories, dating from at least as early as the mid-fifth century? And that some at least could have been based on real people, and maybe corruptions of real events? It all tied up, didn't it?"

"So ...?"

"So, my leap of thought tells me that my slip just now at the Saxon cross reminds me that we named Ellie for that ancestral line through my mother Elaine."

"Except that I thought we named her for Eleanor, your uni friend, because you hardly see her now she's moved down south with her husband and boys?"

"Yes, that's right. But all those names are variations of the same and originate from Vivianne and Nymue, the Lady of the Lake."

Rory squeezed his eyebrows together and shook his head, emanating a sense of confusion and doubt.

"Are you sure you're OK, darling. Only you looked so pale and shocked in the churchyard when you thought it was all happening again."

"It *was* all happening again, Rory. I mean, it *is.*"

"Brought on by what, exactly? Naming our child Eleanor ... Ellie?"

"Oh, I don't know." Viv stretched her back and circled her shoulders. "God, I'm stiff."

"Probably from bending down peering at the Cross."

"Grief, I'm not ninety! Early thirties is hardly the

age for having problems with simple everyday movements like bending down. Especially not when I practice my yoga every day."

"So, what are you searching for?" He peered over her shoulder at the website that flashed onto her screen again.

"I'm learning about Aethelbold the eighth century king of Mercia. Strangely enough, he wasn't really on my radar. But he's rather interesting. And I'm also searching to see if I can find any reference to a possible earlier monument or burial or whatever. I just know there's something there, hidden beneath the carving of the Saxon king. The Celtic type cross at the head of the shaft could indicate an earlier memorial."

"But even if that's the case, that it was originally a monument for an earlier king, why would it be re-purposed for Aethelbold?"

"Well, that's the big question. I really don't know. I don't recall ever hearing of that happening elsewhere."

A little cry issued from the nursery that soon became a demanding, furious yell.

Rory looked at his watch. "I'll go and get her but I think you're going to have to feed her very soon. She's getting raucous. And I need to go out. I've got a meeting in town with The Bish."

"OK," Viv murmured, distracted, her mind engrossed with something she had just found on an obscure academic site.

Rory sighed and squeezed her shoulder. "Did you hear me? Can you hear Ellie bawling?"

"Mmm. Yes, yes. In a minute."

It was a report of an archaeological dig, not one of her parents' digs she thought, but one decades ago on the edge of the current graveyard. In fact it looked as though it was sited where the burial area had been extended many years ago: the new graveyard, the villagers called it, although she was sure that it had been in use since before any of them were born. She frowned and sucked in her breath. So that wasn't so far away from where her parents had led the dig at the place that used to be Cooney's Mere ... well, still was of course, although she would forever think of it as where Lady Vivianne's settlement was in 499 AD. She shivered. Because she had seen it; she had been there and known that world.

Viv felt a chill rise up her spine. What if their Saxon cross was in fact so early it was Celtic-Saxon, and what if it had some connection to the Cooney's Mere settlement? To Lady Vivianne?

As many times before, Viv wished that her parents were still around to talk to, to ask about this other dig, literally behind the garden of the rectory. But they were lost in the plane crash when she was a child and she could no longer ask them anything. How she wished that time could be rewound, that it wasn't linear, but that you could turn back the clock and their history would be changed. But of course then everything would be changed.

She felt that familiar pain deep in her soul, the echo of loss reverberating across the centuries.

CHAPTER 3

LADY VIVIANNE

Cūning's Mere 520 AD

"Oh, my Lord in heaven! How did I manage to breed such a disobedient daughter?"

Lady Vivianne jumped as Nymue slammed the wooden door behind her leaving a drift of anger and frustration behind her across the mead hall. Her shoulders slumped and she clutched the folds of her over-gown in a tight grip in vexation. It was at times like this that she missed her long-ago parents so keenly. Surely they would know what to do with such a wilful child. She felt that familiar pain deep in her soul, the echo of loss.

She swung around as she heard the snort behind her. Sir Roland, her beloved husband, grinned at her.

"She becomes more like her mother every day." He

held out his arms to her. "My love, do you not recognise her strong will?"

She slipped into the warmth of his embrace, but she gently beat her fists against his broad muscular chest. "She is but a child still."

"No, my sweet. She is into her second decade already and has a mind of her own, as you did then and so do now. But calm *your* mind, my beautiful wife. Nymue will too. Let her scream and shout at the hens or the sheep or the pigs until she tires. Then presently we can talk to her about Gareth Swineson."

"But he is the son of the swineherd, Roland! She cannot be consorting with him. Not as the daughter of the chieftain of the settlement, the first ætheling!"

She felt Roland stroke her back gently to calm her. He bent to her and spoke softly in her ear. "My love, it will do no good to cast that at her. She will only want him all the more. She is at that age of questing for freedom, from her parents, from the restrictions of her station in life, from the conventions of the settlement, and so we must act with great care. We cannot afford to drive her away from us. She is our future, the next in line."

Vivianne had fought hard with the thegns of the Witan to secure Nymue's succession as ætheling though she was a woman. Slowly Vivianne steadied her breathing, as she felt his kiss on the crown of her head. He made sense. He always did. He always had.

He had rescued her from the foul clutches of Sir

Pelleas so many years before, when the Saxon usurper had wheedled his way into her late parents' affections and taken hold of the chieftaincy after their untimely death. Roland had been calm and strong and determined then, and now, as her marriage partner, he was still. Strong and supportive through that awful time of losing those dear babies before they could even breathe the world's air. Before her precious ones began to arrive safe and healthy at last.

"You are always so wise," she whispered into his chest. "My strength and stay."

She remained there for a few moments more, as long as she could before the thegns would start to arrive for the Witan. It was the main council of the year and there was much business to settle. Then she reluctantly pulled away from him.

"I will speak with her later when she is calm." She was aware that he drew in his breath sharply and was inclining his head. "We will speak with her together. I value your authority."

"I am glad of that," he laughed. "I have to admit that I do not see that very often!"

She had the grace to smile at his teasing. "Well, all appears to be ready." Her eyes swept the mead hall, laid out for the Witan, the table on the dais at the far end of the hall, the ceremonial battle banner draped over it, the white dragon of her own family intertwined with the red dragon of Roland's, on view for all to see, their fiery breath and sharp claws stretched out towards the body of the hall where all the thegns would stand, the three ealdormen in front of them and the ceorls behind them at the back. They had agreed that the ceorls, the freed men, would attend, as they had been permitted to do in her parents' time, a practice that Sir Pelleas had forbidden along with his ban on women attending, inheriting, or standing in any high office. Only the geburs were absent, busy at their work in the fields, already beginning to gather the early harvest before the Harvest Moon, or in their workshops or attending to their thegns' halls - and of course the watchmen at the boundaries, standing guard and repairing the fortifications.

Lady Vivianne looked up at the wall behind the great long table where they had hung the simple tapestries again, the pictures depicting their battles with the marauding Picts from the north and now more frequently their skirmishes with the Saxons and Angeln from the east and south. She sighed. They needed to add memorials to the tapestries more often now than she would have liked. She feared for Roland.

Many a morning she sat with her ladies in her chamber off the mead hall, helping with the spinning of the wool, which not so long before was warming the sheep's backs in the fields beyond the village. It was not so long ago that she sat with her bone needle and strands of bright coloured wool, making a celebration of the line of shield bearers and spear carriers. She had silently wept as she worked the banner with its red dragon and the figure of Roland, as always leading from the front.

"My lady, my lady!" An urgent cry pierced Vivianne's thoughts, and she turned quickly to see Matilda, her erstwhile under-maid of the chamber and now chief maid of the nursery for the past ... what? ... thirteen years? Since Nymue's safe birth. And, goodness, it seemed like yesterday, and not twenty-one years, that little Matilda, Tilda as she called her affectionately, had been appointed her maid of the chamber after Guin's betrayal and disappearance. Not so little or hesitant now, with her wild fair hair kept under control in womanly braids and her modest cap restraining it all.

Red-faced and clearly sweating with exertion, Tilda was lumbering across the hall towards her, a child hanging on to each hand, heading after young Tristram, named for Vivianne's lost father, who hurtled through the hall, kicking up the dust and floor-herbs from the precious new wooden floor as he went, and finally slipping behind his startled father to hide.

"Tristram!" Roland swung around to catch hold of his giggling son. He was barely suppressing the smile on his face and Vivianne could see the effort her husband was having to keep his expression stern and disapproving. "What *are* you doing?"

"My lord, he says he is attending the Witan," puffed Tilda as she stopped before Roland and gasped for breath, her comforting plump body quivering. "He says he is old enough *and* the male ætheling."

Vivianne smiled grimly. It was barely ten years since she had birthed him, a much easier birth than Nymue's had been. He had slipped out like a wriggly little worm, long and thin and ruddy of face, but his cries were strong and forceful, and she knew that he would be a great warrior like his father. Nymue's arrival had been long and painful, all two agonising sunrises of it, but her appearance, finally, healthy and glowing, so very welcome after the grief of losing the first baby she carried. Little Ana. They had given her a naming ceremony and buried her tiny form at the sacred site at the edge of the settlement, not far from Cūning's Mere. Vivianne was aware that her eyes had grown moist with the memory.

Roland nodded gravely. "Hmm. Well, if he can sit still and not move a finger length during all the proceedings, if he can listen with great seriousness to all that is said in council, if he can stay silent, if he can do without his friends and his gaming counters for a whole day ... then he may sit beside me at the table." Tristram slipped round to face his father, eyes wide with astonishment. "But if there is one thing ... one, mind ... that he fails in, he will be removed from the hall in disgrace in front of all the thegns."

Vivianne could not help but smile at Tristram's expression as he mulled over each of his father's requirements.

"Your father is giving you the chance to show that you are a man now," she said.

Tristram frowned and inclined his head. "But the thegns can move around the hall and stamp their feet and beat their shields in agreement and they can shout and ... even curse!"

Vivianne could hear Roland stifle a guffaw. But she kept a stern face to Tristram.

"Oh, but let me come and ... and I will be a warrior like my father and my grandfathers and all my forebears!"

"Enough now, Tristram." Vivianne turned away, her heart quivering. Her son was growing up and of course he would soon follow his father into battle. It was expected. But she hated the thought, as she hated every time Roland donned his battle gear and raised the battle banner, that awful gleam of war in his eyes. At least Nymue and the little ones would be safe at home.

She crossed herself and whispered a prayer. Thus far the women of the settlement and of the others in the region were not following the ancient example of Boadicea leading the Iceni into battle. Though she had heard tell of women of some southern tribes even now holding their banners and fighting the Saxons alongside their menfolk. Nymue would not be riding to war, thank God. Much as she had promoted the place and role of women in the settlement of Cūning's Mere, there was a line Vivianne would not cross, nor would her daughters if she had anything to say about it. She could do little to stop the fighting spirit of the men, even of her own husband, and she honoured him for his skill as a warrior. After all, their history was in many ways built upon it. The tapestries showed it. She wished it were not so. She wished that there were not the threats to the settlement that seared her soul. She wished that they could be solved by other means than fighting to the death. And for her, the women must be the peace-weavers.

"Thank you, Tilda," she said, smoothing her over-mantle, adjusting her inlaid brooch as she straightened her back and stood taller. "You may leave Tristram to his father's care for now. But first he must apologise to you for his behaviour which is most certainly *not* that of a warrior, and then you may take Launce and little Nini back to the nursery chamber for milk and honeyed cakes."

"Will I get to drink some mead?" asked Tristram eagerly.

Lady Vivianne's eyes cast around the Witan council. The mead hall, great as it was, was full and the noise of so many people gathered together echoed from the wooden walls, bouncing off the golden Christian icons that jostled for space with the pagan symbols. She had insisted many years ago that her mother's Celtic-Brython pagan heritage as well as her father's Romano-Brython forebears were marked here, even though she was herself brought up as a devout Christian. As a little girl, she had watched her mother's pagan rituals and been fascinated by them, although a little fearful if truth were known, especially the rituals at Cūning's Mere, that dark mysterious stretch of water at the edge of the settlement.

Well, her mother's beliefs and practices were understandable, she knew that now, as a descendent from the legendary Lady of the Lake. Mother to daughter. Yet thus far, Vivianne was protected from the most frightening aspects of her ancestors' paganism, through her father's influence, she believed. She had only experienced, once, a strange connection to something, someone, far into the misty future. Once only, and yet that had freed her from the grip of Sir Pelleas, freed her community, and with his drowning in the mere had allowed the settlement to restore the civilised ways of her parents. Not only were the rich tapestries and beautiful Christian icons back again in the hall but the best scōps and glæmen too, with their songs and tales and legends, not the dreadful bawdy ones of Pelleas's rule.

She and Roland sat at the centre of the long table on the dais. Young Tristram sat on the other side of Roland who was engaged in steadying his son with his hand on his shoulder. The head of the council, on

Vivianne's right, rose and lifted the Witan sword aloft. The assembly fell silent.

"Today, we welcome Sir Roland's son, Young Tristram, to the Witan dais. He will be our honoured observer only at this current time, until he grows into his warrior status. Sir, your presence amongst us is saluted." He turned to Tristram and bowed his head.

Vivianne noticed Roland nudging his son to acknowledge the courtesy with a bowed head in return. She was pleased that Tristram seemed to be behaving as he should and following his father's actions. Her husband had instructed him well. She smiled. Apart from the odd naughtiness, as expected from a child of his age, he was a good boy. He caught her eye and blushed as she surreptitiously winked at him.

"And now, to our business." The head of the council raised the Witan sword higher and Vivianne's ears rang with the sound of the thegns' roars of approval as they raised their spears aloft or clashed swords onto shields. Then they fell silent again as the business proceeded.

Lady Vivianne listened intently although she and Roland had already heard it all in their prior meeting with the head of council. She wanted to gauge the feelings of the ceorls as well as the thegns. The women of the village were more difficult to assess; even though their voices were now to be heard in the Witan, as they had in her parent's time, perhaps they had grown used to Sir Pelleas's rule, and even after all these years it was only a handful of ladies who spoke out. Some were still hesitant even to vote, glancing to their husbands first before raising their daggers. Vivianne mused that maybe it was because they did not fight as warriors that they hesitated. But to her, the Witan council was more important than the fighting.

A cupbearer topped up her mead cup and offered a platter of honeyed cakes. She shook her head but glanced down the table to see Young Tristram taking a handful as well as more mead, and she noted that she must speak with him later. Many of the thegns in the hall were taking a moment to receive a cup from their own bearers, and she hoped that they were keeping a clear head.

The business moved on from the building of a new winter shelter for the cattle in the far field, before the snows came, to the issue of the number of battle thegns needed on the north boundary in the light of the constant threat from the Brigantes from the north east. The discussion had just begun when there was a disturbance at the far doors behind the ceorls and Lady Vivianne strained her neck to try to see what was happening. The crowd of thegns in front of her parted to let the newcomer through, and anxious faces watched his progress as he approached the dais. He stopped and bowed. It was one of the guards, the watchmen from the southern boundary fortifications, his shield and spear glinting in the sunshine that filtered into the hall from the great main doors.

"Please, Lady Vivianne, Sir Roland, I apologise for the interruption to the council, but I come with important and urgent news. A messenger from Deorabye in the south has ridden here with news of the sighting of a band of warriors from the Angeln tribe. The carrier was unclear, but he believes they are coming north from the south east land, where more landings were sighted three months since. They are the men of Icel, son of Éomēr of the Angeln, from across the water."

Immediately there was a wave of noise from the body of the hall, thegns and ceorls alike turning to their neighbours and raising their spears to the dais.

Sir Roland stood straight-backed and tall, and reached for the Witan sword. He held it high and the company quieted.

"This is indeed unwelcome news and we must be ready for their attack." Roland's voice was strong and steady. "Both the Saxons and the Angeln are dangerous foes. It was barely last Beltane when we had to ride out last to protect our boundaries thrice from warriors from these same tribes and they were bitter battles." Lady Vivianne shuddered as she remembered the horrors as she had prayed for her husband and his men, and the losses they had suffered, despite their ultimate victory. She looked across at Roland, listening keenly to his words. "If this present danger is indeed from Icel's men then we will have a fierce war on our hands. So I say we divert a large band of our battle thegns from the intermittent Brigantes' threat in the north to this new and more immediate issue from the south. The Pecsaeton peoples up in the Peaks are able, for the moment, to act as a first defence against the Brythonic clan and reduce the threat considerably ..."

"But the Deorabye warriors can be said to provide the same defence to the south!" shouted a new voice from the midst of the crowded hall. "Your plan is absurd! The Brigantes are our greatest threat. I say, rethink your strategy!"

Disconcerted, Lady Vivianne looked over sharply to identify the rude and untoward interruption. Thegns never interrupted the high table. It was against convention. They may murmur and talk amongst themselves at times, if roused, but they never ever shouted out an interruption. And to Sir Roland! Such disrespect. The assembly fell into shocked silence.

Her husband lowered the Witan sword a little to scan the hall. Then Vivianne saw that he had picked out the culprit and his expression hardened; eyes narrowed. She followed his gaze and then she herself recognised the heckler. She would know that handsome but arrogant, scornful face anywhere. It was Sir Aldwyn. Of course. Yes, it would be, would it not? Her heart juddered. The self-proclaimed, yet illegitimate, son of the late Sir Pelleas and Edyth, a gebur's daughter of the settlement, a difficult woman who had always been a source of concern and distress to Vivianne. She was glad that Nymue was not here.

She watched Sir Roland's face and she knew that he struggled with the best way of dealing with Aldwyn. He chose to speak calmly and manifest the courtesy and respect his assailant had not shown.

"Sir Aldwyn, I hear your argument and I acknowledge it. However, it is a pity that you did not wait to hear the rest of my thoughts on this matter. I believe that we must weigh up the level of threat and use our resources wisely. The threat from the Brigantes is intermittent and can be contained reasonably for a while by the Pecsaetons. We can leave a band of battle thegns guarding our northern fortifications. They were strengthened last winter and are at the moment more secure than our southern boundaries that received a battering last Beltane time and that we are still in the process of repairing. That part of our fortifications is the weakest. Thus, that is where we must concentrate our forces and our defences. What say you?"

"No! I say not so," shouted Aldwyn again, red-faced and furious, before the thegns could raise their spears in agreement with Roland. "The Angeln will not be any threat to us for some time and the Deorabye tribe is great and presents a substantial shield to our community. Who wants to send our warriors to wait idly for winter and for Icel's men to arrive when they can be clearing the threat from the north before the snows? Remember that we also have the raids from the

Picts to contend with up there. To the north, I say! How many are with me?" He looked around him, eyes raised, confident in his words.

The thegns erupted into loud opinions, too many of whom appeared to Vivianne to be siding with Aldwyn. Vivianne knew that Roland with all his experience of battle and battle-plans had a better idea of levels of threat than Aldwyn, but she also knew that Aldwyn had a voluble following.

Roland raised the Witan sword again and spoke firmly. "I hear what you say, Aldwyn, and commend your ideas. But there will be no waiting idly. The Angeln can approach fast and will do so to strike before the winter closes in. We already know that from bitter experience last year. Some in the south, west and the east, are reporting that the Angeln and parts of the Saxon armies are also now attempting to navigate the rivers of Dove and Derwent towards the middle lands. On the other hand, the Picts are currently quiet. We have not seen raids from them for some time. I say again, the greatest threat at this time is from the Angeln and Saxons and I say again that we must attend to the south."

"North! North!" shouted Aldwyn, banging his shield with his spear. The cry was taken up by a crowd of thegns around him, and suddenly Vivianne knew in her heart that this was a pre-arranged battle cry and that they had already planned this rebellion, somehow.

Was her husband right? Or was Aldwyn? She must grasp the correct path. She clutched her skirts beneath the table, her knuckles white. She knew who to trust, but according to the ancient Witan rules there had to be council agreement on battle strategy. Roland had to take the council of ealdormen, thegns and ceorls with him.

Lady Vivianne rose slowly, and gripping the edge of the table, hoping that her trembling hands did not show, straightened her back and stretched to her full commanding height. She reached for the Witan sword from Sir Roland. He passed it to her as they held each other's gaze. Vivianne knew that the tension in her eyes was reflected in his. But she took the sword and held it aloft.

"I am your cūning, your queen, the hereditary Chieftain of the settlement. You must listen to my words today, for, as always and by the rules of the Witan, they are final."

When she had finished speaking she ran her eyes across the hall from the foremost thegns to the ceorls at the back. All bowed their heads to her supreme authority. All but one. Aldwyn. He stood upright and did not flinch even when her eyes met his. He glared at her; his eyes narrowed with open anger. She felt the threat and the curse fly as swift as an arrow from a bowman, across the space between them.

CHAPTER 4

LADY VIVIANNE

Cūning's Mere 520 AD

"Did you *see* the way he showed his disrespect to me?" Lady Vivianne was pacing their private chamber, angrily swishing the skirts of her heavy over-gown and raising a thick perfume of purple thyme as she trod the strewn herbs on the floor.

Sir Roland looked up from inspecting his gleaming battle helm and raised both his hands. "Forget him and his childish words. Aldwyn is nothing to us and he ..."

"Childish? He is older than Nymue by several Beltanes. You know that Pelleas was taking Edyth to his bed before my maid Guin. And probably during his association with her too, knowing what he was like. And he has been gone, and dead, these many years, quite some time before we made Nymue."

"Yes, I know that about Edyth – or so rumour has it. Although I try not to listen to such gossip. And you should avoid it too, my love. It only makes you cross. No, I simply mean that Aldwyn is immature for his age and status as a warrior thegn. And, my love, in truth, it is not good for you to be overly concerned for such squabbling. Not in your condition."

He smiled at her and she paused her pacing and stroked her rounded belly. She was glad that he had not added "and at your age", for she was well aware that she was considered quite old for child-bearing, and did not wish to be reminded of the dangers of it. She shook her head. "It is always while I am with child that these battles happen."

"Not last time." Roland inclined his head and grinned. "Unless you withheld news from me?"

"Of course not." She sat on the stool beside the fire pit and sighed. "But what do we do now about the dissent?"

"Well, it is not widespread, and the council agreed my battle strategy at the end. Aldwyn and his clan were kept silent."

"But we have never had such open rebellion before. Oh, I do know that there are always murmurings. It is by men's natures that there is always some amount of personal discontent. There will always be someone who does not like the decision of the council. But this feels different. I fear it."

She warmed her hands at the crackling wood on

the fire, although it was not a cold evening and watched the wood smoke rise up to the thatch, whirling its way through the gap in the roof to drift away on the early autumn breeze. A log of wood slipped, and she followed the sparks as they too rose like fiery stars in the sky.

In her hands she held the gold brooch that she had unclipped from her over-mantle as she discarded it onto their bed. Her fingers stroked the image of the white dragon upon it, her family's ancient emblem. She thought of her parents, their death in the fire that Pelleas had set at the sacred hall when she was but a young child, and the way she had always yearned to establish once again the peace and prosperity of their rule. But these past few years had been increasingly wrought with skirmishes and raids from other tribes, both near and far. And every time Roland and his men rode out to battle her heart broke a little more and her fears rose again.

"Are you not concerned at all, about Aldwyn and his men, about the coming battle, for war it will certainly be?" Even to herself, her voice sounded irritable, but she knew that she was not irritated with Roland – he was only doing what he had to do.

"Of course I am concerned. But it is my role to be your battle-leader, to attend to any threats our settlement may have. However sudden and unexpected. I have to keep this settlement safe. I am the peace-keeper, just as you, my love, are the peace-weaver. And I am not afraid, if that is what you are asking." Roland strode over to Vivianne and bent to wrap his arms around her, kissing the top of her head into her thick bronze-red curls that she had loosed from her braids. He ran his fingers through her hair and pulled her close to his body. She rested the brooch in her lap and reached up to him.

"My steadfast protector," she murmured. "And of the whole settlement. Although we must surely call our community a kingdom now, so large it has grown, with folk fleeing here from war torn villages to the north and south, and all the ceorls and geburs from nearby tribes riven by battle."

"Indeed it is a kingdom." Roland nodded, thoughtfully.

"And you its king ..."

"No, I am no king. Only the most senior thegn, the battle leader married to the queen."

Vivianne shrugged. He would never take that role. He saw himself as a warrior not a ceremonial king. Yet she had argued with him so many times that it was possible to be a warrior king.

"And when do you ride out?"

"The sunrise after next," he said, and she heard the glimmer of excitement in his voice. She hated that: he called himself a peace-keeper, yet he seemed to revel in the fight.

She bit her lip, but she nodded and spoke as strongly as she could. "Then I will get the house gebur to polish your battle helm. And may God will it that you all return safely."

Roland stepped back from her and looked straight into her eyes. "My helm is already gleaming." He saw the expression in her eyes, and he softened and smiled gently. "But of course it can never be too bright." He sighed; his full mouth turned downwards in a grimace. "And you know full well that whatever the outcome, we will not all return safely."

THE WHOLE SETTLEMENT RANG WITH THE SOUNDS OF urgent activity and excitement, the sharpening of spear and seax, the polishing of shield and the repairing of battle dress. Horses whinnied and blew cold breath as they were made ready.

Lady Vivianne sat with her dear Tilda and her new maid of the chamber, Afera, who was not so dear, repairing the banners and re-sewing tears. Later she and Tilda would walk around the settlement with encouraging words, calming the womenfolk and those who needed to remain because their work was to keep the village going – the bakers and the field workers, the crop-growers and the pig-men and cattle-carers, the spinners and the weavers. And they would speak words of pride and urging to the warriors preparing for battle, although their hearts were sorrowful.

"Why does Gareth not ride to battle?" Nymue

asked as she winced and sucked her finger, drawing away the blood from the prick of her bone needle. She peered at the fabric of the banner edge she was working, to ensure there were no fresh red drops on the embroidery, mottled as it was with the dried red-brown of battle blood that had proved too difficult to remove, even with their precious salt.

"Because Gareth Swineson is needed here to maintain the settlement. He is the son of the swineherd, after all. And we cannot let the pigs go wild while the other men are away at war." Vivianne rested her threads for a moment. Her hand was aching. "We all still need to eat, battle or no battle, and the warriors will have great appetites when they return to us again."

"I will wager that Gareth will have the greatest appetite," Tilda winked as she darned the backing fabric. "Even though he does not go to war, he will be running over the fields. Many furlongs now that the settlement has expanded so much. And he is a big strong muscular youth." She guffawed and looked at Nymue. "Handsome, eh, Lady Nymue?"

"Tilda!" Vivianne warned with a frown.

Tilda looked down at the work on her lap, but a grin hovered on her lips.

"Well, I am glad he is not going away." There was a defiance souring Nymue's words, Vivianne thought with a sigh.

"And there will be no meetings." Vivianne turned to her daughter. "We have already spoken of this matter. And my word, and your father's, are final." She saw her daughter's down-turned mouth and steely eyes. "The battle and your father's absence changes nothing, young lady."

"He kissed me." Nymue's voice was belligerent. "So now we must be hand-fasted."

Vivianne looked up in shock and she noticed that Afera did so too. "Kissed you?" She knew that her face was red and her eyes hard with disgust and fear as she stared at Nymue, chin dropping at her impudence and discourtesy.

Nymue knew what this meant and her fingers shook a little so that she could barely thread the needle. Her expression registered a series of emotions: determination, then hesitation, then fear at her own rudeness. "Oh, well, mother, I mean that he raised my hand to his lips."

Tilda giggled and her eyes looked up to the roof. "Pft!"

Afera sighed and shook her head.

But Vivianne did not notice as she exhaled deeply.

"That is, at least, unexpectedly gentlemanly. I do not object too much to that." She glanced at Nymue's flushed face. "But just once. Do not encourage it again. And do not talk more of hand-fasting with Gareth Swineson." She glared at her daughter and rose, slipping her section of the banner onto Nymue's lap. "Tilda, come. Nymue may complete the repairing task on her own. I cannot hear her nonsense any more.

And Afera, be pleased to see that her stitches are straight."

Lady Vivianne swept from the chamber, Tilda following behind. Outside, she halted and turned to her maid. "I do not know what to do with her, Tilda. She is so headstrong. For whatever reason, she has determined to hold to this son of a swineherd and she will not let go. Sir Roland and I have had no chance to speak with her together. His mind is occupied with readying for battle now, as it should be, and so it falls to me alone to deter her. And to be honest with you ... I know not how."

Tilda drew in her breath. "My lady, I have known the lady Nymue since birth, of course, and I believe that she will have many loves before she finally settles." She looked up at Vivianne. "And I know you fear the worst might happen, but truly she is at heart a sensible girl. She is perfectly aware of the consequences of any liaison. She thinks to challenge, as all the young folk do. Were you not the same at that age?"

Vivianne nodded. "I hope and trust that you are right, Tilda. But, no, I don't know whether I was the same at her age. My parents were killed, and I was spending my time fighting off Sir Pelleas, as well you know."

Tilda glanced sideways at her lady. "But were you not like this at first with Sir Roland?"

Vivianne gathered up the folds of her skirts into

her hands and set her mouth in a hard line. "But Sir Roland is of noble birth." She swept onwards along the dusty track through the village.

But she did not see Aldwyn supervising his gebur who was engaged in rubbing down his battle horse. But Aldwyn watched her and he looked after her as she went, his eyebrows raised and his mouth straightened in a thoughtful sneer, full of hatred and opportunity.

She also did not notice Nymue following her out of the chamber and hesitating beyond the outer door. She failed to see the way Aldwyn raised his eyes to her daughter and smiled, an expression designed to demonstrate his admiration as his look swept her body from her head rail to the toe of her fine leather shoes. And she did not see the way Nymue blushed and averted her eyes, only to peep up at him in a manner that could only be interpreted by a young warrior as flirtatious and inviting.

CHAPTER 5

VIV

Derbyshire. Present day

"I'm sorry, poppet, mummy got a bit carried away there." Viv jiggled Ellie against her shoulder with one hand as she slid the paper from the printer tray with the other and ledged it on top of her keyboard. She sat down on her desk chair and slid Ellie down onto her lap, unbuttoning the jersey top that was straining against her full breasts. Goodness, how dexterous she was becoming at this business of caring for a baby.

She studied the print-out while the baby abruptly ceased her accusatory yells, her tiny mouth occupying itself now with latching on to the nipple instead.

"You see, Ellie, this is a plan of the dig site on the edge of our churchyard." Viv turned the paper to peer at it from different angles. "Yes, the location is almost certainly overlapping the current newer part of the graveyard. Hmm, and it's dated 2003. Why didn't I know about this before?" Ellie glanced up at her mother, eyes wide open, then frowned, never pausing from her suckling.

The plan was labelled 'Cooney's Mere' and it clearly post-dated Viv's parents' dig by more than ten years. Viv narrowed her eyes. Was it a follow up to *their* dig nearby? If so, why had she never heard of it? Well, it would have been, what, seven years after their death and she was in her teens, being a pain to her beloved grandparents no doubt. Viv reached for her computer keyboard on her desk beside her and carefully with one hand clicked to retrieve the further information she had found on the findings of the 2003 dig.

"Well, Ellie, we don't have much here. It looks at first glance to have been rather unproductive. What a shame. Oh, wait a minute! Look here. There's some suggestion of a possible small burial with east-west alignment. That suggests a Christian burial. But, oh, they found evidence of some grave goods, not usual in a Christian burial, probably early Anglo-Saxon, pieces of glass and pottery, a brooch and, oh, my goodness, a gold bracteate. Wow!"

Viv hitched Ellie to the other side, her grin widening with mounting excitement. "Do you know what that means, Ellie? A bracteate was a disc pendant worn round the neck maybe on a string of leather, and it was often from Scandinavia. It was usually found in adult graves, women of high status. But, oh dear, this is a small grave, unusually small. The archaeologists' report concludes it was probably a tiny child or even a baby."

Viv bit her lip, thinking of her own baby's burial at the other end of the churchyard under the shade of the cherry tree. Baby Ana. A five-month miscarriage. A shiver ran down her spine. Was this something similar, all those centuries ago? The child of high status parents, chieftains of an Anglo-Saxon or even pre-Anglo-Saxon settlement? Could this possibly be to do with Lady Vivianne?

She scoured the report. The grave goods had been removed and dated as probably early sixth century and were now in the museum. But it was strange: there seemed to be far more than they would normally expect for a baby burial. Was this more than one burial? But nothing else had been found, no evidence of a settlement or further remains. No further burials found. No fragments of bone. Just these simple artefacts in this one place.

Viv quickly searched the museum's website. At last she found the glass and pottery fragments and the brooch from the dig. But no bracteate.

Where was it? And if it was from Scandinavia, how had it got to this spot, in the middle of the English countryside?

She searched and searched until Ellie, replete and

contented, needed to be lifted to her shoulder and burped.

VIV WAS STILL FROWNING IN PUZZLEMENT AS SHE carried Ellie in her papoose to the new section of the churchyard, the print-out of the plan of the 2003 excavation sticking up out of her jeans pocket.

There was no sign of any dig now, of course. The reason for it in the first place was because of the request by one of Rory's predecessors to extend the graveyard eastwards and the subsequent objection by one of the parishioners who remembered Viv's parents' dig and was convinced that an Anglo-Saxon settlement at Cooney's Mere stretched this far.

Now the area just looked like a part of the churchyard that had always been there, and that is what Viv had supposed, until now. She pulled the plan out of her pocket and peered at it.

"This is very strange, Ellie," Viv murmured, distractedly stroking her daughter's little head in its beanie hat, primrose yellow this afternoon. "The Saxon cross, or what we think of as Saxon, but which may be older, pre-Anglo-Saxon, is way over there." She pointed towards the church behind them. Ellie took no notice, continuing to sleep peacefully. "And this burial was ..." she scoured the plan again and began to walk around the modern headstones "...about here."

She looked around her, not really knowing what she was looking for. "Why out here? OK, it's still within the general church area, but on the edge of it." She thought about the missing bracteate, its significance. Then she remembered that she had read in her research last year that often high status people of a settlement in post-Roman, early or pre Anglo-Saxon cultures would be buried on their own, away from other burials as a mark of respect and position. It was beginning to fit together. This would have been a sacred site. But what a shame there was no further evidence of a settlement right here, as she had known and felt at Cooney's Mere that time a few years ago. When she first met Rory.

Ellie began to stir. "You know, Ellie, that the name Cooney's Mere is a corruption of the ancient 'Cūning's Mere' – the king's lake. It's where Sir Pelleas died when he was exiled from the settlement ..."

Viv shivered, a cold mist rising up her spine. She caught her breath. A wisp of a memory. She forced her eyes to focus on the gravestones around her in the churchyard, the concrete reality of stone, of flowers, of the warm gentle breeze. But the air around her seemed to draw in its breath too, and she felt the earth judder beneath her feet.

She was drifting, muzzy, so light-headed that all her thoughts flickered away and disappeared, leaving her with only feelings, sensations. Behind her eyes she saw the mead hall, heard the roar of approval as she lifted her eyes to the rafters. Then an unease stirring her heart, her daughter, older now, flirtatious, an anxiety filling her heart, a chamber of women busying themselves with sewing, repairing. Readying for something that spelled danger, death. Walking along a dusty path, knowing that eyes bored into her back, pressing hatred into her spine. Someone's eyes locked on to Lady Vivianne.

Viv pulled back, shook her head, forced herself to deny what she felt, because she knew what it was, and she could not go with it. Not now, not with little Ellie close on her chest. She struggled, pulling back, then being drawn in again, drifting despite herself. Oh God, no.

A cry seemingly from far away, then becoming louder, more insistent, calling to her for attention. Determined, demanding.

Viv shook her head and her eyes refocused on the consciousness of now, the present moment. It was Ellie, calling her back, dragging her into the present again. Her eyes saw the hard stone and the pots of bright spray carnations and roses with the sharp clarity of tropical daylight, the quality of light she had come to appreciate in Madeira. But here, now, in their country churchyard, and Ellie crying for her whole attention.

"Oh, poppet, thank you." She kissed the tiny head that was now struggling angrily to turn, beating against her chest. "OK, OK. I know. You want to come out of there." She tugged at the papoose and lifted her baby out, resting her against her shoulder. Ellie showed her objection with her little fists, pummelling Viv's clavicle. Goodness, she was a determined little one. She was certainly going to be a strong-willed young lady. "Right, let's turn you round so that you can see everything." Ellie's cries subsided and she began to gurgle in delight, happily waving her hands in the air and kicking her legs out in their pale yellow babygro onesie.

"Right, Ellie, let's go and look at the Saxon cross again."

Viv's fingers traced the image. It was so similar to the Repton Stone, and yet this one had its right hand down towards the seax across his middle. The Repton figure had its right arm raised, holding up the reins of the horse it was riding. The steed was clearly a stallion, from the distinctive carving between its hind legs. When Viv had looked more closely, enlarging the image on her computer it had become clear to her that the whole image was depicted as a representation of masculine strength and power. But this image on their Saxon cross did not appear to be riding a horse. Surely there were his legs standing straight down. As his right hand holding the seax at his waist, or was it something else? Peer as she might, Viv couldn't be sure.

And this suggestion of a figure carved beneath the Saxon one, as well as those runes – she needed to find someone who could investigate that further, an archaeologist and runologist. A name popped into her head, as she walked back to the rectory, trying not to wince at the kicking of Ellie's heels against her lower ribcage.

"COULD I SPEAK TO DR HELEN MORTIMER, PLEASE?" VIV held her iPhone to her ear as she dangled the bright blue stuffed elephant just out of Ellie's reach, so that she waved her hands towards it and gurgled delightedly on her baby gym set up on the carpet of the sunny rectory drawing room. While she waited for the university reception to transfer her to the archaeology faculty, she dropped the little elephant into Ellie's outstretched hands. The baby clutched it hard, waved it about, then threw it with surprising force across the room.

"Oh, hello, Helen. It's Viv DuLac here."

"Viv. How are you? How's ... er, you married the priest, didn't you?" Helen sounded her usual distracted self. She was not an overly social being. But very professional, discreet and reliable. Viv pictured her in her mind, dark cropped hair, very neat, immaculate white lab coat, peering down a microscope, thick muscular arms operating the controls, strong from all the digging Viv supposed, the lab staff around her silent and focused. So unlike her own university room amidst the hustle and bustle of academics and students popping in and out. "I didn't know that was possible. Marrying a priest?"

"Oh yes. Church of England, not Roman Catholic."

"Ah. Right. Don't have much to do with these things. So. Haven't seen you for, oh, must be a year or two – more?"

"I know. Well, you know ... maternity leave, then sick leave, then in Madeira for a year ... and maternity leave again."

Viv could hear Helen breath hard, hesitate as if remembering, working something out, then the scrape of lab stool as she sat back from the bench and refocused.

"Oh. Ah. Does that mean a little newcomer in the rectory?"

Viv smiled down at her daughter. She was sure she was giggling. "Yes, indeed. Little Ellie."

"Ah. Right. Er, well done." Her voice changed gear. "I heard about ... university grapevine ... you know. I was so sorry. But it sounds like you have another little soul to keep you occupied. Presumably, you'll be back to the English faculty at some stage?"

Viv wondered what kind of personal life Helen had. She'd never heard anything about it. All their chats had really been coffee meetings mulling over some academic issue that concerned them both. Always about work. Or about Viv's parents' digs – which was work to Helen.

"Yes, all too soon, I'm afraid. I'm enjoying what I

have now, while it lasts. Soon enough back to the grindstone."

Viv heard voices in the background and Helen whispering 'give me a minute'. "So, what can I do for you, Viv?"

"Well." She told Helen Mortimer about the Saxon cross in the churchyard, describing the runes, the image, and her notion that there was another figure beneath it. "So, I was wondering if there was any way of dating the stone and maybe determine whether there is, in fact, another figure hiding underneath it? And I thought of you especially because of your specialism as a runologist. The runes might hold the key to all this."

"Actually, that sounds rather exciting." Viv didn't think she'd ever heard Helen use the word 'exciting' before. She could hear Helen shushing someone else in the room and detected the frisson of animation in her voice. "Yes, firstly, there are various methods we could use on the stone. Of course, the location and topography of the site in the first place. I assume that it's just the Cross and that there's no burial site to investigate to give us a clue?"

"No, no grave, or at least nothing that's been found, just the Cross like a memorial stone, but we don't think it's marking a burial."

"But it's possible?"

Viv frowned. "Well, I suppose so. But there's no way we can start digging up the graveyard to find out.

Actually, the stone was moved when it was re-erected, I think, in 1919. But it seems as though it was dug up nearer to the church wall, under the south west buttress."

"Ah. Interesting. Have you thought that the burial could be beneath the present church? From what you say it does sound like an early Saxon cross and that would have predated the church by a long way. There could have been a smaller wooden structure there instead if it was some kind of sacred site."

"Right. And that would make it more important to try to date it."

"OK. So, to put it briefly, there is radiometric analysis, electron microscope, etc. But stone itself as a material ... hmm ...the tools we use do depend on the presence of organic material and colour pigment – paint traces, and so on."

"Oka-a-y. So would it be worth someone's while to take a look?"

"Good God, of course. I'll come myself. You're not far away. And this could be a really interesting find. I really want to look at those runes on the Cross. I mean, if we could interpret them this could be ... well, very interesting." Viv could hear her drawing in her breath in something approaching excitement. "And is there anything else in the churchyard to help us get the bigger picture?"

Viv told her about the 2003 dig, the child's grave and the missing bracteate.

"Yes, I do recall the other artefacts in the museum, the ones from that early millennium dig. That was in *your* churchyard, then? Obviously before your time there. But even so ... Well, I hadn't caught on to a missing bracteate though. Listen, I've got a meeting now, but I could free up some time tomorrow, if that's OK for me to come over?"

"I'VE BEEN READING UP AGAIN ON YOUR PARENTS' DIG AT Cooney's Mere back in, what, the early 1990s?" Helen and Viv were heading for the Saxon cross, Helen bedecked with a large camera round her neck and a huge bulging canvas bag, and Viv feeling somewhat odd without Ellie in her papoose on her chest, as though something vital was missing from her. But she knew that Rory had taken her for a walk round the parish again, freeing her up to talk with Helen unencumbered.

"And what did you think? Any connection with this 2003 dig, do you think?"

"Well, yes, definitely could be. There's not much on the 2003 dig, though, so it's rather tantalising. And I can't find anything about the missing bracteate either. It's very odd. But, yeah, the artefacts are dated around the same time as your parents' findings at Cooney's Mere. The theory is that there was an important pre-Anglo-Saxon settlement there, dating from way back when – oh, Roman times, third century AD, and that it was repurposed as a Romano-Brython settlement after the legions left. It seems to have grown and become more important post early sixth century. In fact, it would have been a small kingdom rather than simply a settlement."

"A kingdom? So there would have been a king?"

"Yes. But it would have been what we might think of as regional, not national, of course. Britain, even England, was not united for another three hundred years, under King Alfred of Wessex. Well, at least, he was the first king to style himself King of all England."

Viv wondered about Sir Roland and Lady Vivianne. Was Sir Roland the effective king, then? She frowned. A frisson of annoyance and negation shivered through her mind. Where had that come from?

"Well, here is our Saxon cross," Viv pointed out unnecessarily. It was quite imposing in their churchyard.

Helen stood and stared at it, then dropped heavily to her knees and peered more closely, tracing the figure with her fingers, just as Viv had done. Then she pulled out of her bag a small eye magnifying glass, the kind Viv thought of as being used by jewellers to peer at tiny diamonds. "You know that there is some scraping damage on the surface. I would say that it's from the original discovery. Did you say that the gravedigger found it lying horizontally and dug it up?"

"Yes, that's how the story goes."

"OK. Let's hope there's not too much damage. But I think I can take samples from appropriate areas. Just scrapings. I don't need much."

Samples? Viv had thought she was just going to take some photos of the runes to try to interpret them, and maybe photos of the whole cross for identification. She hoped it'd be OK with Rory to take samples from church property. Or whether he'd have to clear it with the Bishop first? Oh well, Helen said she didn't need much in the way of scrapings.

Viv nodded. "I'm going to enjoy watching you working. You know, I never got to see what my parents did. I was too young when they passed away. I never actually watched them work."

Helen was frowning at the Cross and its markings.

"Well. This is most interesting. These runes ... well, I can hardly wait to get started on interpreting them. Hmmm. As you said on the phone, this figure is very reminiscent of the Aethelbold image on the Repton Stone, but there are those differences that you already noted. You know, my initial thinking is that this is a deliberate attempt to liken the memorialised person here to the King of Mercia. Maybe to reflect the high status of the king it represents. But it is, I would say, a different king."

"So could it be a memorial to a king of the Cooney's Mere settlement?"

"Possibly. But I would need to conduct some tests to look at the actual age of the Cross. And yes, I do think you're right. There may be a painted figure beneath this. Or at least an image scratched and painted onto the stone. I don't know how you managed to identify that, though. There's almost nothing to see. Hmm. But ... we might be able to retrieve some pigment from around the edges of the carving." She stood up, replaced the eye glass in her bag and unhooked the large camera which was hanging around her neck. She took a number of photos of the runes, the figure, and the whole cross from different angles. It reminded Viv of police dramas with SOCO photographers recording every angle of a body. Or Silent Witness forensic scientists. "This is remarkably interesting, Viv. I'm so glad you called me."

"So ... I hesitate to ask – I know you're really busy at the moment. But any chance you could investigate, test – whatever you need to do here?"

Helen smiled – a rare event. "Absolutely. Hopefully, the runes can tell their tale, but that will take a while. So first we need to do some testing on the stone." She carefully placed the camera and the bag on the ground beside her and retrieved the magnifying glass again, fitting it to her eye. Helen peered around the figure again and turned to take from her tote a poly bag, which she tore open and slid out a pair of latex gloves that she put on and smoothed over her hands.

Viv watched her rummage in her bag again and pull out a clear plastic box. Her colleague opened it and took out what looked to Viv like a tiny scraper tool, a pair of tweezers and a couple of test tubes. She placed the box back into the top of her bag that gaped open for access and rested one of the test tubes on top of it.

Bending to the stone again, Helen began to scrape the surface gently into the test tube. Viv watched, fascinated, as she worked, admiring the dexterous way she held the scraper and tweezers in her fingers, working the tweezers every now and then as a fragment from the Cross proved more obstinate. When she was satisfied, she stoppered the test tube and dropped the scraper and tweezers into her bag.

"Right. I think we have enough here."

"But there really are only a few tiny pieces there," said Viv with relief as she watched Helen write on the label.

Helen glanced up. "Oh, that's enough. That's plenty. We don't hack away at an artefact. Only a little scraping. The machine only needs a little material. And it looks like a bit of organic matter here on the stone. If so, that could help us to date and identify the carving." She placed the test tube in the pocket of the bag and took out the second test tube and a new scraper and tweezers. She turned back to the Cross and shifted her position so that she could repeat the process into the very edge of the figure. "I'm retrieving a little of these paint fragments, tiny traces of pigment, which I reckon could be from something underneath the visible carving. Let's hope so, anyway."

Finally, Helen stood up and stepped away from the Saxon cross. She stared at it for a while. "Right, I need to get this back to the lab for analysis. You know, it never ceases to be amazing and intriguing, doing this, investigating a new artefact. You never know what secrets you might uncover." She turned to Viv and smiled again. "The secrets of the Saxon cross, eh? What *are* these runes hiding?" It sounded almost romantic to Viv.

CHAPTER 6

VIV

Derbyshire. Present day

Waiting for the results to come back from Helen's lab was excruciating for Viv. She couldn't wait to find out something, *anything*, that might shed some light on the Cross in the churchyard, and how it might be linked to the little burial to the east, and maybe to the Cooney's Mere settlement. No, not a settlement now, but in all likelihood a small kingdom.

Of course, she hadn't told Helen anything about her time-slips into the world of Lady Vivianne, the way she had fallen back to 499 AD, that she knew about that world first-hand, as it were. She knew that Dr Helen Mortimer, archaeologist and runologist, with all her scientific training would most probably consider it all weird and unbelievable. Most people would, after all.

"Well, you didn't find it unbelievable, Viv," said Rory, swivelling round in his desk chair and watching Viv bouncing a delighted Ellie as she paced up and down the hallway outside his study. Ellie was giggling uncontrollably, a throaty, utterly captivated laugh.

"No, at least not eventually when I'd got more used to what I was experiencing. And then when I found out about my mother and all that ... Oh, and I guess I'm more in tune with the vast possibilities of life and time and space through my work in medieval history and literature. I'm not an objective, factual scientist. I can see other things than the material world." Viv tickled Ellie's chin which sent the baby into paroxysms of delight, kicking out her little legs in jerky excitement.

"Hmm. I'm not sure that all scientists would agree with that assumption. Take Stephen Hawking, for example. Black hole theory had to come from a pretty imaginative place outside what we might normally think of as the physical world. And Einstein and the Einstein-Bridge theory of time and space, that arguably started it all, didn't exactly ..."

"OK. But you know what I mean! I can't wait to hear what Helen's discovered."

Rory's smile morphed into a grimace and his forehead puckered into a concerned frown. "Viv, I don't mean to be a kill-joy, but you need to be careful about what investigation is done in the churchyard. It *is* church property. And any publicity about what's found … we have to handle it all very carefully. We don't want folks coming to sight-see and trampling around causing damage …"

"Honestly, Rory, I watched Helen and she literally took a few grains of scrapings. There was no damage – far less than the grave digger's spade in the first place."

"Right. But do be cautious. We don't want to get up Bishop Jonathan's nose."

The landline telephone began to ring across the hall in the drawing room. Viv gave Rory a rueful grin. "OK, you can get back to your work now without our interruption. But if it's parish business I'll put it through to you. Which reminds me, you really should get that second line set up for all that. Or use your own mobile."

"I know," Rory smiled. "It's on my to-do list. Or rather *your* list for my to-do."

Viv dived off and grabbed the receiver before it cut to voicemail.

The room was suddenly filled with loud shrieks, and Ellie jumped in Viv's arms, startled. "Hiya, Stranger! What are you up to, sweetie-pie?"

"Tilly! Long time, no see. All of two weeks, I do believe." But Viv smiled, picturing her erstwhile neighbour who lived in the flat upstairs to the apartment at the abbey that she still kept as her 'bolt hole'. She could see in her mind's eye Tilly's pretty moon-like face and wild frizzy blonde hair, probably with the phone squashed between unnaturally hunched shoulder and cheek as she expertly painted her toe nails her signature bright sapphire blue. They'd had a catch-up over coffee a couple of weeks ago when Viv had taken little Ellie across the village to Tilly's.

"And how's my little beauty? Sorry, Viv, but I don't mean you. Oh my days, Ellie's such a cutie-pie. My best, bestest, girl. Is she there? Put her on." Viv held the phone to Ellie's face who obligingly made babbling noises into the receiver at Tilly's voice. "Hello, Ellie-Pellie!" Viv winced "What have you been doing, my little precious? Playing with mummy? Tormenting daddy?" Ellie was trying to eat the phone, so Viv moved it back to her own ear. "Oh, your lovely daddy. Oh, is that you now, Viv? So, how's that gorgeous hunky priest of yours?"

"My gorgeous hunky priest is very well, thank you, Tilly. But also terribly busy, what with one thing and another."

"Oh hell, not more nonsense like you had in Madeira?"

"No, God no, thank goodness. No weird embezzling church wardens here. Just normal busy ..."

"And no village tarts trying to get off with him, then? Pinching my pitch! You know, that SS character."

Viv screwed up her eyes as she tried to keep up

with Tilly. "Oh, what – you mean the lovely Sadie Smythe?"

"Fragrant and a bit too hot for comfort, that one! I should watch her, sniffing around your unworldly husband – she's not good-natured like me. Something of the seedy night club about her. Something toxic."

Viv laughed and shook her head in affection. "Honestly, Tilly! She's a newcomer and I'm sure pretty harmless. She doesn't mix much."

"Oh, come on, sweetie-pie! You think she's strange as well!"

An image of Ivy Nettles flashed across Viv's mind. "To be honest, Tilly, so are one or two of our villagers. Goes with the territory, interesting characters."

"Hmm. Well, just watch the tarty one with Rory ..."

"OK. So ... was there a purpose for the call or just a chat?"

"Well ..." Tilly drawled with a slight upward inflection.

Viv recognised that tone of voice. "Oh dear, that sounds ominous."

"Nothing awful, sweetie-pie. Remember what we were talking about last week, or the week before or whenever it was ... Tuesday, no I think it must have been Wednesday because I'd spent the night with Joe and he'd – well, that doesn't matter. *Anyway*, I wanted to ask you something. Something that's come up at work."

Tilly now worked as a designer for television

historical programmes, or researcher, or part-time producer, or finder and creator of replicas, or 'gofer' or some such. Viv wasn't quite clear. Whenever she asked Tilly for enlightenment her friend's explanation was so garbled and complex that she still remained as puzzled as she was before. Tilly always seemed scatty but in fact she hadn't so long ago walked across the university stage for her second degree in historical design. Viv smiled as she recalled that Tilly had dyed her lovely fair hair bubble-gum pink for the occasion. Thankfully it had grown out now.

"OK. Go on."

"We-e-ll. Remember I told you that we were looking for a new project for the History Now series? You know we did the lovely Lucy Worsley and that Tudor dig, Henry VIII's *other* palace? Oh, was that Lucy or was that someone else? That other female historian, whatsername ...? Hmmm."

"Ye-e-s ...?"

"Well, anyway, we were looking for maybe something medieval or earlier – dark ages, or some such. And of course I'm thinking of you, and our amazing adventure a year or two ago."

"Oh no, no, I really don't want to revisit those ..."

"No, but not exactly that. And we want ongoing archaeological work, so that we can film it as it happens. God, Viv, have you never watched the show? Honestly!"

"As a matter of fact I *have* watched it. I saw every episode of the last series and it was very interesting."

"So, a little birdie tells me that you're involved in a new project with Dr Helen Mortimer from the archaeology department at the uni. A Saxon cross right there in your churchyard ... and with some intriguingly mysterious runes on it ... and sample testing of the stone ... and a possible link to a child's burial in said churchyard, maybe dark ages stuff ..."

"Oh no, Tilly." Viv was thinking of Rory's concerns and shaking her head at the empty space in the drawing room, looking out through the French windows to the beautiful rectory garden. "No way. It's at a very early stage of possibility. And anyway, how on earth did you hear about it? Someone spying on us in the churchyard?"

"Ah. You aren't denying the rumour then?" Viv hadn't even thought about denying it.

"It *is* true, Tilly. But, honestly, I really can't say anything about it at the moment because ... because, I don't know, it just feels like tempting fate to even talk about it. I don't know whether there's anything significant in it at all. And anyway, for heaven's sake, it's Rory's church! And it's not an archaeological dig, just a visual investigation of what's on the Cross. There's no burial site to excavate. Nothing much at all."

"Ah ..."

"Tilly, please stop saying 'ah' like that. I have a horrible feeling you're cooking something up."

"I was just going to say ... ah, well, there's a fee involved that would, if Rory wants, go to the church funds. Quite a substantial amount if the episode is strong enough to go out. But we don't necessarily want an actual dig, just an investigation of an ancient mystery. The mystery of the runes on the Saxon Cross. And we'd dress it up with reconstructions of the dark ages or Anglo-Saxon times, or whatever, to make it viewable and 'real'."

"Reconstructions? Not in the church? Not sort of re-enactments? I don't think ..."

"Oh, they wouldn't be *there*. They'd all have to be shot in an appropriate space, not in the churchyard with all the modern gravestones around. Or even in the church itself – that's got all sorts of more recent additions, Victorian even. And I don't think the church dates from as early as the Anglo-Saxon period. No, we'd need to find a location with suitable dark ages atmospherics. And use CGi I guess. But it'd be the story of the dark ages or Saxons."

"We-ell ..."

"Honestly, sweetie-pie, we'd have a single camera for the video of the cross and any testing of it – we're in favour of the hand-held stuff now, it's more realistic, immediate."

"No OB palaver?" She thought of all the huge vans required for Outside Broadcasts that she'd seen on television.

"Viv! You're thinking of Wimbledon! No-o-o! It'd

just be like you taking a video on your mobile, or your digital camera anyway. And then some footage of the testing of samples in the lab. Some talking heads - can be at home or in the lab. The lab technician? Maybe you. Or the divine Rory. Actually, very little in the churchyard. I mean, a stone cross is hardly the raising of the Titanic, is it? No, no. All quite simple."

Viv knew that nothing, especially if it involved Tilly, was ever 'quite simple'. But she thought of the struggling church funds, the need for the organ to be serviced and repaired, something that Rory had been moaning about, wondering how to raise the funds. And the belfry tower needed some renovation work too. He'd said there was no way that the usual sponsored walks or church fêtes would do it, however many homemade cakes they sold, or however much the ever-popular Miss Bates's bric-a-brac stall could hope to raise.

"Obviously, I'd have to discuss it with Rory. It's a church matter. My investigating the cross and getting Dr Helen to take tiny samples is one thing ..." Viv heard Tilly's intake of breath and she knew she was actually inciting even more excitement. "But having film crews trampling around is quite another."

"Look, talk to your sexy priest man about the idea. But, honestly, Viv, it wouldn't be like that. We do this a lot. We've done a whole series with ongoing investigations and in-process digs, and we're extremely sensitive to the locations and surrounds. And this isn't a dig, is it? Just work on dating the cross. Did you hear about the cathedral burial ground investigation last year? That was ours."

Actually, Viv did remember that work and the filming – and also how pleased the cathedral dean was with the work and the funds. She thought there was something about the television company doing some renovation work while they were there, but she couldn't be sure.

"Well, I'll ask him, but I'm sure he'll have to go to the Bishop and maybe even higher for approval. You can't sneeze in church without approval these days."

Tilly laughed, a gurgling infectious laugh that put Viv in mind of Ellie's.

"OK!"

"But Tilly, how did you find out about my interest in this cross?"

"Oh, you know." Viv could almost see Tilly tapping her nose. "Not much gets past me these days."

"And Tilly? You'd need to talk to Rory yourself about details of this programme even if he agrees to square one."

"Mmm, can hardly wait! As you know, sweetie-pie, I fancy the pants off that divine man. As I've always said! Divine. In more ways than one!"" And as Tilly rang off, Viv could distinctly hear her raucous strains of "*How great thou art!*"

It sounded rather interesting – the project, not Tilly's singing. Hmm. And who knows there might be other specialists who could help with identifications. She'd just have to be incredibly careful about how she presented the idea to Rory.

Ellie interrupted Viv's thoughts with her own take on the world, namely that it was time for her own special playtime.

"Right, sweetie-pie ... oh goodness, I'm channelling Tilly now! Poppet, d'you fancy the baby gym again? Or tummy time? Use a bit of that boundless energy up."

IT WAS LATER THAT NIGHT BEFORE VIV FOUND THE RIGHT time to broach the subject of the television programme. They were lying snuggled up in bed, Viv's head on Rory's broad chest where she could hear his steady heartbeat. She felt his breath tighten and raised herself up to look at him and to gauge his reaction. Rory looked horrified at first, his dark eyes widening, then he began to soften his expression and ask questions, a lot of questions.

Viv nodded and grimaced. "I can't answer all these issues. You need to talk with Tilly, I think. She can tell you much more about what they're thinking of and how it would all operate."

"Yes, OK. I can see some benefits of it ... but I can also see some potential problems. I'll talk with Tilly, probably along with Michael. As curate, especially a new one, he needs to be involved. And then I'll obviously have to discuss it all with Bishop Jonathan and if he approves, then the PCC."

Viv knew that his caution arose at least in part from his experiences in Madeira when things had been done by others without consultation or discussion, underhand in fact, and chaos had resulted. So she had sympathy for his hesitation. But she could also detect his undercurrent of excitement as he mulled over the opportunities it might present to their little church in the middle of nowhere, but which clearly had a whole back-story to tell.

Rory fell silent for a while, clearly mulling over the ramifications of the idea. Viv's mind went back to Lady Vivianne and Sir Roland and the connection to that time and place centuries ago. A wisp of air drifted across the room, then settled uneasily.

Viv sat up. She sensed a cold draught shiver into the bedroom. She felt the air whirl around her, a disturbance, a perturbation. Someone, somewhere, was anxious. Then a quietening and a deep silence. A waiting. Something, someone, was discomforted, and was sending a silent warning ...

CHAPTER 7

LADY VIVIANNE

Cūning's Mere 520 AD

*L*ady Vivianne felt discomforted. Something was wrong. The air was disturbed, and she knew of old that meant something bad was afoot. Please God, no.

She knew that it was something a long way away. In distance or time, she did not know. But her thoughts drifted to the approaching forces of the Angeln, marching inexorably northwards towards them. She rose from her little prie-dieu in the corner of her chamber and crossed herself. She rubbed her knees through her gown; the wood of the kneeling ledge was getting rougher although she thought it should be getting smoother with all the praying she was doing now.

There was a movement, a sickness in her belly.

Surely it was too early for this little one to be kicking already.

"Tilda!" she called, thinking that her maid was in the next room at the back of the great mead hall, attending to the smaller children. But there was no answer. Perhaps she had taken them outside. They liked to chat to the baker – and especially if he slipped them a piece of fresh crusty bread. She guessed that Young Tristram was still sulking about their refusal to let him ride out to battle, saying he was too young yet, maybe next time. Roland had been in half a mind to let him go with him, but Vivianne had refused.

But she knew that her discomfort was not about that. She glanced at the icon above the kneeling stool. What was it that stirred her thoughts? She felt a chill drift across her mind, and she shivered.

The stamping of boots on the earth outside warned her of Roland's approach. Not warning her that he was coming to her but warning her that he was soon to depart into danger, again. The time had come.

He swept the door open wide, as he always did. Never a cautious entry but a heralding of his strength, his power, his confidence. She knew that he enjoyed times of danger, that he felt the excitement and that it gave him a sense of purpose and a role to play.

"It is time," he said without preamble. "We are about to ride out southwards. The thegns are ready." He caught her expression and smiled reassuringly. "The banner is wonderful, my love. You and your ladies have worked miracles with it, and I thank you all." He moved towards her and took her hand. "But you most of all because I know how hard this is for you. The weight of it all on your shoulders. I am glad that you have our ealdorman Godwyne as your advisor and protector whilst I am away. I know that he is getting old now but as the senior ealdorman and previously elder thegn he has the wisdom of years."

"And you promise that you will be back before the Hunters' Moon?"

Roland shook his head gently. "You know that I cannot promise anything. We go to uncertain battle, not to do trade. But I am sure that we will be back by then. Certainly, before winter sets in, before *gēol*."

"*Gēol*? You mean Christ's Mass!"

"I beg your pardon." Roland bent in a slight bow. "I used the old term."

"The pagan term, brought in again from the Saxons!"

"Indeed. I hear it from the ceorls and sometimes a few of the thegns too. But, my love, you do not usually turn aside from both terms, especially as your own mother ..."

"Yes. I know. I am a little ... strained just now." She reached out and touched his thick battle dress, his cloak with its large gold shoulder fastening. She drew in a sharp breath. "And likewise I am glad that you have this, at least." She gently placed her slim fingers on his leather over-jerkin with its gleaming gold rings overlapped upon it.

"Indeed! You were very clever to think of such a thing. I do not know what gave you the notion, but it will be invaluable on the battle field." He caught her expression. "Do not worry, this will protect me, not least because it is made from your love. And maybe at some time we will be able to make this battle clothing for all the thegns."

"Yes, indeed. I am only sorry that this present danger caught us unawares and without enough protection for all. Although we have managed without for all these years. At least all the senior battle thegns have them. Perhaps it will keep our minds away from danger whilst you are gone if we try to make as many of these as we can. For the next time." She crossed herself. "God forbid. Yet I know it will not end with this battle against the Angeln. It will then be the Saxons again. And then the Picts." She turned away from his gaze. "Will it never end, Roland?"

"My love." She felt him move close behind her as he wrapped his arms around her. "I must speak truth. It will never end. We will always need to defend our settlement, our kingdom. And we will always protect our way of life. We have here at Cūning's Mere the best of the Roman life and the best of the Brython. And also of the Celtic way. We have chosen and kept the things we hold dear from all of those. And so it will be."

Vivianne turned in his embrace. "Yes, we do, my dearest love. And of course we must protect it all." She smiled. "And add new things, new ideas, new ways too, when we come upon them from our traders and travellers."

"Of course. And we are well placed to be receptive to the new, and to absorb it into our ways, as we have always done."

Roland bent to her and his mouth was on hers, pressing into her the memory of their love and their life. Just in case.

Then he stepped back a little and, pushing aside his cloak, he opened the large pouch that hung from his wide leather belt. He drew out a piece of cloth, a delicate square of pure silk. "I had it embroidered for you."

Vivianne took the token from him and gasped at the delicacy of the stitching. "It is wonderful. Who worked it, may I ask of you?"

"Your own nursery maid Matilda," he grinned. "For all her ungainliness, the work with her hands is unsurpassed."

"Thank you, my love. I shall keep it next to my heart until you return safely to me."

LADY VIVIANNE WATCHED WITH UNEASY BREATH AND held up her arm in blessing as the battle horses kicked up the dust from the tracks through the village, and the crowd of ladies and the remaining older ceorls stood lining the road with a melée of sobbing and cheering. Even many of the geburs were there, taking a few minutes from their work in the fields to wave the thegns off to battle.

She noted that Afera, whom Tilda had trained to take her place after several disastrous maids, was standing amidst the jostling crowd, wide eyed and awe-struck at the sight of the battle-geared thegns. She was so impressionable. As her lady, she must keep a strict eye on her. She did not want any ill-advised liaisons while she was under her care. Not that she had succeeded too well with her own daughter. Vivianne turned to the parade before her. Soon, when they were away from the village boundaries, she knew that a stark seriousness would descend upon them all.

As ever, Sir Roland rode in front on his great battle horse, his banner guards with him. He passed Vivianne with a slight bow and she was sure that he winked at her as he rode by. She kissed her piece of embroidered silk and held it up towards him. He smiled but she could see that his sights were already away from her and focused on the matters ahead. He rode on and she tucked the silk token back into its gold pin. She watched as the red dust kicked up around her from the horses' heavy hooves. But he was soon too far away for her to see him properly and her heart trembled.

Her hand pressed the token pinned at her chest. It was what they always did but this time somehow it seemed special, as though this battle was somehow different from the others. She knew with foreboding that it would be a big and bloody battle. She could not pretend otherwise. The Angeln were a hardened and determined force. Her heart felt heavy and her stomach churned with unusual dread. She hoped to God that her sense of foreboding was not one of her premonitions. She prayed that Roland would be coming back to her, and soon, before the Hunters' Moon and the prospect of the bad weather that heralded winter. It seemed suddenly a lot to pray for.

She was aware of a movement beside her and turned to Nymue. Her daughter was raising her hand to her lips and then towards a thegn in a dark red cloak, not unlike Sir Roland's. Vivianne squinted in the sunshine. It was Sir Aldwyn who signalled back at Nymue and who smiled as his eyes flashed cunning. His gaze flicked momentarily to Vivianne and his eyes hardened with threat.

She waited until the horses had passed and then the striding, jostling company of ceorls who accompanied their thegns to the battle. Then she took Nymue's sleeve to guide her back towards the mead hall.

"What do you think you are doing, Nymue? And what is that in your hand?" Vivianne hissed, gesturing towards Nymue's hand, a tight fist clutching something dark blue.

Nymue frowned and turned down her mouth. "It is a token."

"I can guess that, my child. But who gave it to you?" Yet she knew, and her heart dipped.

"Sir Aldwyn." Nymue's voice was hard.

Vivianne stopped in her tracks. "Why? I do not understand. Why are you receiving favours from Sir Aldwyn? I thought that Gareth Swineson was your love?"

"Oh *him*! He is not riding to battle, is he? And anyway, you did not approve of him. You wanted me to love someone of a higher standing. You yourself said so." Her eyes flashed and she tossed her thick red hair. "You said it had to be a thegn or a king of another settlement. Because I am the daughter of the chieftain. The first ætheling! You said so!"

"Nymue, anyone who stamps their foot like that must still be a child, and one too young to exchange tokens." Her heart twitched. "Nymue, what did you give him, Sir Aldwyn?"

Nymue pouted and flicked her overgown in defiance. "My gold finger ring."

"Oh, no, Nymue. What have you done?"

"The other girls have a love already and I wanted one too. And he is most comely and an important thegn. And he made eyes towards me."

Vivianne stared at her daughter. It seemed not long

ago that she had birthed her. She had played with her when she was but a small child and taken her round the settlement to introduce her to the thegns and ceorls and even the geburs working in the fields. They had run in the wheat fields together and fashioned dolls from the corn, just as she had done with her own mother. She had taught Nymue to ride and to hunt for boar. She had taught her to become skilled with the bow and arrow, even as a little girl.

And now she was speaking of 'love'?

"Oh, Nymue, I have surely taught you how to behave as a lady, as an ætheling? How to remain distant and unattainable." She frowned. "Even though a man might make eyes towards you. And this ... this Aldwyn ..."

"Why are you so fixed against him, mōđor? He is a worthy thegn, much higher than Gareth Swineson. It is surely what you wanted. He says that his father was a high-born noble although he never knew him before he died ..."

Vivianne shook her head, in turmoil as to how she was to explain to Nymue the dangers of such an association. "My dear, let us return to the privacy of my chamber." She clutched Nymue's arm as tightly as she dared and took a deep breath as she dragged her daughter away. "His father was not a high-born noble. He was a Saxon runaway, or rather he was turned out from his Saxon tribe, and my father in all his kindness took him in and raised him as a son. He was Sir Pelleas."

Nymue turned towards her mother, a look of surprise crossing her beautiful features. "The traitor we know from tales and legends?"

"Yes. And his mother, Edyth ..."

"I know of his mother. She is a poor daughter of a gebur of the fields. That is not her fault."

"No, indeed not. But she is not of good character, and always ready to cause trouble. And Sir Aldwyn is a thegn only because Sir Pelleas made an entitlement before the Witan council just before his death, when he thought his Chieftaincy was secure, and Aldwyn was his only son, as far as he knew. But things changed."

Nymue was silent for a while as they entered the chamber and then she turned on her mother. "Mōđor, to my mind, it is not fair or just to speak so against someone who has had such an unfortunate beginning. He *is* of noble birth, his father *was* the Chieftain, however you may think that your family was wronged." She drew back at Vivianne's raised eyebrows and hard-set mouth. "And of course they were wronged in a way. But that is hardly Sir Aldwyn's fault. A son cannot be blamed for his father's misdoings, nor his mother's low birth. I think you are being unjust and ... and intolerant ... and I love him all the more!"

And with that, Nymue flounced away out of the

chamber, with Vivianne calling vainly after her, "you do not understand!"

How could her daughter understand the dangers that Pelleas had put them all in, all those years ago before she was born, and therefore her mother's fear of his kin, and that the darkness was in his bloodline? How could she explain to Nymue about Aldwyn's behaviour to her own father in the Witan?

How could she tell her that Sir Aldwyn's father Pelleas had killed her own grandparents?

Lady Vivianne sank onto the stool by the hearth in her chamber. She thought of her opposition to Gareth Swineson and wondered why on God's earth she had imagined that association was bad when this was so unimaginably worse. She had tried to explain, carefully, rationally, to Nymue, the reasons why there could be no hand-fasting with Sir Aldwyn. She thought she had been cautious and that she had trodden sensitively with her daughter, difficult as she seemed to be these days. But Nymue was the first ætheling, she would continue the royal line, whoever was her husband would sit beside her, would be first protector of the kingdom, would give her children ... and Aldwyn with all his bad blood from Pelleas ... no, it was unthinkable.

Why had she got it all so wrong?

She was still sitting with closed eyes, horrified at the images her mind drew, of disaster for the settlement, for the kingdom torn apart by Aldwyn's manipulations, for a return to the dreaded rule of a new Pelleas, when she heard the door open and the shrieks of her younger children.

Launce and little Nini rushed in, with Young Tristram close on their heels, brandishing a wooden seax.

"What on earth ...?" she began as Tilda staggered inside, out of breath and clutching her chest. "My goodness, Tilda, what is going on?"

Tilda leaned against the wall and steadied her breath. "Oh my!"

"Tristram! Are you terrorising your little brother and sister with that seax?"

"It is only wooden, a play thing." Tristram thrust out his lower lip. "I was only chasing them."

Vivianne gestured to her children to come and sit at her feet by the hearth. Little Nini snuggled into the skirts of her overgown and glared at her older brother, while Launce shrugged and pulled out his counters from his pouch, shuffling them nonchalantly. She looked sternly at Tristram. "Why?"

"Because ... because I cannot go with the thegns to battle."

"Yes, I see. But surely it would be more useful for a young thegn to practise his skills with the battle trainer, so that he might be more able to join the battle thegns next time? Do you not agree, Tristram?"

The boy hung his head for a moment, thinking, then he rose to his feet and straightened his back, flashing a defiant look towards his mother. "Indeed. I will go to find him and do my practice. And then I can go to battle!"

"Come, come, young thegn!" said Tilda as she held the door open for him, her normal breathing now returned. "Go and do your practising." She winked at Vivianne. "Oh my, oh my. I do not know how you wheedle them around, my lady."

But Vivianne had caught the look in Tristram's eyes. She bit her lip and bent to ruffle little Nini's shock of dark hair, so like Roland's, and she could not help but smile at Launce's concentration as he arranged his counters in a battle formation, one thumb firmly in his mouth, a habit he had never lost even though he was now all of seven years. "It is not so hard when they are little. I wish I could wheedle the lady Nymue a bit more!"

She felt a twinge and rubbed her belly. Their future was around her and inside her, and she wondered how it would all develop. For the first time since she and Roland had become hand-fasted, then married by the church, she felt an ominous heaviness that weighed down her heart. More than the feelings of anxiety she had whenever Roland had ridden out to battle before.

This one was different; this battle was different. And it was all bound up with Nymue and her sudden obsession with Sir Aldwyn. At this moment she felt more than ever how fragile their life was, how uncertain their destiny. The way she and Roland had talked before he rode out, about the security and strength and unity they had made together for their kingdom – was it all only a dream, an insubstantial hope against what was *really* about to happen, something that was out of her control?

She shuddered. She felt a cold air shivering around her and she saw in her mind a vision of falling, walls crumbling, wood on fire, and she seemed to hear the clash of swords, steel against steel, and battle cries, the howls of fury, the yells of agony, roars of anger, the anguished neighing of horses. The clash of battle as their kingdom fell. Those strange feelings again, reminiscent of the ones she had before, of touching another world many centuries into the future. But that was oh so many years ago.

CHAPTER 8

LADY VIVIANNE

Cūning's Mere 520 AD

*L*ady Vivianne held her skirts up above the dust and dirt as she made her way to the sacred hall for the first time since her thegns had ridden out to battle. It was already the time of the Harvest Moon and the sky above her was heavy and ominous. It was one of the first acts when she became the chieftain queen of the settlement after Pelleas died by his own hand in the mere, to build again the sacred site that her parents had held so dear. And where they were so brutally killed in the fire that Pelleas had set. It was a memorial to them as well as a place of prayer and reflection. She had kept her father's Christian altar and her mother's more pagan icons to mark them both, the merging of their two cultures and tolerances.

As she stepped quietly through the doorway and

into the peace of the sanctuary, Vivianne felt the spirits of her parents, Sir Tristram and Lady Nymue, for whom her oldest two children were named. They swept around her as she entered, enfolding her in their embrace. She looked to the altar and the icons and raised her face to the thatch.

"I can tell nobody else, for I need to be the strong leader, but ... but I am truly afraid," she whispered to them. "There is something in the air and the wind that I cannot see but only feel. Something new, something different ... and something that breaks my heart. This battle with the Angeln, this rebellion from Sir Aldwyn ... is it all a curse from Sir Pelleas that has been silently creeping since his death, a revenge on us all because he was thwarted in his ambitions? Is he worming his way through Nymue to threaten the very foundations of our kingdom? Is the settlement we made and grew to be undermined by an evil man's legacy? We wanted only peace and stability and tolerance. We wanted a community of peoples who melded together their different backgrounds and beliefs. Was that too much to ask? Or is it because of our success that Pelleas has returned from the dead to haunt us ... and to destroy us all?"

She felt a tear slip from her eye and fought to harden her breath against it, knowing that it was up to her to be brave. She had to be as courageous as the thegns, as her husband, who rode out to battle ... she who had only to stay at home, safe, while they risked their lives for her. They had ridden to battle so many times before, so why was this one so different? This time she had watched each sunrise, the lightening sky each dawn streaked with the garish red of blood and she had felt the dread sink her heart.

"What should I do?" She raised her cupped hands to the roof. "Tell me, I beg of you. How can I avert disaster if this is what may come? Though I am the chieftain queen, and have given my women voice, in the Witan, in the decision-making, I am but a woman and women do not ride out to battle as warriors. Women do not lead the thegns, as Sir Roland does for me. I fear for my kingdom yet am helpless. What do I do?"

Lady Vivianne heard a low noise behind her and turned sharply. But there was nobody there. Instead a drift of warm wind circled around her and the far-off sounds of the village muted softly. She turned back to the altar. A wisp of air gently touched her upturned palms and stroked her hair, loosening her braids.

A voice, calm and slow. "Your time will come."

She closed her eyes tightly. "When?"

"Soon. Quite soon." The voice she recognised as her mother's, but it was thin, insubstantial, and she had difficulty in catching it and holding on to it.

"But what will I need to do? How will I know?"

"You will know the call when it comes. Be still."

She remained for a few moments, eyes closed, face

uplifted to the thatch above, breathing deeply to calm her fears. "I will. Thank you," her heart whispered.

Silently, she went to the altar and lit a candle, staring into its flame until that was all she could see, a bright light consuming the shadows. Then, following the custom that allowed no flame to be left unattended since the fire that took her parents, she softly blew out the light and watched the drift of smoke that whirled around her in farewell and rose to the roof and beyond, into the heavy sky.

And she stepped out into the daylight again.

MY TIME WILL COME. THE THOUGHT REVERBERATED across her mind and would not leave her, even as she made her way around the heart of the settlement, calling in at as many workshops as she could, trying to raise the spirits of those ceorls left behind to keep the vital services of Cūning's Mere going while the battle thegns were away. They all knew there would be hardship.

"Good day to you, Edgard," she called as she finally stood in the doorway of the leather tooler's hut. She loved the rich smell of the polished leather at the selling front of the shop and breathed it in deeply. The old man appeared from the shadows of the back of the shop, face as lined and tanned as his leather, wiping his stained hands on his yellowing apron. With him drifted the smell of the tanning urine out at the back. Vivianne stepped back a little onto the roadway. "I came to see that you are well provided for, and to ask if there is anything you might need at this difficult time?"

"My lady," he bowed. "I trust you are well. Yes, indeed I have everything I need at present. My wife is at the baker's helping out in exchange for our bread, but she will be back to her wool spinning soon and my children are with the metal worker…"

"Ah, yes, Edgard, that is what I wished to ask you about."

"My children, my lady?"

"Well, not exactly your children. But something that I have been thinking about a great deal of late." She frowned and peered around the shop for what she wanted. "There," she pointed. "The leather over-jerkin."

"Ah, yes, my lady. I made one for Sir Roland with the metal rings at your request. A new invention, from our traders from the east, I believe you said. I hope that Sir Roland was pleased with my work."

"Indeed he was, and I am pleased with it too. You were kind enough to make more for the senior battle thegns."

"Kind, maybe, but I made much coin for them and I thank you for that, my lady. My children were well fed and well clothed as a result! Especially now that hard times will come if the battle southwards continues for long. Then there will be little trade to be done without the thegns and horses here for repairs and replacements to shield straps and belt pouches for their weapons. And if ..." He stopped suddenly and blushed. "Oh, I beg your pardon, my lady. I did not mean ... I mean to say, there will be work enough when they all return and need their new leather. But for the moment we are well."

"Good. I am glad to hear of it. But I want to ask you to do more whilst work is slower for you. I would like *all* our battle thegns to be equipped with these over-jerkins. And that also means extra work for your children to make the metal rings for overlapping onto the jerkins. Can this be done, Edgard?"

The old leather worker raised his eyebrows but smiled. "Well, my lady, they cannot all be made with gold like Sir Roland's. But we could make them from other metals. Hmm, I will speak with the metal worker and together we will see what we can do. Is this the way we are to be now? For all the battle thegns?"

"So I would like. If they have to ride to battle, we must see that they all have as much protection as we can make for them. If it saves even a few lives it would be good. I will send my household ceorl to discuss payment with you and the metal worker. You will be paid well, Edgard, never fear and our gratitude will be great, mine and Sir Roland's. When he returns, before the Hunters' Moon," she added with emphasis.

Lady Vivianne turned and breathed in the fresh air as she tried to clear her head of the smell of urine. The stink had overwhelmed the comfortable smell of polished leather and as she hurried to distance herself from the workshop, she heard the rough voices of the geburs at the back, steeping the skins in the troughs of waste from the middens.

She looked up at the sun, weaker in the grey glowering clouds above, and guessed that there was just enough time now to seek out Gareth Swineson in the pig field before she needed to be back at the mead hall for the midday meal.

It was muddier and more difficult to walk on the rise above the village, and she needed to hold her skirts up higher until they were well up above her ankles. But she had to speak with him, so she navigated the wet rutted earth to the pig pens. She was concentrating so hard on keeping her balance on the drier ruts that she did not hear her maid's call until the girl was almost upon her.

"My lady! My lady!"

Vivianne halted, wobbling a little, and turned. "Afera! Whatever is the matter?"

Afera gasped as she bent her small slim frame, then caught her breath and smoothed her skirts. "Oh, my lady, I did not know where to find you and ..."

"Afera, I told you that I was walking around the village to see the home-ceorls and the field geburs, and that I needed no assistance to do so. Is there something urgent that you run after me?"

"My lady, I was not happy that you were alone and

unaccompanied through the settlement. I cannot think that Sir Roland would be pleased."

Vivianne shook her head. "But that would make no sense, girl! I have been out these past hours around the village before you come rushing headlong up to me in the fields?"

"Oh. Well ..." Afera peered slyly up through lowered eyelashes and Vivianne turned to see the object of her attention. Gareth Swineson was striding towards them. Vivianne looked upon him with greater attention than before. She could see that he was indeed someone whom her nursery maid Matilda had said was 'a fine figure of a man'. He was broad of shoulder and chest, muscular of leg and most handsome of face. But he brought with him the rotten smell of the midden.

"My lady Vivianne." He bowed his head and gave a shy smile. "What might I do for you?"

Vivianne could sense the heat from her maid at her side. "Afera, please to stand back further." She watched as her young maid stepped back a pace, still holding her head to one side coquettishly and glancing up at the swineherd. "Gareth, I ... er, I ..." For a moment she could not think why she had come. She frowned and looked down. Why did she imagine she needed to come up here? She thought of her daughter Nymue who had loved him and then dismissed him, all with the quickness and disregard of youth. He was her swineherd, after all, and especially important to the village with so many gone to battle. She needed him to be on her side, not resentful of her daughter's fickleness. But she, for once, had no idea how to start.

"My lady, might I guess that you were on your usual walk-about around the village to check that we were all well?" he offered gently.

Vivianne blinked and recovered her power of speech and thought. "Yes, yes indeed. Is all well? Your father, does his back still trouble him?"

"He is well, my lady. And he speaks often of your kindness in giving him the soothing potion in the spring. And the draft of camomile drink. They have helped greatly."

"Oh, I am so glad. And ... and you are well?"

"Indeed I am, my lady, very well." Did she see a frown behind his words, a sorrow?

"And not ... pining ... after the battle thegns' departure, I mean?"

Gareth looked at her strangely, then Vivianne saw a glimmer of light cross his eyes and he smiled again, softly. "All is well, my lady. We are grateful to you and although I would have liked nothing more than to ride out as a thegn, yet I know that is not to be, not ever."

Vivianne nodded. So, he knew that there could never be any liaison with Nymue. He accepted that. He accepted his place. All was indeed well.

But as she turned away and Gareth bowed his farewell, she felt her heart twisting a little. He seemed a good man. For a swineherd. But all would settle down and be well; all would return to the proper order again.

She became aware that Afera was mythering at her side. "Yes, Afera? Something else?"

"My lady, I had to tell you that Young Tristram has gone missing again. Tilda sent me. After his training, his tutor said he …"

"Why on God's earth did you not tell me this in the first place?"

Afera fiddled with her skirts. "I … I was distracted, my lady."

"I could see that," Vivianne called back as she hurried away down the hillside back to the mead hall, Afera scampering behind her.

"Tilda, what has happened?" Vivianne closed her eyes and sighed loudly. "What has Young Tristram done now?"

"Oh, my lady! He has disappeared. I do not know where he is, though I have scoured the village while you were away. A few of the villagers have seen him heading for the roadway south but …"

"And nobody thought to stop him? To enquire where he was headed?"

Tilda hung her head. "No, my lady. I guess they did not realise he was off with nobody knowing. He was cross with his training tutor and he ran off. I did not know myself until his tutor came looking for him. He was giving him time to cool down before he came. But Young Tristram did not return here. I have sent a party of geburs out to look for him. Do you think he has gone south to find his father and the battle thegns?"

"I sincerely hope not. But what makes you think so?"

"Oh, my lady, but he has taken his tutor's seax and sword."

CHAPTER 9

VIV

Derbyshire. Present day

"Wow! Am I allowed to hug a man of the priestly persuasion?" Tilly looked Rory up and down appreciatively as he stood in the hallway of the rectory, in his clerical gear, ready for Wednesday prayers across at the church.

"Well," Rory said solemnly, adjusting his dog collar, although Viv noticed the amused glance he gave to her crazy friend. "Only if you put my daughter down first."

Tilly gave little Ellie a big kiss on her head before reluctantly handing her back to Viv. "You gorgeous extra special person. Oh, sorry, I meant Ellie, not you, Rory." She clasped her hands to her ample bosom. "Although of course you too, Rory! I mean ...Oh, I'm all of a fluster now!" She fanned her hands in front of her face. "Woosh!"

Viv laughed and Tilly opened wide her arms to envelop Rory in her embrace. She kept hold of him and patted his broad back as Rory glanced in mock desperation over her shoulder at Viv.

"OK, OK, Tilly. Enough." He disentangled himself and drew back, running his hands through his thick curly dark hair.

"Gosh, is that like hugging God?" Tilly giggled. "Hmm, rather too sexy for God, I think."

"If I didn't know you better, I'd be a bit worried for my husband," Viv grinned, handing a wriggling excited Ellie back to her Godmother.

"Oh, you scrumptious little thing. I could eat you up," Tilly cooed, "Um, Ellie I mean, not you Rory. Although ... hmmm. One very sexy priest there! But hey, Viv, sweetie-pie. Hang on a minute." She peered at Viv over Ellie's growing thatch of curly auburn hair and pouted. "You mean you're not jealous? So, I'm not the tempting siren I thought I was?"

Viv shook her head with a smile and reached up to kiss Rory goodbye.

"Sweet," Tilly said, head to one side and closing her eyes. "Still in love after all this time!"

Rory winked at Viv and disappeared through the front door. Viv closed it gently behind him. "Only three years. You make it sound like we're an old married couple of pensioners!"

"Oh, but if I could go three weeks of relationship bliss, I'd be a happy woman!"

"But you *are* a happy woman, Tilly!"

Her face fell. "Seriously, I could do with a better track record with men. The sex is great at first, every time ... then woops, goodbye!" She followed Viv into the kitchen. "Be honest with me now. D'you think I should lose some weight?"

"Tilly," Viv said and realised she sounded like a school-marm, "You are lovely just the way you are." She filled the coffee maker and took a couple of mugs from the cupboard above the counter.

"*I love you just the way you are!*" sang Tilly in a strained falsetto as she jiggled Ellie who roared with delighted laughter and clapped her hands to Tilly's chest. "And this is one beautiful happy baby. Viv, you are one lucky, lucky lady."

Viv grimaced. "Yes, I know. It hasn't always been easy, but yes, I am." She poured out the coffee, plenty of milk and sugar in Tilly's, and put the mugs and a plate of home-made flapjacks onto the wooden tray. "OK, let's go through into the drawing room, and sit in comfort to talk about the television stuff."

"Drawing room! Hey, get you!"

"Sorry, yes I know. But it's always been called that."

"I know. I'm only teasing, aren't I, little sweetie-pie Ellie?" She turned to Viv and swapped the baby for a mug of coffee. "You know, I want one of those."

"I think you need a man first." Viv settled Ellie in her baby gym on the old worn carpet that had certainly seen better days. At least it was clean, but they really ought to get round to replacing things. "So, this television programme. I've talked to Rory and Dr Helen Mortimer, our archaeologist and runologist, about the idea and in principle they're OK with it but obviously both want to ask a few things about how it will operate in practice. Rory will have a chat with you when he gets back from the service and in the meantime – because he'll be a good hour and a half knowing how his parishioners like to chat afterwards – I thought after our coffee we could drive over to the university to see Helen. She told me this morning that she'd got some news, so she's expecting us."

"Ooh, yes, that'd be great. Then I can see the lab and report back to the company."

HELEN MORTIMER MET THEM AT THE MAIN DOOR TO THE lab block in the archaeology department, hidden away at the back of the university buildings.

"So, there's some new equipment you'll be interested to see, Viv."

"Great. Is it OK if I bring the baby in? She's asleep." Ellie was in the papoose at Viv's chest, although she was getting rather too big and heavy for it now. "She won't make any noise."

"Yes, that's fine." Helen waved her hand in dismissal. She wasn't really a baby person. But then neither was Viv before ... well, before Ana to tell the truth.

"Wow, this is fantastic." Tilly gazed around the lab. "It'll make some great shots."

"Well, I wanted to ask you about that, about the process and exactly what will happen, what you'll want to film, who you'll want to speak with, and all that. Perhaps we could have a Skype conversation or maybe a Zoom meeting set up along with my head of department? But first, let me show you this." She led them over to her work station.

"OK, so let's start with the figures on the Cross you wanted me to look at. Now, the stone itself we can only date to the age of that stone in geological time, Viv." Helen clicked on an icon on her computer screen and an image composed of numbers and lines and a kind of graph popped up. Viv made appreciative noises but hadn't a clue what on earth she was supposed to be looking at.

"And that means ... what?"

"So, we do it by radiometric dating. Now, the problem is that it doesn't date the stone itself but the organic material on it. The process is based on an assumption that all living matter absorbs carbon C_{12} and radioactive carbon C_{14} into their living tissue ..."

"Yikes!" said Tilly. "So there's radioactive ... *stuff* all around us? And ... *in* us?"

"Well, yes, in a sense. But it's not radioactive

material that's dangerous in itself, though. It's what the living world's made up of."

"My God." Tilly shuddered.

Helen shrugged. "OK. So, to put it simply, from the moment living tissue dies, the $C14$ begins to decay and as this is at a known rate, we can use the missing amount of $C14$ to determine the date of the material."

"That means you can use it to assess the date of the material, which century it existed in?" Viv frowned. As a non-scientist, it was hard to get her head around this. She glanced at Tilly who was staring agape at the computer screen.

"That's right. But – and it's a very big 'but' in this case – it's only possible on organic material, ie, not stone. And therefore of course the same applies to the carving *on* the stone."

"And what am I looking at here?" Viv peered more closely at the screen.

Helen flicked to bring up two screen images side by side. "Here is the dating of the stone itself, the limestone the cross was made of. But the dating is in geological time, the geological era which is not what you're interested in. We don't need to know when the limestone rock was originally laid down according to the parameters of your research. Likewise, the dating won't tell us when the carving took place either – we can only estimate that by looking at the form and style it takes. And we want evidence from organic material." She indicated with her cursor. "So, here ... the data from my scrapings of such material. We were able to see from the variation on your carved figure, that this part here," the cursor waggled again, then clicked back on the data screen, "has more recent organic material deep within the etchings. I need to take this further, but at the moment, Viv, it looks like your figure was carved around the 8th to 9th century."

"In other words, around or just after Aethelbold's time as king of Mercia?"

"It looks a possibility."

"Oka-ay. So that's not a surprise. The carver was commemorating Aethelbold's life, like the Repton Stone, maybe after his death?"

"Yes, could be. But at this stage I don't think it's actually Aethelbold that's being commemorated here. Look at the figure. Here, let me enlarge the image ..."

"What am I looking at?"

"So ... here, the chest, and here, the legs. Not only are they standing legs, whereas Aethelbold on the Repton Stone is shown riding a stallion ... these seem to be a woman's legs – look at the curving - a woman's torso. Breasts were not shown on a male figure."

"Not even man boobs?" Tilly laughed.

"Well, they had other ways of showing a masculine figure, if they wanted to represent manly power and virility." Helen frowned. "Like the horse on the Repton Stone."

Tilly opened her mouth to respond but Viv leapt

in. "Wait a minute. So, you're saying that this is the image of a woman? What, a queen maybe?"

"Yes, and more than this. This is where the runes come into play. Now, I can't at the moment say whether these were carved into the stone at the same time as the figure carving, or later or before."

"But you have some indication of the dedication?"

"Ye-es." Helen hesitated and looked at Viv with a frown. She clicked onto yet another page and the screen showed a set of runes. "There's a name, which is exactly as you might expect. But it's ... look, how much do you know about runes?"

"Nothing." Tilly said happily, "but it all looks very mysterious and magical!"

"Well, a little," Viv added. "But not enough to be confident of an interpretation – which is why I called you in."

"Only," Helen began carefully, "only ... Um, let me explain." She turned to Tilly. "Runes are basically signs that are representations of voice sounds, sort of like the Roman alphabet but they vary with dialect and pronunciation differences, so it's often difficult to interpret the meaning of individual runic 'letters' or semantics. It's the way we wrote before it was replaced entirely by the Roman alphabet ABC etc which is what we know and use now."

"OK, I think I'm with you ... um, I think," said Tilly.

"Basically, it was an early form of writing. So, it's rather like writing down the speech sounds you hear, using the only signs you know – for us, it would entail the Roman alphabet. You make a stab at choosing the nearest Roman letter you know to what you think you hear. Phonetics."

"As do young children when they first learn to write," added Viv. "They write exactly what they think they hear. Phonetic spelling. So it can reflect local pronunciations."

"Exactly. Except of course children in our culture are using the Roman alphabet. So it's easy for us to read or interpret. Well, usually."

"And these ancient scribes are using runes to reflect their variation of speech."

"Yes, but with an added complication ..."

"Oh God!" Tilly sighed loudly.

"Symbolism." Helen glanced at Tilly's puzzled expression. "OK. Look, runes as letters, if you like ... runes continued to be used in some circumstances long after we'd adopted the Roman alphabet and often developed with a mixture of Roman letters and runes, mainly because they wanted to represent sounds in their language of use that weren't represented in the Roman alphabet . There's an early Anglo-Saxon variant from around the fifth to the twelfth centuries and I think we have an early example of this here. It's called the 'futhorc' or 'fuÞorc' if we use the Anglo – Saxon letter 'thorn'."

"Erm ..." Tilly frowned.

"Right." Viv bent to peer closely at the screen, one

hand protecting Ellie. "Tilly, here's the linguistic science bit ..."

"Oh God!" Tilly grimaced.

"... OK, I'll summarise. In the early Anglo-Saxon language, they used signs we don't use now to represent sounds that were important to them to distinguish. For example, they distinguished between the sounds of a hard 'th' as in 'those' and a soft 'th' as in 'thing'. For the hard 'th' they used the symbol 'eth' that looked like a barred 'd'. Here's one: 'ð', look. And for the soft 'th' they used a 'thorn' – like this one here, 'Þ'. See." She pointed at the symbols on the screen as Helen enlarged them further.

"Oh God, yes. Wow! Ooh, I could say those now!"

"Helen," Viv frowned. "I can recognise some of the Anglo-Saxon symbols here and I can see them clarified on screen here better than on the stone itself. Or even enlarged on my phone. This is much clearer. I know about the 'uu' rune, the one that looks like a sharp angled P and became our letter 'w'... here's one ... and of course the 'æ' diphthong ... um ... like this one here .... But yes, they do seem to be a mixture of the Anglo-Saxon symbols that I know and those early, rather primitive looking, signs scratched on the stone. Those are the ones I don't have a clue about. Like these strange distorted 'F's with the horizontal branches slanting up or down ...here ... and these like crosses ..."

"So, they do represent sounds 'f' and 'n' for example here, but also many of the symbols are also literally symbolic, and those ones are certainly. They represent things in the world known to the scribes – trees, cattle, wealth, kings, Gods. And this is why people associate them with magic signs and ancient curses. Especially as they aren't always clear. But look, these scratchings here are really worn in many places, as we would expect, although it looks as though there was some possibly deliberate but abortive attempt to scratch some of them out."

"Like erasing the words?" Tilly peered closer to the screen.

"Yes, exactly. Like using an eraser or tippex corrector on paper. That makes it more complicated because some runes are very alike, so if we lose one stroke of the chisel, it could mean something quite different. I'm afraid that runology is not an exact science."

"Which parts are indistinct then?"

"Here," Helen indicated with her marker. "Basically, it's saying it's a memorial to this person named here." She selected the symbols and enlarged them. "This could be a 'feoh' or a 'thorn' so it could be what we might think of as a soft 'th' or an F that represents the 'F' sound and also symbolises wealth, cattle, or it could be an F 'ōs' rune that symbolises a God. Either way it signifies someone high-born, a royal personage, wealthy and respected much like a God."

"Wow!" Tilly gasped.

"The thing is, the name as spoken would have been

something like 'fifia' or 'thithia' or 'thithiaen' with a soft 'th' and it appears to be feminine."

Viv gasped. "Say that again!"

"I said 'thithiaen'." Helen frowned.

"Vivianne!"

Helen looked at Viv. "Does that mean something to you?"

"Goodness, yes!" She glanced at Tilly who cocked her head to one side and raised her eyebrows knowingly.

Helen nodded. "Interestingly, the same name is woven through the script as well." She clicked to the top and the screen changed to one that again showed the rune script but this one with certain runes highlighted in red scattered through it."

"Oh, my goodness! That's what Cynewulf did with one of his poems in the 7th century!" Viv said shaking her head. "So there's a precedence a century or so before ... at least, if this *is* Lady Vivianne."

Helen narrowed her eyes in query but continued. "Um, this also emphasises the importance of the named person or claimed authorship or maybe requested prayers for their soul. And of course, that could correspond to the figure, if we are right in thinking it represents a woman. And if the runes were carved at the same time as the figure. Although rune stones were more usually raised for men and by men, so this is a strange one." She paused.

"Raised for a woman?"

"Hmm. And also they were usually for dead men as a memorial, but this one ... basically it suggests something raised as a 'praise' to this person rather than necessarily a post-mortem memorial or commemoration of an important life. And of course, we can't automatically assume that it was a headstone for a burial. But this one, it's not something I've seen before. Interesting. So, all in all, I'd prefer to call it a Rune Stone rather than a 'Cross', although there are Christian elements too."

"Gosh, my mind is whirling!" Viv straightened up and rubbed her back. "I wonder if ... oh, wait a minute. Didn't you take a sample of pigment as well?"

"Yes, indeed I did, and this is another interesting finding. There is an indication, as you thought, Viv, of a painted figure beneath the warrior carving that's visible on the surface. I found traces of fairly rare, luxury pigments, purple, red vermilion - a bit like gold today. It would have been imported and therefore expensive and reserved for especially important people at this time ..."

"What time are we talking about?"

"We could analyse the pigments with our electron microscope. These have an interesting chemical composition and probably date to something like the early Anglo-Saxon period, the late fifth or early sixth century AD."

"Well, that fits what I'm thinking." Viv felt a rush of heat suffuse her body, and her hands felt clammy.

"This really is exciting." She could sense Tilly looking at her quizzically. She wouldn't tell Helen about her time-slips to that time. But Tilly knew and she touched Viv's arm in recognition.

"Of course, it may have been the pigment of kings and the Gods, but it was rather dangerous to use because of the mercury content."

"Ooh, I remember something about that!" exclaimed Tilly "Oh, was it the Romans, maybe it was at Pompeii, I can't quite ...but yes, the artist making the murals snuffed it, didn't he ... he died ... oh, what am I thinking about?" She nudged Viv.

But Viv was deep in thought, trying to put all these findings together in some sort of logical interpretation. Hmm, better to focus on Helen's work and think later.

She twisted round to Helen. "So, what would the painting underneath have been, then?"

"Well, I don't like to surmise, Viv. I'm really only interested in the concrete physical evidence."

Viv detected the hesitation in Helen's voice and maybe a frisson of excitement. "But if I pressed you to surmise, to put together a possible theory?"

"Well," Helen began slowly. "Putting it all together, my guess – and it's only a wild romantic guess at the moment before I do more analysis, you understand, so don't quote me – is that because of the positioning of the pigment traces, the painting could be of the same person as the later carved figure, the woman, the female warrior. But ... do the runes possibly date from the same time as the painting, around the turn of the sixth century? Or the same time as the figure carving on the surface? Maybe the carving of the warrior that we can see is the memorial some couple of centuries later after her death, when for some reason they wanted to represent this legendary figure as on a par with Aethelbold."

"God, so she was quite something then," said Tilly. "A top broad!"

"Seems like it. But that's all I've got at the moment. More work to be done on it all, especially in a couple of major areas. I'll let you know when I have anything else." Helen stood and clicked off the screen. Clearly that was the end of their session.

"Very exciting and food for thought." Viv straightened up and adjusted Ellie's position, "That's wonderful, more than enough for me. Hmm, a Rune Stone rather than a 'Cross'. Interesting. Thank you so much, Helen. We must treat you to a special meal out."

"Oh, it's my pleasure. What a find. In principle, I'm happy to contribute to your filming, Tilly, but we do need that Zoom meeting to look at some of the detail."

Tilly grinned and scrabbled in her copious hobo bag for her card. "There's my email. And thanks. We'll talk soon. Or should I say, my people will talk to your people? Ha ha!"

Helen stared at her with a puzzled frown. "Um. Yes. OK. Hopefully, we can work together. Maybe in return for a contribution to the lab's work?"

"I think we can manage that. And thanks from me too."

"Well. We'll let you get on. I think little Ellie's beginning to stir." Viv turned to go.

They were opening the door when Helen called out. "Oh, just one more thing ..."

"You sound like Columbo!" Tilly laughed.

Viv turned back. Helen looked even more confused. "It's OK. Don't worry about it."

Helen nodded sharply. "I was just going to say ... One more thing about the runes ... there's a bit at the end I'm struggling to make out. You know I said many centuries ago they could have been used as – or interpreted as – magical signs? Well, there's one bit that indicates a message, a warning ... to anyone damaging or interfering with the Stone."

Tilly turned to Viv and her eyes were wide. "What do you mean, like a curse?"

"Oh, I don't believe in curses," said Helen sharply. "Not through all this time, through all these centuries. This isn't some American horror movie on Netflix."

CHAPTER 10

VIV

Derbyshire. Present day

"*O*h my God!" shrieked Tilly as Viv pulled up outside the rectory and lifted a grizzling, obviously hungry, Ellie out of her baby seat in the back. She helped Viv to close the doors and tickled Ellie's head. "That's a great thing for television. Although a little frightening at the same time. But ... wow ... a curse!"

"No, Helen didn't say it was a curse ..."

"A curse?" Rory emerged from the rectory doorway and took Ellie from Viv's arms. The baby immediately stopped grizzling and beamed at Rory, reaching out her hands to his clerical collar and patting it. He smiled at her, but he looked flustered. "What's all this about a curse?"

"Oh, nothing, really, just something that Helen

couldn't interpret in the runic inscription on the cross."
Viv glared at Tilly. At this rate Rory would cancel the
whole thing and she really did want to know more
from Helen's further research. "Oh, and we need to call
it a Rune Stone now."

Rory pulled at his clerical collar and Viv thought
he looked flushed.

"Did you have a good Wednesday service? Was
everything OK?" she asked as they crossed the gravel
drive.

"Hmm. Well, fine until ..."

"Rory, is that lipstick on your face? Ooh, it is! And
it's not Viv's!" Tilly gasped. She peered more closely at
Rory and he stepped back. "Good God, it's not that tart
Sadie Smythe again, is it? Sexy Sadie?"

Viv scanned his face. Yes, a definite lipstick mark
on his mouth. Hot pink. Definitely *not* hers. "Oh Lord.
Rory? What happened?" She reached out and rubbed
it off with her finger.

"Sadie Smythe!" Tilly guffawed and looked across
at Viv with a 'told you so' expression. "Ha! You know,
even her name sounds like something out of a Jilly
Cooper novel!" Tilly winked at Ellie who giggled
delightedly, waved her little hands in the air and
reached out wildly across Rory's shoulder towards
Tilly's hair.

Rory smiled ruefully. "She ambushed me in the
church porch when I thought everyone had left. That

woman is ..." He took a deep breath, "well, a bit of a menace."

Viv remembered what Tilly had said before. Images flashed now across her mind of Sadie on Sundays standing far too close to Rory at the church door, holding onto his hand far too long to whisper her thanks for the service. Maybe Tilly was right about her. An image of Sadie leaning over him with her cleavage on display in her far too tight and low-cut top, as he tried to kneel with the 'tiny tots' in the kids' club area at the back of the church. Sadie, whom nobody seemed to know at church before Rory arrived. Sadie whom nobody seemed to know at all. Who diverted every question about where she came from or what she did for a job. Even to the village's most persistent busy-bodies. Yet she clearly wasn't shy. Hiding something sinister? Should she feel annoyed with her or sorry for her? No, annoyed that she was making everyone uncomfortable. Yes, Tilly was right all along.

"You need to tell her straight. Honestly, Rory, this is a bit ridiculous."

"I know." He sighed.

"Well, if you *have* to be such a gorgeous priest ... what can you expect?" Tilly giggled, setting Ellie off chuckling again. "I speak as a friend, of course!"

"I'm afraid that I may have made it worse." Rory grimaced. "I did kind of tell her to get on her bike. Or words to that effect, anyway."

"Right. Well, hopefully that'll stop her." Viv

snorted, knowing that Rory's words would have been much milder than that. "I mean, she isn't really even a church goer. Well, at least she wasn't until you came along and then suddenly she's at every possible service and grovelling around you to be on the PCC and God knows what. And she won't do anything like the flower rota because she knows you won't be around when she does it. Welcoming new members of the congregation is one thing, Rory, but it's so obvious she's only interested in one thing, *you*."

"I can't stop her coming to church, Viv, and I wouldn't want to. I had to encourage her to ..."

"Well, not that way and not that much! There *are* limits. I'm not saying you encouraged her to behave like that – obviously – but it looks as though she's taken your patience as a green light. It's gone too far. The woman has to be told. For goodness sake, Rory! You're quite right to tell her to take a hike! She's a nuisance. Always hovering around you."

"I know. But don't get worked up about it. I just ... I guess I feel a bit sorry for her. And I didn't want to, you know, put her down. I know this is a bit of amateur psychology but I think maybe she's had too much rejection in her life already."

"Um." Viv grimaced. "There's not much you can do other than reject her, though, Rory, can you? I mean, you're not exactly available, are you, so what else could you do?"

Tilly laughed. "You could always have an affair

with her!" She was enjoying this far too much. Viv glared at her. "OK, OK. Just joking! And I must be going now. Off out tonight. New boyfriend. Well, date anyway. And maybe a sleep-over. Who knows? May get lucky this time. Eh, sweetie-pie, what d'you say?" Tilly tickled Ellie's cheek over Rory's shoulder and was rewarded with a gurgling giggle.

"And we must feed this starving 'sweetie-pie'." Viv air kissed in the vicinity of Tilly's cheek and Rory waved, as Tilly scurried across the gravel to her car, tooting the horn as she swerved around and roared off down the drive.

"So, tell me all about what you discovered from Helen at the lab," said Rory as they grabbed a quick lunch at the breakfast bar in the rectory kitchen.

"Quite a lot, actually. For starters, the Saxon cross isn't entirely Saxon. It looks as though the original stone was a memorial to ... well, some – probably – female ruler in the sixth century, so very early ... Lady Vivianne maybe? We know that the Cooney's Mere settlement under her was at the end of the fifth century into the sixth, and that it was not a Saxon settlement at all then but Romano-Brython, although we don't know whether it ended up being invaded by the Angles or Saxons later on."

The doorbell rang: a loud insistent ringing as

though someone was just standing there on the rectory doorstep with their finger pressing the bell angrily again and again. Viv went to the window that overlooked the front doorstep and peered out.

"Oh God, it's Sadie Smythe."

"Oh dear," said Rory, looking sheepish and flushed – looking guilty.

"What? What's the matter?"

"I ... er... when I told Sadie effectively to get on her bike, I also said ... but if you ever wanted to talk to me as a priest, that's fine." He glanced at Viv's expression. "Viv, I felt guilty for making her feel bad – I didn't want that. But I thought she'd understand that I meant counselling, not anything of a personal relationship."

"Oh *really*, Rory! Look, take her into your business office then, while I clear up the lunch things."

"No! Yikes. I think it'd be better if you were there. Oh goodness, I don't know what I was thinking!" He raked his fingers through his hair and grimaced. "It was just like saying, you know, we'll have coffee sometime when you know you never will. I never thought she'd come round to the rectory the same afternoon."

"Well, *honestly*, Rory! You'd better open the door to her. She'll know we're in because the cars are there in the drive."

"Couldn't we just hide behind the sofa?" Rory grinned, took a deep breath and made for the hall. He opened the front door, a little hesitantly Viv noticed as she followed him through. Sadie was standing on the doorstep in full make-up, long blonde hair gleaming, slim white trousers, a tight low-cut top, vertiginous heels. The whole show. Very glamorous. She glanced at Viv who was hovering behind Rory and frowned, her mouth set in a straight line, then she looked at Rory and her expression softened into a pouting smile. Viv wondered if she'd had botox or just a very clever lipstick.

"Hi Rory, I have tried to …"

"Oh, Sadie?" Viv exclaimed innocently, peering around Rory. "Have you got a problem? Already? Rory, I can hear our daughter waking. Shall I go and fetch her down or will you, *sweetheart*?"

Rory turned and raised his eyebrows at her. She never called him 'sweetheart', not in that exaggerated fashion.

"Er …" He was flushed with embarrassment and bewilderment. At that moment, the landline phone rang.

"A rector's business is never done!" said Viv with forced bonhomie. "Look, you take Sadie into the drawing room then, rather than the office, and I'll bring a pot of tea for us all when I've answered the phone. Actually, Ellie's stopped crying so we've got a few minutes. Leave the door open, please, darling, so that I can bring the tea tray in."

Rory gestured Sadie into the hallway and through to the drawing room with a rueful smile at Viv as she picked up the phone. It was the lead bell-ringer wanting to ask Rory his advice. She laid the receiver down on hall table although it was cordless and she could easily have taken it in to Rory. Viv went into the drawing room and saw them standing together by the French windows. Sadie was tossing her long blonde hair and reaching out to touch his arm. Viv had the distinct impression that he was trying to step back except that the old oak bureau was in the way.

"Darling, it's Chris about the bell changes. And he says that Bill's also been trying to get hold of you about Sunday's hymns, but your mobile's been off."

"Yes, it was!" Sadie fluttered. "I tried to say, I've been trying to ring you for the past hour!"

"Well, that's probably why he switched it off."

Rory grimaced and escaped into the hall.

"So, Sadie, what exactly did you want from my husband that you didn't already ask him after service this morning?"

Sadie glared and Viv saw the spite in her eyes. "It's confidential."

"Ah. Well, you know there's nothing confidential between a man and his wife, even when he's a rector. It's not a confessional."

"I just wanted to ..."

"Look, I do know what you're doing. But my husband is, as you can see, terribly busy with church business, as always. And he does have a private life too. He's not always available at the drop of a hat for everyone that knocks on the door. I'm afraid that I have to be a bit of a gate-keeper. Could I suggest that in future you make an appointment before you come to the rectory, as everyone else does. It would save you a wasted journey." She mentally crossed her fingers, as she knew this wasn't strictly true. He had a fairly open-door policy, although most people did have the courtesy to call first.

"But this is a personal matter. Between me and Rory."

"Personal? Between you and Reverend Netherbridge? Whatever could that be, Sadie?"

"Rory and me ... we are very close and we ..."

"Sadie, I'm sorry. I don't know what you imagine is going on here, but I can assure you that my husband has no *personal* interest in you in *that* way, only as one of his many parishioners. Look," Viv lowered her voice and softened it to sound like a concerned friend, "I know he's a good looking man and it's his job to be empathetic and sometimes girls can imagine that they're ... well, *closer* to him than is the case, that he might actually ..." she laughed, "*fancy* them! But I can assure you that this is never the case."

"Oh, you make it sound so *sordid*!" Sadie flashed; eyes narrowed. "I know you're his wife, but I think you need to know that he ... we ... have something ..."

"Sadie, I'm sorry to burst your bubble, but you really must stop this. It's a fantasy. Please get help or something. And not from my husband. You need counselling maybe?"

Sadie's cheeks turned puce and her eyes black with fury. She hissed through clenched teeth. "How dare you. I don't need counselling, you... you bitch. There's nothing wrong with me. And actually ..." she pulled back her shoulders and thrust out her chest, "you need to know that Rory's *seeing* me behind your back ..."

"No, Sadie, I'm sorry but I'm not *seeing* anyone other than my wife, and you know that!" Rory was standing in the doorway, a startled look on his face. At that moment, Ellie began to cry again.

"So," Viv said firmly, "if you've no actual church business or an emergency, then please leave us alone."

Sadie began to march into the hall, brushing past Rory, who smartly stepped aside, then she stopped and turned on Viv.

"Just you wait. You think you've got it all, don't you? Well, it'll all come tumbling down around your perfect smug little ears. You'll see!"

She pushed past Rory and rushed out, slamming the front door behind her.

"My God," Rory exclaimed. Viv raised her eyebrows. He never used the divinity's name in that way. "Was that some kind of curse?"

"Well, I hope not." Viv tried to laugh lightly but her heart was thrumming loudly in her chest. "Was it something I said?"

CHAPTER 11

LADY VIVIANNE

Cūning's Mere 520 AD

*T*he darkening clouds felt heavy on Lady Vivianne's shoulders as she returned to the mead hall and her chamber, and a sense of doom filled her heart. She had a strange feeling of a cursing pressing down upon her head. Was it Aldwyn's curse? She remembered the look in his eyes and bit her lip at the thought of his unspoken threat that had hung in the air between him and Sir Roland, and that spelled itself out as he had looked upon Nymue. She shuddered as she reached home.

But she saw with relief a group of ceorls approaching along the dust road, and Tristram in their midst. She steeled herself and signalled to them to follow her through the mead hall. At her antechamber doorway she nodded her thanks to the ceorls and led Tristram within.

Lady Vivianne took a deep breath and frowned at her young son, standing awkwardly before her in her chamber as she sat heavily.

"What do you think you were doing? Running away like that?"

Tristram hung his head and mumbled, "I wanted to join my father. I wanted to fight the Angeln. I want to be a battle thegn."

His face was so flushed and his chin trembling so much that it was not hard for Vivianne to quell her anger and her fears. She reached out her hand to him.

"Oh, Tristram, my little man, my little thegn, I know you long to be grown up, but you are not yet ready. Come." He moved to her and she held him in her arms. "You must wait a little. And please to remember how frightened you made your poor mother."

"I only got a short way down the road." He looked up at her through his long still babyish eyelashes, even at ten years. "I am sorry, mōđor. I did not think." She thought she saw wetness on his lashes.

"Well." She patted his hot sweaty back. "Just remember that when next you are tempted to do such a silly thing." She sighed and straightened her back, holding him away from her body. "And, more importantly, remember also that your actions have taken my ceorls away from their work to look for you and bring you back. Do not forget that. Think always about whether your actions will affect others. That is a really important lesson for you to learn, my son. Hmm?"

"Yes, I know, mōđor."

She could not help but smile fondly at him. He had not yet grown into the belligerence of his older sister, thank the Lord. She guessed that would come soon enough, but for now he was quite amenable and still had that childish fear of her disapproval. That would change in time. "Now go back to your training tutor and apologise. You should be good at apologising by now. You seem to be making a habit of it these days."

In the corner of her eye she saw that Matilda was at the doorway, grinning ruefully, waiting to take Tristram off to his tutor, and she smiled at her with a shake of her head.

If only Nymue was so pliable. She was keeping to her chamber and Vivianne could hear her sobbing at night. She tried to comfort her, although she hated the idea of comforting her daughter for the loss, albeit temporary, of such a man as Aldwyn. Even thinking of him, let alone thinking of him with any attachment to Nymue, made her nauseous. During the day, Nymue found every excuse to avoid Vivianne, knowing her deep disapproval of her infatuation with Aldwyn.

AND SO THE DAYS PASSED SLOWLY, DESPITE LADY Vivianne's many duties and cares which helped to keep her mind distracted. Sir Roland and the thegns had not returned before the Hunters' Moon and she was desperate for the news which never came. She knew that they must have ridden far, for many moons, but she had never journeyed that distance south, and knew nothing of the wildness of the south, except from the tales the messengers brought back. Every time she heard the sound of a rider she ran outside to see if it was a messenger come to tell her of Roland's progress, his victory, or even whether he had by now joined her forces with the Deorabye tribe to the south, whether they had ridden to meet the Angeln, whether battle had been joined. Whether they were alive or dead.

Why was there no word? Every day she prayed for their safety, for some word. As she closed her eyes at her prie-dieu each morning she knew in her heart that she was becoming more and more resigned to whatever happened. More and more understanding that she could do nothing but wait. She could not alter whatever may befall. She could not send further men out in to danger to seek the truth, not with the increasing number of raids not far away to the south of Cūning's Mere. She could not lose any more of her people. She hoped that she had not lost any already. She prayed that she had not lost Roland.

She felt as though they were living on an island. She felt trapped – no, imprisoned. If only she could ride out herself, even into danger, to find her battle thegns, her husband, to see for herself that they were safe. Yet her first duty was to her people, here at Cūning's Mere, the people who relied on her for everything. She was their queen, the mother to them all, and she could not abandon her children with danger all around. She must keep them all safe and at peace.

Her daily councils with ealdorman Godwyne, her elderly advisor, white haired and bent of body, were of some comfort, if only as a confirmation of her own decisions. But still she constantly felt anxious, waves of fear sweeping over her and a sense of doom resting heavily upon her head. She wondered if Godwyne was telling her the whole truth of their situation or keeping something back so as not to worry her unduly.

The weather had turned, and the rains and cold winds had come with the Hunters' Moon. At first it was a welcome drenching for the crops after the intermittent rains of the equinox, but as it continued and became more torrential each day that passed, she knew that the field geburs were becoming anxious. But Godwyne seemed to make light of it all, telling her often that "it would all come good in the end, never fear." But she did fear.

Finally, Acton, the ceorl who supervised the geburs in the arable fields, spoke quietly to Vivianne in the mead hall on the fourteenth day of continuous heavy rain and unusually bitter winds. She had been about to return to her chamber and the accounting book. Godwyne was still at her side after their council and he paused and turned, his old wrinkled eyes raised.

"My lady, my lord," Acton bowed. "I wonder if I might speak to you a moment?"

"Of course." Lady Vivianne turned to give her full attention to him. She saw that Acton's old eyes mirrored Godwyne's and betrayed his concern. "Acton, you have served us well for many years and we have been most pleased with your work, the way that you have organised the crops and the geburs. Your loyalty and conscientiousness are acknowledged. What can I do for you?"

Acton sighed and fiddled with a scroll clutched in his hands. "My lady, I hate to add to your concerns at this time. I am aware of how difficult it is with the thegns away and fewer hands to work and direct. But with the cold and the rain, many of our late crops are ruined. I must warn you that the harvest stores will be thin. Many of our roots are washed away or rotted, the carrots, parsnips, and turnips. We have the early harvest - although it was not as plentiful as in past years. We have the wheat and oats in storage from before, but they will not last long if we have need to rely on them before this winter and then we will have no reserves of food. I know too, from the herdsmen, that the animals have suffered for lack of grazing, so the meat will be scarce. They talk of a shortage of salt so preserving the meat we do have will become more difficult as the days go by." He shook his head. "Also, the hunters and trappers on the uplands have brought home little because the wild creatures are suffering too. Whatever they have caught, the wild deer and boar are so thin and scraggy the hunter geburs have barely enough for their own use. There is some fish in the river, but the salmon, trout and oysters only feed their own families." He took a deep breath. "So ...there is little for the markets."

"Ah, I see. I thank you for being so forthright with me. I do need to know the truth and you are wise to tell me." She glanced sideways at Godwyne. "I must know, however hard, however dire, otherwise how can I act in our best interests? Very well. So we must be diligent and careful with the stocks we have currently?"

"Yes indeed, my lady. The bread will be scarce shortly. Would you consider a ration so that all can have a share?"

Vivianne paused for a few moments in thought. "I think that is the only course of action we can take. Everyone must share the depleted resources we hold. Have you drawn up a schedule for sharing?"

Acton held out the scroll and offered it to her. His thin wrinkled hands were shaking. Godwyne stepped forward to peer at the scroll alongside Vivianne.

"Thank you." Vivianne unrolled the document and scanned her eyes over it. Experienced as she was in quantities and proportions needed, she blanched at what she read. She heard Godwyne's intake of breath beside her. "This is bad news indeed. Are you sure this is accurate?" Acton threw her a glance that was startled and disturbed. She shook her head and drew in her breath. "I am sorry. I did not intend to question your competency, Acton. I mean that I am shocked. I knew that there were problems, but this does not augur well for this coming winter."

Godwyne grunted. "Thank God that we moved further over to grazing from arable land use."

"Yes, indeed," Vivianne agreed. "At least we have our meat."

"But as I mentioned, my lady, the animals are suffering shortage of fodder too," Acton reminded her.

"Of course. So you said. Perhaps Gareth Swineson or one of the herdsman geburs can attend an audience with me to tell me their present accounting situation. And Godwyne, even though we have more grazing now than arable, we still need crops, our cereals for the bread and ale, vegetables for the table so that our villagers do not get the sickness."

"My lady, I am wondering ..." Acton frowned. "I apologise if I am being forward or speaking out of turn ... but I am wondering whether we could perhaps manage our food systems more efficiently at this difficult time, with your gracious permission?"

"What are you thinking, Acton?"

"My lady, do you think ... could Gareth Swineson become the chief herdsman for all the pigs, cattle, sheep and fowl? He is an accomplished swineherd and our stocks in the sties have been thriving under his sight. His pigs are doing better than the other herds with his husbandry. His father, as you know, my lady, is becoming too old, infirm and blind to cope as are some of the livestock geburs and, frankly, many of the other chiefs. A number of the geburs left in the fields are struggling with age and weakness of limb. But Gareth has been a stalwart worker, often spending more than his working day helping the others."

"I see."

"My lady, I am thinking that if he could take charge of all the grazing lands whilst I do my task of looking after the arable, the two of us could work more efficiently together in order to make a new balance of available food stocks."

Vivianne frowned. Reports she had received of Gareth's work at the sties had all been excellent. And he appeared to work well with all the other geburs, gaining their trust. "Gareth has the respect of the field workers? If I were to make him their chief, he must be able to command respect. And he is still young."

"I beg your pardon, my lady, but he is a little older than your dear daughter Nymue."

"Yes, of course. I forget how they grow." She glanced at Godwyne who, almost imperceptibly to anyone other than Vivianne, nodded his approval. "If you think that this is wise, then I will be guided by you. I trust your judgement and of course you know his work much better than I. So, I will grant Gareth chief of all the herdsmen. You may see to that at once, Acton. But of course he is gebur. I will retire to give thought to how to give him the status of ceorl if he is to be the chief herdsman. It is a considerable and responsible work."

"Thank you, my lady."

Vivianne inclined her head and thanking both Acton and Godwyne, dismissed them both and swept out to her chamber. This was the right thing to do. From what little she knew of Gareth, she was sure that he would repay her faith in him, and she trusted Acton's opinion. He had never been wrong before.

But when she returned to her room in private, she sank onto the stool by the fireside and fought back the tears. Problem after problem. What would become of them? Was she strong enough to hold this settlement together without the support of her dear Sir Roland and of course the other thegns who all played their part? Of course, she had Godwyne but that was not the same. He was old and she had never been so keenly aware that she was a woman. And women had weaknesses that men did not have. Her hand strayed to her belly. She had always felt strong enough for her role, and in her heart she was still as strong as any man, but in these dark days she wondered if she was in fact too weak and feeble in body. She closed her eyes and prayed for strength and resolve in the face of what was to come.

❀

EARLY ONE MORNING, A FEW SUNRISES LATER AND MANY sunrises since the battle thegns had left and Vivianne had ceased counting, she was so distracted that she did not hear Afera's words until she had repeated them. She became aware of her maid tugging and mumbling as she dressed her, pulling her light blue kirtle over her head and smoothing it down to skim the little bump of her abdomen.

"My lady, I am asking you which overgown you want today?" Afera was fiddling impatiently with the folds of the soft kirtle. "I laid out the burgundy you like so much but then I remembered it was your Saint's day and wondered if you want the dark blue for your Saint?"

"I am sorry. I am in a dream world! Yes, goodness, of course it is. Well done for remembering, Afera." Vivianne sighed. "I have so much on my mind at present. Yes, my dark blue would be appropriate today, although I do not feel like celebrating, I must admit."

"Well. I will fetch your dark blue from the chest, my lady." Afera's tone had an edge to it.

"Oh dear, Afera." Vivianne chose to ignore it. "I am so distracted." She looked to the door of the chamber, but her eyes were seeing far far away and she murmured to herself. "How long has it been since they left? And still we have heard nothing." Was that good news, then, or bad? Her fingers clutched at the fabric of the kirtle and crumpled it into ridged creases.

"Oh, my lady! Please! You are spoiling the fall of the cloth!" Afera grumbled as she bustled in from the ante chamber, the dark blue overgown, fresh from the chest, carefully draped across her arms. She laid it on the bed and turned to her mistress, smoothing the kirtle, tugging out the creases with something less than gentleness.

Vivianne smiled but raised her eyebrows and drew in her breath sharply. "Thank you, Afera. I am ready for my overgown and all the rest now. I will stand still and patiently and not move a muscle!" She held up her arms for Afera to slip the overgown over her head and drape the over-mantle across her shoulders.

With fixed lips hardened in a straight line, Afera brought the wooden board and held it out for her lady to choose the mantle brooch. Vivianne picked up the large gold piece that was decorated with the curled white dragon of her family and Afera fixed it in place. She gestured to Vivianne to hold up her arms again a little so that she could slip the leather girdle-belt around her thickening waist and loop it through the buckle and back around its length to fall at the front.

Afera paused and stood back, checking her handiwork, just as Matilda used to do. The belt was becoming tight. She would need to ask the leather worker to make a new longer one soon.

"My pouch?" Vivianne prompted.

"Yes ... my lady. I do know. Matilda taught me well."
She reached for the tooled leather pocket and hung it
from the girdle.

Afera moved behind her and dragged the harsh
bone-comb without mercy through Vivianne's long
hair that reached to her hips. She winced.

"Matilda will also have taught you that I like a
gentle touch on my hair. What is the matter with you
today?"

Her maid paused and Vivianne felt relief as the
comb ceased to rake her scalp.

"I am just trying to hurry this morning."

"Why?"

Afera resumed her combing and Vivianne could see,
as she glanced sideways at her reflection in the precious
glass propped on the table, that her maid began to hold
each hank of her curly flowing locks carefully as she
teased the comb through – as she had been taught to do.
The daylight was only just beginning to penetrate the
room and Vivianne smiled with satisfaction that her
hair shone bronze-red in the flare of the flames lit in the
wall sconces on either side of the hearth. Even now, after
four children her hair was not yet losing its rich colour.

"Hmm?" she prompted again.

"Well. I thought perhaps I might be able to get up
to the swine field before Gareth has to take ..."

"I see," Vivianne interrupted her. "That is assuming
you have completed your duties here, is it not?"

Afera's fingers stilled. "Of course, my lady."

"And you still have to arrange my hair and my head rail and veil, and help Matilda with the food to break the fast." Vivianne turned slightly towards her maid and smiled. "I do not wish to deter young love but complete your duties properly and *then* you can go to your lover. I was under the impression that was our arrangement. But of course, if you wish to amend that contract, then we can discuss it?"

Afera resumed her task and began to scoop Lady Vivianne's hair up to pin under her veil and fillet. "No, I am happy enough with my position here with you, my lady."

"You are treated well, surely?"

"She most certainly is, my lady," came Matilda's voice from the doorway. She ushered the children in bearing baskets of food, jugs of watered ale and wooden bowls. They laid them on the little table by the hearth fire. She glanced up at Afera. "You would not want to be like your sisters I am sure of it, sweltering in the heat of the furnace at the metal worker's hut, would you?" Afera shook her head. "You become more like Guin every day and look what happened to her! Ungrateful wretch! I apologise for her, my lady. She has much to learn!"

"Ah well. Nothing is spoiled. Afera, please to go to the bakery for the fresh spelt bread, and then you can take yours up to the swine fields. And see that we do not take more than the share. Small loaves, if you please. We will manage."

Matilda clucked at her young apprentice and gestured her away impatiently. "Do as my lady says." She pulled a handful of purple thyme from one of the baskets and laid it in the fire amidst the pine logs, before turning to lift the wooden boards away from the window openings, letting the weak light filter in.

Vivianne breathed in the comforting aroma of wood smoke tinged with the sweetness of the thyme and sat on her stool at the hearth.

"My lady, I have laid out for you some honey from the hives – thank goodness the bees are still providing – with the cold meats left over from the meal last night, and fresh hedgerow berries, as you requested. There is even a little butter from the dairy. Here, Young Tristram, Launce and little Nini, come to the fire and break your fast with your dear mōđor. Afera will be back shortly with the warm bread from the ovens."

"Thank you, Tilda. And Nymue?"

Matilda shook her head and her plump cheeks wobbled. "Still sulking in her chamber, I fear. I have taken her food through, but she says she will never eat again." She gave Vivianne a wink. She gave the children their bowls and poured each some of the weak ale.

But she nearly dropped the flagon as they all heard the commotion outside the doorway. "What on God's earth is that? Not Afera being stupid again, surely?

That girl!" She straightened her back with a sigh and made for the door. "Hopefully she has brought the bread with her from the bakery."

"Come, children, eat. It is long since time you broke your fast and ... Tilda! What is the matter?"

Matilda rushed back inside, white faced. She clutched the door lintel and gasped for breath. "Oh, my lady! It is our guard just ridden in with news of a messenger come from Wermunds Low ..."

Vivianne looked up from the roasted chicken leg she was nibbling. "To the east?"

"Yes." She struggled to control her breathing to a steady pace. "He says that the messenger rode for two sunrises to our border and that he brings news ... my lady, I did not want him intruding on you at your breaking fast ... but should he come in?"

"Yes, yes," snapped Vivianne, standing and smoothing her gown as she approached the doorway. The guard appeared at the entrance, red-faced and wet from the rain and the sweat, his boots muddy and torn.

"I am ..."

"Yes, I know who you are, Cerdic the Guard from our eastern border. What news have you brought me?" Hopefully news from Roland ... but why would that come from the eastern border? Matilda was hovering beside her. She signalled to her to return to the children by the hearth in order to distract them.

"Lady Vivianne, I am sent to tell you that Wermunds Low has suffered raids in the past five nights. The raiders are fighting men from the Angeln pushing in from the eastern coast, but they have not joined battle, but raided the stocks and the crops in the fields under cover of darkness. They must be camped somewhere further east."

"Is anyone killed?"

"One of the sheep-men who was in the fields with his flock, but the alarm was raised, and they were driven back. But they have stolen or destroyed many of the crops, as if there were not already a short supply and worse to come with this weather. Wermunds sent a rider to our eastern guard post with the warning to be cautious for other raiding thegns that might be gathering forces."

"As if we did not have enough disasters," she muttered. "But thank you, Cerdic." She dipped into the pouch at her belt and drew out a small metal disc with deep cross-ways scouring. She did not break it but offered Cerdic the whole. "Here is coin for your efforts. Well done."

She dismissed him and turned to see the worried faces of Matilda and the children.

"Shortly I must gather the remaining thegns and ceorls so that we can make ready and have a plan if indeed there are raids on our depleted crops or animals. And Tilda ... bring Gareth Swineson to me with all haste. He has been chief herdsman for only a short time now, but I promised to think about his status. Whether he has to join a battle force ready to defend our settlement, may God forbid, or continues to command the herdsmen to make the food for our sustenance, he will be needed as a chief ceorl."

Matilda raised her eyebrows. "Indeed, my lady?"

Vivianne chose not to enter into a long explanation as her breathing felt harsh and her trembling hands clutched at her skirts. "And send to Acton the crop-ceorl and to all the other chiefs of the ceorls, and as soon as the children have broken their fast, I want them and all the remaining thegns who did not ride to battle, to join me in the mead hall for a general moot and a minor Witan council."

CHAPTER 12

LADY VIVIANNE

Cūning's Mere 520 AD

"We are gathered here in the Witan for a most important ceremony." Lady Vivianne had placed her children either side of her: Young Tristram with Nini on one side and Nymue with Launce on the other. Ealdorman Godwyne, her advisor and protector, the elder from the remaining thegns, was also on the top table on the dais and Acton at the far end to represent the chief ceorls. Gareth Swineson stood at the side, eyes to the rushes on the floor. The other chiefs of the ceorls and the other remaining thegns turned to each other with puzzled expressions and there was a general murmuring echoing around the mead hall.

She raised the Witan sword for quiet and the company bowed their heads then looked up at her expectantly. "My people, I asked you to be here to witness, as is customary, the granting of the status of ceorl and chief herdsman to Gareth Swineson. He will from now on take charge of all cattle, swine, sheep and fowl. My chief crop-ceorl, Acton, has spoken with all my geburs who look after the different grazing animals, and all are in agreement, and in fact welcome an overall guiding hand who can coordinate all the grazing lands. In these days of bad weather and hardship, we need to keep even greater care and management of our resources. Gareth is much respected by us and we have pleasure in granting him his own seax as the right of a free man."

Gareth stepped forward, with a shy smile and a bent head to hide his blushes. Vivianne placed the Witan sword back on the table before her and lifted the seax in both hands and offered it to him formally.

"Here is the sign of a free man. Use it wisely. And I have granted you the use of the house that is presently unoccupied and stands below the swine fields. Your father may choose either to stay in his hut in the fields or come down to live with you." She reached out and touched his shoulder.

"Thank you, my lady. I am honoured and ... and rather overcome!"

He looked up then and caught Nymue's eye. She blushed, shrugged her shoulders and looked away. Gareth turned back to the assembled chief ceorls and they raised their own seaxes in appreciation.

"And now," said Vivianne, relieved that there was no disagreement in the Witan. Acton had done his work well. "Now we must all work together. We have outlined to you the news from the eastern guards with regard to the raids on Wermunds Low, a day or so's ride to the east. These raids seem to be for food. All are hungry these days. We believe that there is no immediate cause for concern here at Cūning's Mere in terms of any prospect of a battle. Thank God, because we all know that we do not have the man-power to engage in battle now that so many of our thegns are away to the south."

There was a rumbling of murmurs at that but Vivianne raised her hand. "But we must stay vigilant and I am asking the border guards to reinforce their numbers and to double their watch. I want no creeping up to our settlement at night to raid the little food we have. We cannot afford to have our crops or animals stolen away. Our trading thegns will be out gathering information as well as making trade with our neighbours. But we are reduced in number, so we all have to play our part in watchfulness. Our metal and leather workers are busy making ringed jerkins for the battle thegns, but I have also directed them to provide more weaponry in case it is needed for our defence. Swords and seaxes."

There was nodding and a few raised seaxes as the assembly realised that this meant more coin for them and their families. Vivianne's eyes swept the hall again, pulling in their attention to her words for she was aware of how important the next message was to them all. "And finally, you are all aware now of the need to ration and share our resources from the fields. Acton has spoken to you about that. In these difficult times, it is even more important than usual that we pay regard to each other and see that everyone has enough. There will be nobody who goes without. *Nobody*. Not a single ceorl or gebur or serf. The rations must be strict. And if they are broken there will be consequences and we will all suffer. So, look to your neighbours. I do not want to hear of anyone taking more than his share. I have placed Acton in charge, and you all know he is fair and just." She paused and looked around her. "Are there any questions?"

Her eyes swept the hall. She could see the shuffling and unease amongst the gathering, but nobody looked rebellious. They were frightened, not angry. In her mind she silently crossed herself. She took a deep breath and squared her shoulders.

"We will protect our lands with every muscle and sinew. We will together do all we can to look after each other and to keep each other safe. I, as your queen, promise you that I will do all I can to keep us all safe and bring better times. Can you make the same promise?" She raised the Witan sword.

Before her in the mead hall ceorls raised their seaxes and thegns beat their spears against their shields in a clamour of agreement and respect. She closed her eyes and exhaled.

∾

"Mōðor, that was amazing!" Young Tristram held his arms wide and gaped. "It was just like when my father spoke in the Witan."

Vivianne smiled. "Well, I should hope so, since I am the queen ..."

"And he is not the anointed king. I know. Although he *is* the chief battle thegn. And that is almost the same."

She raised her shoulders and slowly shook her head. Little Nini was clinging to her skirts and Vivianne ruffled her dark curls. "Yes, indeed he is." But anyone vigilant would have caught the flicker across her eyes as she thought of Sir Roland away to battle. Where was he and was he safe? There was still as yet no news. Why had he not sent word even now?

A tentative clearing of the throat made her look towards the doorway. Nymue was standing there, tall and straight, her hand on Launce's shoulder. "Am I permitted to go to my own chamber now?" she asked with an impatient toss of her head.

"May I come with you?" asked Launce. Peering up at his big sister. "You said you would tell me a tale of thegns and heroes and dragons ..."

Vivianne inclined her head towards Nymue.

"Yes, I did promise you. And you may come with me. But you must leave me in peace without stamping your foot when I say so. Anyone who stamps their foot is a child who will not grow into a battle thegn."

Smiling at the same words she remembered speaking to Nymue as they waved the thegns off to battle, so long ago it seemed, Vivianne caught Nymue's eye and saw her blush.

"Thank you, Nymue, and you all, for supporting me in the moot Witan."

"Oh, I did not ... I mean, you are welcome." Nymue shuffled and took Launce's hand in hers. "Well then, come."

She has not yet quite forgiven me, Vivianne mused. Well, it will take time.

Nymue paused at the doorway and glanced back. "I ... I thought that Gareth Swineson looked ... I am glad that you made him ceorl." Vivianne puckered her eyes at her daughter's blush. "Oh. I mean that I hope perhaps now he will have so many duties that he will forget me."

"I think you may rest assured that he may have already, Nymue." Vivianne said as gently as she could. "Does he not have our maid Afera as his love now? She seems to think so."

Nymue frowned quizzically. "Oh."

Matilda stood aside for Nymue and Launce to leave and made her way to the fire to prod the flames into life again. "You tease her, my lady. But she perhaps has need of reminding at times that she is not the only one." She poked the iron into the pine logs, dropping a fresh sprig of purple thyme into them, and a comforting aroma drifted through the air towards Vivianne. "Where is that silly girl Afera to attend to this fire? Too busy drooling even more over Gareth now that he is made ceorl and has his own house, I will be bound. The sconces will need to be lit too, there has been so little light today, and now the day is drawing in."

Vivianne sat on the stool by the fire, so tired now after her efforts in the Witan. She gathered Nini to her lap and turned to Young Tristram who was fiddling with her queen's head rail that was lying on the bed where she had dropped it. "Tristram, please to go to find Afera, will you?"

"Yes, mōđor."

"I will stake my life on her being up in the field with Gareth, forgetting her duties again." Matilda grumbled, standing back from the fire, hands on her plump hips.

"I hope not." Vivianne snorted. "The skies are darkening."

Matilda gave a knowing look. "That is probably exactly what she hopes."

"Tilda, my stomach is sore and murmuring. Could you find me a draft of chamomile? I think that Afera put it in the box in the ante room." She winced and rubbed her abdomen. It was most likely the stresses of the day.

"Of course, my lady." Matilda threw an anxious glance at Vivianne and bustled out to the ante room.

"Mama," whispered Nini, wriggling off her lap and staring at her mother. "You are not ill, are you?"

"No, of course not, my little love. Do not fear. I am simply tired and ... and hungry I am sure."

"I am hungry too. Will Afera be coming soon with milk and cakes for us?"

"I am sure she will."

Matilda bustled back with a draft of chamomile in Vivianne's small cup for herbal infusions and handed it to her with a frown.

"Are you sure you will be well for tonight, my lady?"

"Of course, Tilda. It is but the child moving I am sure. He is giving me indigestion."

There was to be a meal in the mead hall that night as always after a Witan. These days it would be far from lavish, with the battle thegns away and the stores too low for a proper feast. But the remaining thegns would be there and many of the ceorls, and she had asked geburs too, who would usually be serving at the tables, to join for the eating. Only the serfs who were learning to wait on tables under the geburs, would attend them to serve the food and drink, and would eat their portion later. At least it would be a sharing. Vivianne knew that she herself would eat little.

"Tilda, please to take Nini with you and gather Launce from Nymue's chamber. Find Afera for the children's milk and cakes. Nymue and Young Tristram may join me at the meal in the mead hall. But now I have a private council with Godwyne."

CHAPTER 13

VIV

Derbyshire. Present day

"*J*'m off for a meeting with Michael. We're meeting across at the church. As my curate he needs to be in on this." Rory waved the email print-out in the air.

Viv looked up from her laptop. "I know. Thanks for forwarding it to me just now. I don't know what to think. The Bishop says the complaint is from one of our parishioners – well, the attachment suggests it is, although it's anonymous. To be honest, I suspect it's come from Sadie Smythe, frankly."

"I'm afraid of that too. I've spoken to as many as I could round the parish about the complaint, and of course the PCC, but I didn't have any indication of anyone being against the filming of the investigation of the Cross. Most people seemed to find it rather exciting. I was quite cheered by their responses." Rory ran his fingers through his hair. "But I haven't made any contact with Sadie – I daren't! Have you heard anything ... unofficially? You're in a better position than me to pick up anything on the rumour mill."

"No, nothing has gone round on the grapevine objecting to it. Not a word or rumour. Nothing round the village at all. But, no, I certainly haven't approached Sadie! It's all rather odd, don't you think?"

"Certainly the way the attached message is worded sounds like someone with a serious grudge." He peered at the print-out. "I mean 'the rector's arrogance' – goodness, that hurts, I hope I'm not arrogant – and 'be warned' ..."

"Horrible. Sounds just like Sadie. No, sorry, I know that's a horrid thing to say. But what did she say the other day when she came round here? 'Just you wait' and 'you'll see'. The tone is very much the same here in this email. Similar threats."

"Well, we don't know, we're only guessing. So I don't want to accuse anyone – Sadie or anyone else – unless we know for sure who the anonymous writer is. And frankly, Viv, I certainly don't want anything about the reasons we might suspect her emerging publicly!"

"God, no! Although ..." She reached out for his arm. "Rory, none of this is your fault, don't think that. If it *is* Sadie who's the unnamed writer of the threats, you have nothing to blame yourself for. It was *she* who was pestering *you*. There's no disgrace in that. You didn't encourage her, quite the opposite. Which of course may be the reason for this. But, on the other hand ... I know what you mean, some people might say there's no smoke without fire, or just wonder about what's going on. The village gossips would have a field day!"

"Exactly. But I will tell Michael about the problem we've had with Sadie, just so that he's in the picture. Under strict and absolute confidentiality. I need to have a quiet word with Bishop Jonathan as well ... just in case."

Viv sighed. "Well, this is the problem with having such a sexy priest ... and me being married to one!"

He grinned. "Yes, indeed."

"Hmm, very modest. I'll ask Tilly to hold fire on the planning for the filming, but I'll just say that we've received a complaint and are investigating."

Half an hour later, Viv clicked on Tilly's number saved in her contacts on her mobile. She briefly explained the bare bones of the dilemma about the email complaint. But Tilly, as always, had other ideas.

"Oh my God! Sweetie-pie! Hey, it isn't that Sexy Sadie person is it – after the divine Rory told her to get on her bike?"

Viv was nonplussed for a moment. "Oh, Tilly, we really don't know who sent it so ..."

"Ooh, OK. I get you! I'll keep schtum. But I guess it is. Rest assured, sweetie-pie, I won't whisper to a soul. I'll just tell the powers that be there was a negative reaction from some person in the village and we're on hold for a bit until it's sorted out. I won't even say it was an anonymous message. Er ... but wait a minute, couldn't you tell who it was from the email address?"

"No, sadly. Whoever it was used an address with no clues to a name and unless someone has had an email from that source before and knows who it is, we can't trace it. At least, not unless it was serious enough to involve the police. And of course we're not going to publicise it."

"God no! You don't want to frighten the villagers into thinking there's a mad person around threatening all and sundry. You know what people are like in little villages like this one."

Viv laughed. "No. Although I don't think it's quite that bad. But I take your meaning. We wouldn't want anything to escalate. And if it is Sadie it would only involve us, not anyone else."

"So you think it *is* Sadie taking revenge at Rory's rejection?"

"I'm not saying that, Tilly. We don't know. Just keeping everything low key until there's any reason for it not to be."

"Rightee ho! I get it. Mum's the word and all that. Listen. Gotta go – I'm due at a site in an hour and I haven't got my mascara on. And there is a very gorgeous producer there. Toodly-pip!"

Viv was trying to spoon a little pureed banana into Ellie's mouth when she heard Rory close the front door of the rectory and throw his keys onto the hall table. Ellie was twisting her head away from the baby food.

"Ellie, poppet, come on! You loved this when we tried yesterday." She scooped up the fruit from Ellie's chin that she'd spat out with a disgusted expression on her red face. "You're not coming down with something, are you?"

"She looks flushed," said Rory as he came into the kitchen. "Is she hot?"

"No, not really." Viv felt around her head and neck. "I think only the heat from getting angry about the banana."

"Annoying stuff, banana!"

"Well, clearly! Honestly, this weaning lark isn't all it's cracked up to be. Perhaps it's a bit too early yet. Just thought I'd try and see." Viv gave up and left Ellie to wriggle in the high chair and bang the spoon on the dish. "At least she's enjoying making a musical instrument out of it. Squelch, squelch, bang. Great game, hey, little madam!"

Ellie abruptly stopped her angry objections and laughed delightedly.

"So, what's the news?"

"I've invited Michael over for supper. I hope that's OK. He hasn't been round for a while."

"Of course! You know how much I like him. Quiet,

a bit nervous maybe, but steady. And he always seems so respectful."

"You mean he keeps calling you 'Dr'?"

Viv laughed. "Of course! It's good that *someone* sees me as something other than a vicar's wife and a mother of a baby."

"Hmm, sucking up to you!"

Viv ignored him. "I'll make his favourite chicken casserole. I've got some white wine and cream I can use. It's no trouble to bung it in the slow cooker. I wonder if he has a partner?"

"Great. But no, he hasn't mentioned a partner. Oh, and I had a word with The Bish on my mobile too. He and Michael have both been supportive. Bishop Jonathan said it happens all the time – well, I think that's a bit of an exaggeration, but ..."

"God, you mean there are so many sexy priests around these days?"

"Ha! Well, what can I say to that? He said there have always been people fancying their vicars. Goes with the territory. But I don't know ..."

"Oh, Rory! I for one have lost count of the ladies of the church falling at your feet! You really haven't noticed?"

Rory shrugged and grimaced. "Well, who am I to ... aaagh! Ellie!" He stooped to pick up the bowl and spoon that she had knocked across the room with her flailing hand, banana puree splashed all over the floor.

Viv tore off some sheets of kitchen paper and handed them to Rory to mop up.

"The joys of parenthood," Viv mused, and turned to Ellie who was chuckling and banging her little hands on the shelf of the high chair.

"So kind of you to invite me again, Dr ... er, Viv," Michael said shyly as he shook hands with Viv in the hallway. He stood tall and thin with a narrow but pleasant face, slightly ginger close-cropped hair, beard neatly trimmed. His V-necked sweater revealed a mismatched shirt beneath, and his trousers had been ironed rather strangely with a wobbly double crease running down the leg. But at least he'd made an effort. She noticed the tick at the side of his eye and tried not to look at it. She had been aware of it on previous meetings with him, but it seemed particularly pronounced tonight, poor fellow.

"No problem. You're very welcome. Come into the kitchen while I finish off and then we can sit down in comfort in the dining room. To be honest, Michael, it's really good to have adult company. I miss the little dinner parties we used to have. Life has seemed to be so full of baby stuff!"

"Well, she's a lovely little girl." He spoke slowly, hesitantly, as though unsure of the words he needed in a social situation.

"Hmm, you've only seen her when she's asleep! But thank you. We adore her."

"Red, white, beer?" asked Rory, wielding the bottle opener. Michael gestured towards the bottle of burgundy on the counter top.

"You know, Michael, you're always welcome to bring a girlfriend ... boyfriend ... partner?" Viv was aware of Rory shaking his head and smiling indulgently at her attempts to wheedle information from him.

"Oh, er, that's very kind. Rory did suggest that." Viv raised her eyebrows at Rory with a look of irony. "But sadly there isn't anybody ... um, any girlfriend," he smiled ruefully, "in my life at the moment."

"Do you wish there was?" Viv ignored Rory's gestures. "It can be a very lonely life as a curate."

"Oh." Michael blushed. "Um, well, I'm fine on my own. The single life suits me OK. As you know I have my music group and choir ... and I guess you get quite selfish when you're used to living on your own, doing your own thing ... not having to refer to anyone else."

"There's certainly something in that!" laughed Rory, and Viv biffed him on the arm.

Over supper, Viv quizzed Michael about the investigation into the Saxon cross in the churchyard, and the complaint about the filming.

"I think it's a ... a fantastic idea. I love history. My first degree was in history, not theology, you know. Well, obviously you don't know! Sorry." He blushed, and Viv noticed that his hand shook a little as he clutched his wine glass. "And this complaint ... no, it's odd. I can't see the real reason behind it. And, you know, I really can't see that it's anything to do with Sadie Smythe ..."

Viv passed the vegetable dish again to Michael and Rory topped up his glass.

"Do you know her?"

"Oh, er, no, not really. I've chatted to her at the church door a few times as she's left service. But she's always seemed a little ...er ... distracted elsewhere."

Viv glanced at Rory. "Hmm. What do you make of her? Or do you not really have any particular impression?"

Michael's blush deepened. "Well." He looked down at his plate. "She seems nice."

"And ...?"

"Um, well, she's attractive. Er, I suppose."

"Viv!" Rory shook his head at her. "Stop tormenting the poor guy!"

"I'm sorry, Michael. I'm just interested in people."

"She does it to everyone," Rory smiled at her indulgently. "But you know, there's one thing about it - she keeps me up to date with my parishioners!"

"Oh, it's fine. It's quite ... nice ... for someone to bother to ask. I sometimes think we clerics are seen as, well, somehow not really human!" He snorted abruptly as though he was surprised at his own thoughts and words.

Viv smiled at him. "I know what you mean. I sometimes think the same about academics. I think students imagine we actually live at the university – always available, you know. Oh, was that the sound of something being pushed through the door? Funny time – eight o'clock in the evening?"

"I'll get it." Rory rose from the table. "Probably something for me anyway, some leaflet about an event someone wants me to open or officiate at."

"And I'll get the pudding. Michael, I've made a fruit crumble. Is that OK for you?"

Michael helped her to pile up the plates and serving bowls to take into the kitchen. The plates rattled together as he manoeuvred them.

"Oh, for heaven's sake!" Rory shouted.

"What is it?" They both stopped and looked up. Viv heard the front door open and then silence, as if Rory had been looking out down the path. A moment later she heard the door close again.

He came into the dining room, a piece of paper in his hand. He stared at them, face pale.

"It's another anonymous note. But this time it's personal, it's … I'm going up to check on Ellie."

CHAPTER 14

VIV

Derbyshire. Present day

"What? What on earth do you mean? A threat to Ellie? She's a baby, for God's sake!" Flushed and heart pounding, Viv ran upstairs behind Rory, with Michael following behind, hot on their heels.

As she turned the bend in the staircase, she could see that Rory was standing in the doorway of Ellie's bedroom, and sensed that his breathing had stilled.

"She's fast asleep," he whispered. "All's well."

Back in the dining room, Rory shook his head and poured himself another glass of wine, gulping it down. "I'm so sorry for panicking you both. I guess I'm a little on edge at the moment. I don't usually react so anxiously."

"No, you don't. You're normally the calmest person I know. What on earth does the note say?" Even though she knew that Ellie was fine and safe, she could still feel her heart pounding in her chest and a tightness in her throat.

He handed it to Viv, and she held it out so that Michael could also read it. Her hand was shaking and her breath raw.

"It's weird, Viv. Look. What do you think?"

Viv squinted at the paper. The typing was full of mistakes as though the writer was shaky and furious, hitting the keys almost haphazardly, and not easy to make out. "Oh God. It says ... "the runes on the cross" ... something ...something ...magic signs" .... What's this? ... "ancient curses". What? Is this person cursing us?" She struggled to draw in her ragged breath, and frowned across at Rory. He grimaced.

"Or perhaps it means that the runes themselves are curses that we've somehow unleashed. I ... I guess people used to think that signs they couldn't understand must be magical, perhaps some kind of ancient curses, didn't they?"

She nodded slowly, pulse slowing now. "Assumed by association. I'll bet Arthur Bone's grandfather and the grave digger would have seen them as curses too. But aren't people a bit more understanding these days, surely?"

Michael sighed. "Please. If I may. Unfortunately,

um, there are many folks who are still superstitious about these rune signs. And, er, I suppose ... especially in small village communities where ancient folk memories still ... um, linger."

Viv calmed her breathing, deeply, in for four, hold for four, out for six. Try to be rational. She saw that Rory was flexing his hands, moving his fingers as if to bring back the circulation. "Hmm. Well, this stuff, the tone – it's nasty, threatening. But, let's think ... it's about the runes. I mean, runes really are just the origins of our known languages. Representing the sounds of the old languages and items that were familiar to those people ... oh ... a thousand, two thousand years ago. Nothing magical. Not curses. That's also what Dr Helen Mortimer said as well."

"Dr Helen ...?"

"Oh, um, Michael. She's a colleague of mine at the university. An expert on runes. It's a fascinating study. But yes of course they look strange and so in the past people have been very wary of them. And tales of magic grew up around them."

"But ... this mentions a specific, quote "ancient curse", though." Michael peered at the note. "It doesn't say what it is exactly ... but then it refers to children."

"Yes," said Rory, "That's what spooked me."

"You said it was personal, Rory. What did you mean?"

"Because it quotes a biblical verse. So immediately

I'm thinking it's me, my job. It's from the Old Testament. Exodus. The note says, here, look, "Sanctify to me every first born … she belongs to me." Rory sat down heavily and gulped the rest of his wine. "You see?"

"*What*? '*She belongs to me*'? Does it mean sacrificing children? To God? To the devil? What?"

"Um, well …" Michael took the note from Viv's trembling hand. "You see ––"

"–– actually, you know, it's misquoted." Rory looked up hopefully. "The biblical verse in fact says 'it' - not 'she'."

"And Ellie isn't our firstborn. But maybe the writer didn't know that." Viv wondered whether Sadie, if it *was* her, would have known about the loss of their first baby. Probably not. Or maybe the writer, whoever it was, didn't count that as a 'first born' because Ana didn't go full term.

"Yes, but I guess that's not really the point, Viv. Not whether it's accurate or not. Maybe we're over-analysing it. It sounds as if it's *meant* to be personal to me. Or that's how I read it first off."

"If I may interject," Michael said hesitantly. "If that's alright? The fact is, however it was intended, it's not a curse at all. The quotation, I mean. It's not about sacrifice. It's about dedicating the firstborn child to God. Even in biblical times, it surely wouldn't be interpreted as a threat … um, but a promise that the first child is in God's grace, is … er, special."

"Yes, indeed." Rory took a deep breath. "Of course you're right. I'm panicking. Confused. It *is* a blessing. *But* isn't the point that the writer herself or himself interprets it as a curse, because it's in the context of this blurb on the note about the rune curses and magic?"

"Yes, I can see that ... hmm, so if it was intended ... what should we do about it?" Michael looked at Rory with narrowed eyes and raised shoulders.

"D'you think it's Sadie?" Viv grimaced.

"Oh, er, I don't think ..." Michael began.

"We-ell." Rory sighed. "Right. Let's think objectively ..."

Viv stared at the note in Michael's hand, frowning. "OK. So let's just stop and think a moment. To be perfectly objective, there's nothing here that is actually a threat or even a warning. It's the tone that's threatening. I'm trying to separate it in my mind from anything that's gone before. The stuff with Sadie, I mean." She bit her lip. She hadn't done that for a long time. "If we'd got this before her little outburst, we'd simply have thought it was someone who passionately objected to the investigation of the Rune Stone. Someone superstitious, maybe. Someone ... frightened?"

"Of magic, of ancient curses?"

"Yes. I mean the Sadie stuff irritated you, Rory. It was unnerving. But dangerous? Is she really capable of something so nasty? This is quite cruel in intent, isn't it? Or amazingly thoughtless. Actually, we were taken aback by Sadie's anger, but we laughed about it afterwards. A woman scorned and all that."

"Well, my main concern was about the objection to the filming of the examination of the cross ... trying to deal with that, but wondering if it was related to her fury at me, which was, you must agree, a little threatening! That's why I needed to let you know, Michael ... and the Bishop."

"I'm glad you did." Michael nodded. "And, er, we must keep an eye on that. It's always best for people around you to know anything that might ... well ... potentially develop further. If you don't mind my saying so?"

"Not at all. I guess I'm putting two and two together and making ten."

"Not like you, Rory."

"No, not at all. OK. Flash of madness and assumption over! So ... Do we think it's the work of the same person who sent the anonymous email to the Bishop?"

"Too coincidental not to be, surely?" Michael shrugged. "But ... on the other hand ..."

Viv frowned. "It's typed so we have no handwriting to go on. In an old who-dunnit there would be a faulty letter on the typewriter so that the sleuth could identify whose machine it was written on. But this is word processed of course so we can't even do a Miss Marple. *Could* it be Sadie, do you think?"

"Oh, I wouldn't think ..." Michael blushed and looked down at his plate.

Rory shrugged. "I really don't have a clue. We're only thinking of Sadie because of her fury over ... well, you know. But that's a very tenuous link. Objectively ... it could be anyone, I guess."

Viv sighed. "Look, let's get our pudding. There's nothing we can do just now. So don't let it spoil the rest of the evening."

But, however hard they tried to resume their chatting, with Rory and Michael arguing amicably about church matters and Viv lightening the atmosphere with village affairs and talk of the research into the cross, at the back of it all was the tremor of concern for all of them.

It was something of a relief to Viv when Michael looked at his watch, sucked in his breath at the lateness of the hour, and said his goodbyes.

"Phew," puffed Viv as she swung her legs into bed an hour later, having looked in on Ellie for the hundredth time, checking her presence, her breathing, her comfort. "What a night!"

"Yes, indeed. But Michael's a good guy. Glad we've got him here. Just hoping he'll stay and not be tempted elsewhere."

"Elsewhere?"

"To his own parish."

"Ah. Not sure he's really ready yet."

"He'll grow into it. He's not so long out of college."

"He's sweet, but very nervous."

"Just feeling his way." Rory stretched his long body in the bed and turned to Viv, curling his left arm around her chest to cup her shoulder and draw her closer. "As I am." He grinned and moved his hand to her breast.

"Hmm." Viv turned in to Rory's body. "Well, I hope he finds a nice girlfriend."

"He may not be looking."

"Oh yes, he's looking."

IT WAS A FEW DAYS LATER THAT SADIE SMYTHE LODGED A formal objection to the filming of the Rune Stone. Her email was sent to the Bishop with Rory copied in. At least she'd signed it.

"Well, not unexpected I guess," Rory said as he twisted round from his computer to take the mug of coffee from Viv.

"No, but a bit annoying."

"She says that she is not the only one who objects – there are "many others" who agree but don't want to speak out."

"Do you think she's right? I mean I spoke to as many of the villagers as I could, well the congregation anyway. I didn't think that others who don't come to church would be interested or that bothered, frankly, about what happens in the churchyard. And nobody raised any objections to me."

"Same here. Although I did speak to some who are not church goers, just to get an idea of the village reaction in general, wider than the church. Nobody objected to me, although they may possibly have not liked to object to my face – above a dog collar. But I guess we need to know, now it's been raised. Diplomacy and all that. Don't want folks complaining about the village church."

"What do we do now? I've put it all on hold with Tilly but of course we can't do that for long because the TV company will need to know one way or another, or they'll go with something else that crops up."

"That's true."

Viv sighed deeply. "That anonymous note's still bothering me, Rory."

He smiled at her, but she saw the lines of his frown across his forehead. "I know. Me too."

"Sadie's now made her opposition to the filming clear, and despite Michael's doubts I can't help but feel her hand in all this. I do see that note as a threat – I mean why else would it be anonymous. It's all so odd. Why do that – just for revenge? Or is there anyone else in the village who might be superstitious about investigating the Rune Stone and is trying to warn us off?"

"I know. It's going round and round my head too. But we do need to deal with this objection head on."

"Hmm. I wonder if we should do some sort of survey through the whole village – ask for a yes/no approval. Or bring it to the parish council?"

Rory took a gulp of his coffee. "Yes. I didn't really want to make a big formal deal out of it because it's not as if it's on public land, the village green or something, and it's not as if it's going to be disruptive to village life or any villagers. It's on church property and they've said it'll only take a day – less than – to do that bit of the filming, and perhaps talk to me in the churchyard, about the history of the church. I never imagined that it would be anything to do with anyone else, and Bishop Jonathan didn't suggest anything wider. But now of course it's a whole different ball game. And I really don't want to cause friction in the village."

"D'you think we should cover all bases and push a yes/no survey through people's doors, giving them the details of what the research and filming is all about? And organise a short meeting in the village hall where we do a PowerPoint about the historical significance of the cross, I mean the Rune Stone, and the mystery that surrounds it? We could then answer any questions and they can give in their surveys? That'd raise interest as well. Couldn't hurt?"

Rory raked his hand through his hair. "Yes, maybe. I'd have to run that past The Bish. And maybe have a meeting in the church so that they can see the venue –

and perhaps that would drum up some interest in the church and the whole project as well. Otherwise we'd have to pay hiring fees for the village hall and possibly get into all the organisational madness of providing refreshments."

Viv cocked her head to one side. "Hey, that's not a bad idea! Refreshments I mean. But in the church. That would get people into the building, people who might otherwise feel daunted about venturing into a church."

"Ah, I see what you mean. Could be ... since we don't even have a church fete in the church grounds – mainly because there isn't a suitably large enough flat area that's unencumbered by gravestones."

"We've got the little kitchen area at the back that we use for coffee after the services, and I'm sure people would help. I can buy packets of biscuits and coffee. Hey, I'll even offer to print out slips to post through doors and put posters on the village notice boards about the meeting!"

Rory smiled and reached out to her. "I do believe you're getting quite excited about the prospect."

Viv laughed. "You never know. I might surprise you and organise a church fete in the rectory garden some day!"

She was still musing about her suggestions as she took Ellie for a walk that afternoon in the watery late summer sunshine. Goodness, was she really turning in to a stereotype of a rector's wife? All baking and church fetes? She'd be running the Mothers' Union next! Hmm. Viv shook her head, chortling to herself.

"Honestly, Ellie," she whispered to her drowsy child. "What's happening to me? I'm getting dangerously into all this church stuff!" She sighed. "Maybe I just want to compensate for all this weird business at the moment, with something comforting and cosy and rural. What with curses and veiled threats and the wretched Sadie Smythe ... and these glimmers of time-slipping again."

They were returning from the woodlands that fringed the fields between their village and the next, on the way home. They had admired the stream that wound its way through the dell between the trees and played 'Pooh sticks' from the rickety wooden bridge. Or at least Viv had, and Ellie had smiled sleepily and obligingly waved her hands a little in the air. Viv had pointed out to Ellie the pink abundance of herb-robert, the wild honeysuckle and several sluggish browny green frogs. They were making their way back uphill along the 'coffin road' – a narrow dusty rutted path, really – when Viv looked up towards the church.

Something caught her eye. A movement, a shadow. She stopped in her tracks. A drift of wind swirled up behind her and as she swung round, something unseen, a misty presence, passed her and made up the coffin road to the churchyard, as if joining something, someone, up there on the brow of the hill. Yet there was nobody in sight. But there was a shimmering up ahead in the new part of the churchyard, a gentle silent crying, a quiet merging of souls. Viv screwed up her eyes and saw that it was just about where the dig had been and where the child's burial had been found.

Ellie murmured a little and Viv stroked her back. It felt warm – too warm? No, probably only the cosiness of sleep. Viv moved on slowly uphill to the small back gate of the churchyard. Her hands were trembling as she unlatched it and her eyes sought the site of the burial. There was nobody there; all seemed peaceful. But yet, Viv sensed a presence, a wisp of something that disappeared amongst the gravestones. She breathed in deeply to calm herself and made her way round the corner of the church to the Rune Stone. Little Ellie mumbled in her sleep. She would wake soon and want to be fed and entertained.

But for a moment, Viv stood before the ancient monument and as she stared at the mossy symbols carved there, she felt her eyes shift out of focus. She heard her own voice deep inside her head. *What secrets can you tell?* Her words echoed through her brain and a soft answering sigh and a gentle whisper crept across her consciousness.

She sensed someone close by and as she stilled the thumping of her heart she heard a soft rustling of fabric, the skirts of a robe, and from the corner of her eye she saw a flash of deep blue, the glinting of a large gold brooch bearing the image of a white dragon, and the gleam of burnished bronze-red hair. A movement towards her. An opening of arms. Viv caught her breath.

Ellie stirred and cried out, and the moment passed. Viv drew her breath in deeply and cradled her child closer to her breast. Then she hurried back to the safety of the rectory and to Rory, still bent, oblivious, over his computer.

CHAPTER 15

VIV

Derbyshire. Present day

It was an odd incident in the churchyard the following week that sunk Viv into an even deeper spiral of unease.

She had taken a short cut through to the other side of the village to take some posters advertising the meeting about the Rune Stone to someone on the PCC who had offered to laminate them for the village notice boards. Her suggestions about a meeting in the church had been enthusiastically received and a date and time agreed upon. A couple of people had happily offered to share making refreshments and Rory was having a great time creating a PowerPoint presentation about the history of the church and the Rune Stone specifically. Before she left the house an hour before, Viv heard him rehearsing it to Ellie who was having 'tummy time' beside his desk with her activity toy and chime ball. Viv hoped that he wouldn't get so engrossed that he forgot the Skype meeting he'd scheduled with the PCC Chair at twelve.

She rounded the corner of the church and stopped in her tracks, her attention caught by the unmistakable filthy old raincoat on the hunched body of Ivy Nettles, grey hair sprouting wildly from under her woollen hat. It was the smell that hit Viv before she even recognised the figure standing in front of the Rune Stone gesticulating and pouring forth her usual foul language that passed as conversation. It sounded as though she was ranting amiably to someone, but Viv couldn't see another person in the vicinity.

She grimaced. Ivy was something of an enigma, one moment the pious congregant and the next the violently swearing harridan, hitting out at anyone she felt inclined to cross swords with. Her outbursts were legendary and intimidating. But even her 'friendly' chats were swamped with language that would make an inner-city drug dealer blush. Her stench was even worse.

Viv wondered if she should check inside the church that Ivy couldn't possibly have entered. She had a habit of using the nave as her personal toilet. Viv was just contemplating the awful prospect before realising that the church must actually be locked, thank goodness, when Ivy, sensing a presence behind her, swung round.

"Ey, Mrs Rev'rend!" Ivy's beady eyes pierced Viv's immobility. It was strange how any confrontation with Ivy swept Viv with embarrassment and inaction. She felt guilty that she had such an aversion to one of Rory's parishioners but at the same time she found her behaviour disgusting. Perhaps she should have more Christian charity. But ugh, the things Ivy did were beyond the pale. "Ey! Over 'ere!"

There was no way that Viv was approaching any nearer. She spent an inordinate amount of her time trying to avoid Ivy without being downright rude. Not that Ivy apparently noticed if anyone was indeed rude back to her.

"Hello, Ivy. How are you today?" Viv pulled her tote bag closer to her chest as though that were any protection against Ivy's pervading odour, a mix of sweat, unwashed body parts and dirty clothes, and other unmentionable bodily fluids. "Admiring our Stone?"

As soon as she spoke, Viv realised her mistake. Ivy's face darkened.

"Admirin' it? What'cha talkin' aboot? These 'ere signs, they be the signs of the devil. D'ya not know they be the devil's ancient runes, curses?"

"Well ..."

There was a movement behind the Stone, and it was only then that Viv realised there was indeed someone else there too, someone Ivy had been talking to. Was that person hiding from her, or merely crouched down scrutinising the Stone.

There was a flash of scarlet and Sadie slipped into view. Ivy turned her attention to her.

"Ey, *you*, ah'm jes tellin' Mrs Rev'rend 'ere about them magical signs cut into the Cross. Like I was tellin' ya jes' now."

Sadie flung Viv a strange look, and it seemed to Viv that it was a blend of anger and scorn. "I have to go. I'll see you later, Ivy, and you can tell me more about those ..." she paused and glanced at Viv, "er ... what we were discussing."

Viv, astonished, watched her stalk off down the gravel path out of the churchyard, high heels unsteady on the uneven ground, and wondered how the seemingly fastidious Sadie could bear to meet up with Ivy in close proximity, although maybe she intended it to be outdoors and upwind.

"Funny lass, that," frowned Ivy, totally unaware of the irony of her words. "Any road up, ya don't wanna be a-messin' with these 'ere signs." She glared at Viv and pointed her bony finger in her direction. "I 'eard all about it, ya know. All this stuff about interpretin' the runes. Ya canna mess with the devil's own runes."

"Ivy, I really don't think they are the devil's runes. They're ancient signs, yes, but they're just like our writing as it was many centuries ago. They're part of our history. The history of England."

"Vikings!" shouted Ivy abruptly, adding a few

choice colourful adjectives. "Effin' heathens! Oh, beggin' ya pardon, Mrs Rev'rend."

Viv shook her head. "What?" Sometimes it was difficult to keep up with Ivy's thought processes. "Vikings?"

Ivy planted her feet in their heavy wellington boots firmly on the ground and thrust her hands on her wide hips. "Vikings," she nodded briskly. "It's them. They come 'ere, rapin' and pillagin' an' leave the devil's own runes an' the devil's curses an' 'is evil magic all around. On our sacred land. In our sacred village." She hawked and spat a thick gob heartily onto the ground and Viv found herself looking anxiously to see if the spittle had landed on someone's poor grave.

Viv held up her hands. "No, no. Ivy, stop it, that's not true. I mean, this cross, this Rune Stone, is early or pre-Anglo-Saxon, way before any Vikings invaded. Yes, you're right that the Vikings used runes, but these runes are much more ancient than that."

Again, as soon as she said it, she realised that it was a mistake. Ivy's face turned even more puce, her eyes narrowing. "Even more ancient, eh? Then ah'm reet, Mrs Rev'rend! Ancient magic. They carved them signs with evil an' darkness in their souls. Mark me words, them be powerful magic that'll come down the ages an' back to the village an' destroy us all."

A thought struck Viv. "Ivy, you haven't been writing messages again, have you? And pushing them through doors? Because if you have, you must stop making threats to people before something awful happens."

Ivy's face screwed up, eyes puckered and mouth quivering. "What messages? What doors? Threats? I ain't made no threats. What'cha talkin' aboot?" She began to stomp off down the path. Then she turned abruptly, finger pointing. "An' don'cha make them acc-a-sations ta me, even though ya be Mrs Rev'rend an' all. Ya can be Mrs Rev'rend all ya like. Ya canna cross the devil's runes."

Viv watched, blinking, as Ivy stalked her way out of the churchyard, muttering. What on earth was that all about? Her head spun with the strange conversation. Clearly Ivy was unhappy about the investigations on the Stone, that was obvious, but the flash of insight Viv had suddenly thought she'd had about Ivy, not Sadie, being the writer of the message pushed through their door, had fizzled out. Ivy appeared to be affronted by the very idea that she had made threats. She seemed genuine. But Viv knew her to be cunning at times in between a naive innocence. Hmm. What to think? She thought for one moment she'd solved the puzzle, but perhaps it was Sadie after all. Or someone entirely different?

Glancing at her watch, Viv realised it was half past eleven and she needed to get back home to relieve Rory of Ellie's care before his Skype meeting. She hurried along the path in the direction Ivy had taken and the ghost of her stench still wafted there amidst the prettily tended graves and beautiful flowers, overpowering their usual sweetness.

As she swung the rectory's garden gate behind her, she played the disturbing incident in the churchyard over in her mind. What did it mean? What was Sadie doing there, crouched behind the Cross? Ivy may have been rambling, but she really did sound fearful. Yes, she was clearly superstitious and muddled, but somehow it preyed on her mind.

Viv let herself into her kitchen and breathed in the smells and sights of their normality: the array of soft toys scattered on the large farmhouse kitchen table, the comforting lingering aroma of the remains of their breakfast bacon, the jam jar of wild dog roses wilting on the window sill, starting to drop their petals. She scooped them up and held them up to her face, breathing in the sweet earthy scent. The house was noticeably quiet. Oddly so, perhaps?

"I'm back!" she called to Rory. "I'll come and get Ellie. Don't forget your Skype!"

There was a moment of time when a flutter of unease shivered Viv's heart. Was it too quiet? She couldn't hear Rory's typing or Ellie's gurgling as she played. Why was she so discombobulated at the moment, as if she was waiting for something to happen? Something frightening. Something very disturbing.

Then, thank goodness, a noise from the study.

"OK." Rory's voice was low and soft. He was

standing at the study doorway, glancing back inside. "Ellie's just gone off. Dropped asleep in the middle of playing with Sophie the giraffe. I don't want to disturb her."

Viv smiled with relief. "That's OK. I'll come and check on her. Do you want me to bring you a mug of coffee?"

"You're an angel."

"Yes. I know."

"And I've pretty much ascertained from the scant evidence that the church dates from the time of Edward the Confessor, so sometime around 1042 to 1066. So what we thought originally was a cross hugely predates the church although apparently there may have been a wooden structure there long before the 11th century or even the Vikings ... and before that the Anglo-Saxons, even back to Celtic times."

"So, the early Saxon baby's burial in the new part of the graveyard would predate the stone church building too. A sacred site there originally, do you think? What about if part of the Cooney's Mere settlement, or kingdom, or whatever, stretched right across where the church stands now – under the church and the churchyard that now exists?"

"Hmm. Right from where your parents held their dig all those years ago. Right from where you first fell, and time-slipped ..."

"So," Viv bit her lip. "So, our baby Ana and a baby from Lady Vivianne's time, maybe a baby of Lady

Vivianne's herself even, were buried near each other. All within the kingdom marked by the cross - Rune Stone as it would have been then"

"Perhaps the Rune Stone, as it was, marked the centre of the kingdom."

"And if the female figure on the Rune Stone was someone significant to the kingdom, and therefore central to it, it does seem quite plausible that it was Lady Vivianne herself. The runes that Helen identified seemed to suggest that was a possibility, or even a likelihood in terms of general dating."

"Well, that's certainly a reasonable theory."

"I wish we could find out whether there *is* a burial beneath or near the Rune Stone. Or even beneath the church! God, Rory, it could be Lady Vivianne's! Imagine!"

"But if so," Rory rubbed his chin, "why would the child burial be way over east of the Cross memorial, if there was a family connection, or at least some kind of kin, at the Rune Stone itself? Wouldn't kin have been buried near each other?" He frowned. "Oh, wait a minute, didn't you say that often high-status people were buried further away from the others of the settlement? Didn't you say that was a possible reason why the child burial was away over where the new graveyard is? In which case, *that's* where Lady Vivianne's burial would be, and Sir Roland's and ..."

"Hmm. Yes. And we'll never know because we can't dig it up now. Anyway, the 2003 dig didn't find any other burials in that area. It's just a bit odd, don't you think? I guess I'd really like the Rune Stone to be marking a significant grave." Viv smiled ruefully. "But, OK, a memorial stone is next best. I wonder why the memorial, though. I wonder what Lady Vivianne – or whoever is commemorated here – did that was so remarkable that she should be immortalised here? And for a *woman* to have this, well, it's apparently very unusual, so really important. My God – what did she *do*?"

"Yes, well, it had to be something pretty momentous! But I need to ..."

A bump came from inside the study, and a sharp cry from Ellie. Rory swung round and Viv wasn't far behind, heart pounding at how long they had left her without checking.

CHAPTER 16

LADY VIVIANNE

Cūning's Mere 520 AD

It had been too long for any good news. Already it was nearing the Mourning Moon and surely her heart was in mourning too. Change was coming; she had seen the waxing moon in the afternoons, ascending in the east amidst the parting clouds, and the wolves had begun to howl in readiness for the arrival of the full moon. She knew that it signified adjustment, a recognition that things do not always work out for the best, as you want them. However hard you pray, God does not always grant your wishes to be fulfilled.

Lady Vivianne knew it and her heart was so heavy that she felt it was hard to rise from her bed in the mornings, hard to move and face the day ahead. Too many days and nights had passed by while she worked on the settlement's business and rubbed the noticeable little mound of her belly waiting for news. And yet increasingly she dreaded what that news might be. In her mind, she went over and over the significance of the absence of a messenger bearing tidings. Surely even in defeat some of the thegns would have managed to return by this time. Surely word would have come, somehow, from someone, even if only from the Angeln boasting their victory. And what about the thegns from Deorabye who were supposed to be joining them – why was there no news from them either?

At the same time, even in her numbness of spirit, she was restless, often walking around the tracks of the settlement, greeting the workmen and women who toiled at their wood and leather and cloth, even trudging up to the fields in the cold rain to try to keep her geburs cheerful, despite the news of sickness and hunger, while she tried to ignore the breaking of her own heart. She tried to pretend that Sir Roland had merely gone to the south border to speak with the guards and would be back in time for evening feasting in the mead hall. That was the only way she could cope with the bleakness in her mind.

She walked and busied herself with the everyday business of Cūning's Mere as if to show her people that nothing was amiss, even as they sickened in the bad weather, as if to prove to herself that everything was as it should be and always was. And she came back to her hall, numb to the cold and her wet clothes and skin, hardly noticing the discomfort above the clamour of the thoughts in her head: how to keep her people safe, how to keep her children happy, how to live without her one true love.

Only that morning, she had returned to the hall from the livestock fields, shaking out her mantle and scattering a great shower of rainwater onto the herb strewn floor. Matilda had berated her for her muddy skirts and rain-soaked head rail and veil.

"My lady! You are wet through! You must be more careful, or you will catch your death of cold. Let me take your robes off to dry. I do not know where that silly Afera has got to, probably sneaking stolen moments with Gareth Swineson if I know anything at all, but we cannot wait for her. You are soaked. I will do it myself," she clucked. She pulled the mantle from Vivianne's body and untied the robe and kirtle, ushering her nearer the fire. Vivianne stood still, letting herself be undressed and wrapped in a warm woollen cloth. "Let me fetch you a dry kirtle and robe from the chest."

"Oh, Tilda, thank you for your care. But I am afeared. There is much shivering sickness in the village, and we have lost many lives to the illness. And to hunger too. Despite all our efforts there is little to go around. Two of Edgard's leather geburs who work with the tanning are burning with the fever."

Matilda stopped in her tracks, garments dripping

in her arms, and swung round to Vivianne. "You did not go near them?"

"No, it was Edgard who told me at the doorway. And they are not allowing anyone to go to them for fear of the infection. A little food is left outside the hut in a chest at the door."

Matilda exhaled a sigh and nodded. "Then I will make an infusion of wild basil with a little honey and take it to their huts," she said gravely. "And I think some garlic too."

"I hoped that you would do so." Lady Vivianne tucked the rough cloth firmly around her and bent to the fire that was roaring strongly in the hearth, warming her hands.

"And, my lady," frowned Matilda severely. Vivianne looked up at Tilda's unusually sharp tone. "You must stop going to the fields in the storms. I must speak straight. I am sorry if I appear disrespectful, but I have to speak truth to you. You cannot catch the sickness. Remember who you are. What would we do if you caught the sickness? What would we *all* do if we lost you ...?"

Vivianne stopped rubbing her cold arms and grimaced, pierced by her maid's words. It seemed to her that Tilda in her rising intonation was about to say: what would we all do if we lost you *too*? What? As well as Sir Roland and the thegns? For one moment Vivianne's heart seemed to cease its beating, froze, and her blood pounded only dread. It was what alarmed her heart, yet she feared to form into words. And then her pulse began again as her body was washed with a new realisation: it was all down to her and her alone. Never had she been obliged to rule on her own; Roland had always been by her side. But truly it was her rule, not Roland's, no longer her dear lost parents' rule, nobody else but her. She may have Godwyne and Acton – yes and even Gareth – but it was, at the end, on her shoulders alone. With or without Roland, though her heart was breaking, she knew that they all relied upon her. That was how it had to be and that was what she must face, with grace and strength.

Matilda must have seen Lady Vivianne's deep pulling in of her breath, the settling of her shoulders, the drawing up of her spine to her full height, the set of her expression. She nodded and turned to drop the wet clothes in to the washer woman's basket and carefully lift the dry robes from the chest. She chose the rich burgundy red robe and the purple ermine-edged mantle, the colours of kingship.

Gareth stood before Lady Vivianne in the mead hall. She sat on the bench on the dais with only the small trestle table in front of her on which was ledged the accounting book, the parchment, and her nibbed reed for writing. Nymue sat at her right side and Tristram at her left. Godwyne as always stood to her side a little behind her as was correct and watched quietly as her chief ceorls approached her for guidance and report. She sat with her back straight and her head high, feeling the weight of her gold circlet heavy on her thick auburn curls. She felt hot in the heavy robes and the fur that trimmed the purple mantle around her shoulders. The golden flames of the fire in the great hearth were high, and the gebur tending it was stoking it up further. She signalled to him to pause a while.

"My lady Vivianne," Gareth began, bowing slightly to her. Vivianne felt Nymue draw herself up on the bench beside her and Tristram wriggle, impatient after having to sit still for so long. She had told them that from now on they must attend the ceorl councils with her in order to prepare themselves for their future roles. They were æthelings, after all, and needed to start to behave as such. Nymue would be cūning after her, as the Witan had finally agreed, and Tristram in reserve, if, God forbid, this was needed. The others were too young but if the need arose when they were older then they too would be attending the ceorl councils and the Witan.

Lady Vivianne put her hand gently on Tristram's hose to still him and glanced at Nymue. Was her colour a little raised? She hoped that she was not coming down with a chill. Or maybe it was just the roaring fire. She turned back to Gareth Swineson.

"And my lady Nymue, my lord Sir Tristram."

Gareth bowed to Vivianne's companions. "Sir Godwyne."

"Gareth Swineson, we are pleased to see you. What do you have to report to us?"

"My lady, you will have heard from Acton already that a certain amount of our root crops have been washed out. The cereals were brought in before the worst of the weather, but the harvest was thin." Despite the bad news, Gareth stood tall and firm, hands at his sides, no longer twisting his fingers in awkwardness as he used to do. Vivianne thought how his promotion to chief ceorl had given him confidence and a new dignity.

Vivianne sighed and nodded slowly. "And what of your own livestock ceorls? How do the animals fare?"

"A mixed report, my lady. We have lost a number of the pigs and their young. Several sows have been overlying their new born litters, and we have too many older boars that we had brought in from the wild who have ceased bearing. But the pigs generally are more able to withstand the cold and torrential rains and we have food for a while if this weather continues. And we have a number of sows in gestation, if we can birth them and stop them from overlaying."

"Good, good."

"But the hens have not been laying as they should and some now have the scraggy sickness. We have had need to separate them from the others, but I fear they will have to be wrung and destroyed for fear of spread.

We have only just enough for our needs in the settlement, but it is close. The cattle are well, their thick coats keep them warm and we have many in the shelters, but we cannot shelter them all. Their milk is more sparse and thin because their grazing is poor in these storms."

Lady Vivianne scratched brief accounts onto the parchment. "You will give your full accounting and numbers to Sir Godwyne presently, but I thank you for your general report to me today." She rested her reed carefully for a moment, then looked up to Gareth and smiled. "You are doing as well as can be expected in these difficult times. I know that you will mitigate the effects of the storms as much as you can, and I am confident that our food is in safe hands with you."

Gareth bowed to her but Vivianne could see the blush rising to his cheeks. She caught his glance towards Nymue and turned slightly to her daughter. She could see Nymue's head bent but she could also see the way she peeped up through her lashes towards the chief livestock ceorl. Was Sir Aldwyn less in favour, then? She hoped that passion was waning. But Nymue was so changeable these days. She rose and signalled to Godwyne to take her place at the table and the accounting book.

"That is all the business for me this day. Come, Nymue, Tristram." As she swept out of the hall to return to her own chamber she did not turn around but she sensed the sweep of Nymue's robes behind her and the barely restrained impatience of Tristram's keenness to get back to his battle training or his sword play.

Afera was tidying Vivianne's robe chest as she and Nymue sank on to the stools beside the fire in her chamber. Vivianne unclasped her heavy mantle and cast it aside. Afera picked it up and laid it on the bed, but Vivianne thought she caught a strange look her maid cast towards Nymue. Vivianne sent Tristram off to his play and he ran off with relief. Ah well, she sighed, he was young yet and with the grace of God he would grow into his position.

"My lady, do you require refreshment after the council? Shall I bring you ale and cake?"

"Yes, if you please, Afera. We are both in need of something to revive our spirits after the accounting."

Afera nodded abruptly and left the chamber.

"You are tired, mōđor."

"Yes." She did not want to make her children anxious and so did not speak what was in her heart. Nymue was old enough to guess but she would not speak it. She turned instead to the fire and held her hands up towards the flames, although she was still warm from the great fire in the mead hall.

Afera returned with the bowls of ale and the honey cakes. She placed Vivianne's bowl carefully in front of her on the little table but Nymue's she set down gracelessly and some of the ale splashed onto her lady's pretty purple robe.

"Pfft! Watch what you are doing, Afera!" Nymue exclaimed sharply. "For heavens' sake! Have you not been trained properly? Or have you not been listening to Matilda's instruction?"

Vivianne opened her mouth, expecting to reprimand Nymue for her cutting words and soothe Afera's embarrassment. But she saw that her maid of the chamber was scowling angrily.

Without a word of apology, Afera stomped rudely out of the hall without a backward glance and Vivianne looked after her, mouth agape.

"What was that about?" she turned to Nymue whose face also glowered.

"She needs to know her place!"

Vivianne reached over and patted her daughter's knee. "I think it was but an accident, Nymue. You were harsh."

"It was not an accident! She did it deliberately. I saw her face as she bent over me with the bowl. She means to be disrespectful. She meant to ruin my royal council robe."

"But why would that be? She is maybe a little flighty and silly at times, but disrespectful I think not."

Nymue scowled and shook her head. Vivianne remembered the flickering of Nymue's lashes in the mead hall and her words when Gareth was given his seax some time before. She remembered her daughter's face when she herself remarked that she understood that Afera and Gareth were lovers. But she also knew that Nymue kept Sir Aldwyn's dark red token at her breast. She sighed.

"Oh, Nymue."

THE BABY WITHIN HER MADE HER FEEL WEAKENED AND nauseated, and she could not recall feeling so unwell with the other four children she had borne. Yet it reminded her of the first baby she carried, not long after her hand-fasting with Sir Roland: little Ana whom they had lost before her time and who they had buried at the sacred site beyond the Mere. Even then, Matilda had plied her with herbal teas to try to stop the baby coming too early, even though it was surely far too early for that. She was barely showing.

Now Matilda brought her so many draughts of chamomile that she was beginning to feel queasy at the very smell of it.

"I cannot," she said, shaking her head at the cup her maid carried towards her as she sat before the fire, shivery even though it was the first bright morning of the Mourning Moon.

"My lady," Matilda said, setting down the cup on the table at the hearth and clasping her hands before her as she bent towards her mistress. "You are not well. Your countenance is too pale, and I swear your wrists are thinner." She clucked and sighed loudly. "Your belly is the only part of you that is full. The rest is wasting away. That is not right. Not right at all."

"I concede that I do not feel as strong as usual."

"Is it the baby, my lady? Is it like the other time …?"

"Please, Tilda, let us not talk of that loss."

"No indeed, and this will not be that way. But perhaps the baby is lying awkwardly inside you, making you feel ill. Or you are feeling keenly the absence of Sir Roland and the battle thegns?"

"Very likely both, Tilda. It must now be time that I send out messengers to bring news back to me." She bit her lip. "I am afraid I fear the worst. Why else have we not heard from them? Are they in storms and floods there too? Yet I hesitate to send messengers into this present danger. Would I be sending more men out to their deaths? I cannot bear to pile more evil upon that we already most likely have wrought on our number. But it has been too long that we have heard nothing from the battle fields. No news has come from the south to the other villages either, or so the border guards say."

"No. But the weather has prevented travel and the messengers have not been able to get through, my lady. The rain and the storms have been unceasing until the calmer weather today. The roads have been flooded and no way through could be found. Trees are felled across the holloways and no men spared to clear them. The horses could not make a way through, though many have tried for the past weeks."

"I know. It has been bad enough right here in the settlement, with so many crops spoiled, and animals lost in the flood. We have been like an island in the ocean cut off from the rest of the world."

"But there has been nothing else we could do but wait on the better weather to send any of our precious ceorls out, my lady." Matilda peered out of the window opening. "Disease from the cold and the rain and hunger has taken so many." She sighed and shook her head, then turned away to stoke up the fire in the hearth and add another log to keep her mistress's chills away.

"Acton tells me that rations are depleting rapidly. With the crops so poor we have needs used the resources in the stores. When they are gone, we will have nothing to replace them." She rose from her stool and went to the window. Even though the sky was lighter, and the rains had stopped for the moment, the high road through the settlement was washed into deep ruts by the recent torrents. The buildings huddled in to themselves, thatch dripping and bedraggled, foul water from the middens flowing out onto the highway. There was no hustle and bustle yet, no sounds of the villagers going about their business, as they sheltered within their homes away from the storms that had rocked the settlement, afraid that they might start again. Only the geburs high in the fields desperately fought to tend the animals that had survived and the crops that were so battered down, rotting where they struggled for life. Acton and Gareth tried to be positive, but she knew that they tempered their reports to her. She wondered how bad it was, because she had not been able to make it up the slippery hillsides for a while.

She closed her eyes. She had failed to keep the settlement safe – how could she keep it safe from the floods and winds?

A cry made her snap her eyes open again. A figure was splashing his way through the waters, long hair soaked to his head, cloak hanging wet from his back. He appeared to be carrying a bundle under each arm. A handful of people began to emerge from their huts and their shouts rent the still air. The excitement was almost tangible. The baker had left his struggle with his ovens and was running out with his children, singing and leaping. The metal worker outside the forge was raising his hands to the sky.

Matilda had heard the noise and came back to Vivianne's side to look. She peered out; eyes narrowed against the light. "I swear that is Gareth Swineson coming down from the husbandry fields!"

"Are those young swine he holds under his arms, Tilda? I do believe that he is showing the villagers that there is new hope."

CHAPTER 17

LADY VIVIANNE

Cūning's Mere 520 AD

The piglets were squealing and wriggling under Gareth's tight grip, their little trotters kicking to be freed. He bent and put them to the muddy ground, and they scampered to the nearest filthy water-filled ruts in the roadway and began to wallow and head butt each other. Matilda followed Lady Vivianne outside the hall to watch in delight at the side of the lane. Lying rain and mud soaked the hem of Vivianne's robe but she scarcely noticed, and Matilda stood by her side, clapping her hands and laughing loudly as though it were festival day.

Gareth straightened up and grinned, gesturing towards the swine. "My lady, new birth. I came down to let you know that we have had quite a number of successful breedings up in the stock fields and the hens are beginning to lay again. These are but two of the welcome breeding from the sties." He looked up to the sky, and Vivianne could see that the clouds looked lighter. And was that a glimmer of watery sun? "If this brighter weather continues and the pastures become drier for the livestock to graze, we may hope for even more."

He was staring over Vivianne's shoulder and she swivelled round to see Nymue standing just in the doorway of the hall. He nodded towards her and she smiled shyly and bent her head. Vivianne turned back towards her swineherd and had to remind herself that he was now a chief ceorl, of course, the head stockman.

"Thank you, Gareth, this sight has certainly brought some cheer to the villagers as you can see." Vivianne said, acknowledging his kindness with a brief incline of the head.

But a rustle of robes and a low growl to Vivianne's right made her turn. Edyth, Sir Aldwyn's mother and the erstwhile lover of the appalling Sir Pelleas, was with Afera outside the metal worker's forge. She did not look happy or cheerful. In fact, her face was riven with scowls, her mouth down-turned and her hands were fixed on her hips, gripping her rough worn tunic. Afera was speaking low to her, but she too looked cross.

"Edyth, Afera, is something amiss?" Lady Vivianne

spoke gently but kept her distance. She had no notion that the two had grown so close, but truth to tell she had been most distracted of late. "What ails you?"

Edyth took a deep breath and narrowed her eyes as she looked over to Nymue. "Yes, indeed something is amiss, and something surely does ail us," she said curtly with no regard for courtesy and convention, not even acknowledging Lady Vivianne's status. She gestured towards Nymue. "Your daughter is betrothed and beholden to my son Sir Aldwyn. And here she is making eyes at Gareth Swineson." She spat out her words. The villagers scattered at the other side of the roadway let out a communal gasp, though whether it was for Edyth's disrespect or the news of Nymue's misbehaviour it was impossible to tell.

Betrothed and beholden? Vivianne gasped and shook her head. "No, no. That is not so. Lady Nymue is not betrothed to Aldwyn and neither is she looking kindly at Gareth. You have no right to speak so to me." She turned to her daughter in puzzlement. "Neither do I understand what you are saying."

Nymue looked down to her feet shod in their fine leather and in danger of being ruined if she stepped into the roadway. She shook her head slowly as though in pain.

Edyth began again with a satisfied set of her thin mouth. "They were betrothed as Aldwyn rode out to battle. She should be keeping modest until he returns."

Betrothed did she say a second time? Her daughter Nymue? Of course not. She had authorised no such betrothal. And why was Edyth preaching of modesty to her? She herself had not been modest as the existence of Sir Aldwyn clearly demonstrated. Why would she *dare* to speak of the lady Nymue in such a way? Nymue with all her faults, her crossness, and her belligerence, was never immodest! She would never have gone behind her back, either with Sir Aldwyn or with Gareth. Would she?

Vivianne looked to Gareth who was shaking his head in concern. "I ... I did not know, my lady. But I have not invited the lady Nymue's attentions, and neither has she offered them to me. I do not know what Edyth is saying." He spread his hand wide in a gesture of helplessness.

"My lady." Afera stepped forward and her simple homespun robe swept the mud. She kept her head bent. "I will take care of my words as I am only too aware that I am your maid of the chamber and that I owe you for my position. But it is true. I saw your daughter give to Sir Aldwyn a token. Her gold ring. She pulled it off her finger and gave it to him. I saw it. A gold ring is a betrothal token, not a battle token."

Vivianne knew that this was true, but it did not constitute a betrothal, not in this settlement and not between a thegn and one of the royal blood. "There is no betrothal. She may have given him a battle token, or she may not, but that does not indicate a betrothal. As the daughter of the cūning and as the first ætheling, she hand-fasts only to the one I have chosen for her. You must know that. So I want none of this nonsense."

"I came here to Cūning's Mere from Wermunds Low and there we respected the betrothal token." Edyth tossed her head and her wispy fair locks slipped from her cap.

"It was many a year since you came here from Wermunds Low, Edyth, and you were but a child. What would a child know of the conventions and traditions of her own settlement, let alone someone else's?" Vivianne took a deep breath to still her fast beating heart. "I will not argue with you about our traditions nor about my daughter." She turned to the hall.

"My lady," Afera's voice stopped her. "Perhaps you do not see. But the lady Nymue has indeed made eyes at Gareth Swineson while Sir Aldwyn is away fighting for the settlement as a noble battle thegn." She nodded at Edyth. "I have seen it all. And more than that, Gareth is my lover!"

"That is not true!" Gareth objected, arms held wide in confusion. "Afera, I like you, of course I do. But we are nothing more. We have not exchanged rings or any other token. We have not held each other." He gulped, his face reddening. "We have not lain together."

Vivianne heard Nymue behind her let out a sigh,

and she thought it was one of relief. She was aware that the villagers had stopped their talking and all eyes and ears were fixed on the little group by the hall. She closed her eyes for a moment, trying to clear her mind. "Hear me. I will not listen to any more of this gossip and tittle-tattle." She set her mouth in a hard line. "You will not speak of any one of my family – your royal family – in this way again. I will hear none of it. If you have any complaint you must use the proper channels, speak with Ealdorman Godwyne, and ask to come to the mead hall for a private audience with me. In the meantime, you will not speak the name of my daughter and Sir Aldwyn or Gareth Swineson in the same breath ever again." She stopped to draw in a deep ragged breath.

Vivianne could hear only the young swine splashing in the water of the roadway ruts. The earth seemed to stand still, holding its breath. "Edyth, you will return to your weaving shed and Afera be about your business – you are not engaged to spend my time – *my* time – in idle speculation about your mistress. Gareth Swineson, you will take the piglets back up to the sties and come back down to the mead hall to speak with me."

Her voice softened as she looked around her at the groups of ceorls and geburs, huddled around the workshop doorways, mouths agape, eyes fearful. "Everyone else, please kindly be about *your* business too. I am sincerely sorry that this moment of joy and hope has been spoiled by this incident." She turned. "Come, Nymue," and she swept into the hall past Matilda who stood aghast at the door, aware that Nymue was hurrying behind her, and aware too that her heart beat fast and loud in the chest and her hands trembled. She barely heard the muffled applause that arose behind her on the roadway and she certainly did not see the bitter glare that Edyth shot towards her back.

In front of the blazing hearth, Vivianne paused then swung round to her daughter. Nymue stood just inside the doorway hanging her head as Matilda closed the heavy wooden door behind them. Her voice was low but slithery as an adder.

"What was all that about, Nymue?" she hissed. "Whatever you have done, or not done, for me to hear something like that *in public* is outrageous! What am I to make of it?"

"Oh, mōđor, I ... I do not know what to say." She stared at her feet. Vivianne had to strain to hear her daughter's words, so quiet and thin they were. "I did indeed give Sir Aldwyn a token and it was my gold ring. You knew that. But it was a battle token not a betrothal token. We have barely spoken together, let alone ..." She bit her lip. "I wanted to be like the other girls and have a sweetheart. They were always boasting of it. I so much longed for a love of my own, and you did not want Gareth Swineson." Vivianne opened her mouth to speak but Nymue raised her hand. "I know why. I accept that. But then when I looked upon Aldwyn ... so handsome and a worthy thegn ... oh, I know you do not approve of Aldwyn because of his father Sir Pelleas. But when he looked kindly at me and his eyes were smiling at me in that way of lovers, my heart felt so full. A man, a thegn, loved me!"

Vivianne felt her anger dissipate. She closed her eyes and sank onto the stool at the fireside. "Oh, Nymue. You are so much between a child and a woman. It was not so long ago that your courses began. And yet ... I think there is the understanding of a woman beginning to take hold in your head and your heart. Come sit before me here."

Nymue sat on the stool facing her mother and as she lifted her head, Vivianne could see the tears coursing down her cheeks.

"Mōđor, I do not know what I want. My head is in a whirl every day. I do not know who I should love."

Vivianne reached across the table, smiled, and patted Nymue's knee. "Well, I hope it is myself and your father and your brothers and sister that you love!"

"Of course. But I mean ..."

"Yes, I know what you mean, Nymue." She sat back. "I think that today has shocked you and that you have realised how the actions of this family matter so much to the people of our settlement. It may be gossip but it is important gossip and it matters to the villagers. That is what it means to be of this family. As well as our privileges we have responsibilities. We need to set an example. We do not have the luxury of privacy and the freedom that our people have. We cannot always do what we want to do. That is what we have contracted to give up, for the sake of this status and position."

"But I did not ask for that."

"No, Nymue, but neither did I. It is handed down to us from our forebears. It was handed down to me from my parents after the settlement rejected Sir Pelleas. Perhaps at some time in the future it will be different. Perhaps another king will appear because he wins a battle over us and gains our kingdom. But until then, this is what we have." She sighed. "Sometimes I feel deeply sorry that this is so – that I have handed down to you this responsibility, one you did not ask for. But you have privilege. You are truly fortunate." Vivianne gestured around her to the riches of the chamber: the roaring fire, the beautiful hand carved furniture of the richest woods, the wall hangings, the fine robes they wore. Knowing that, whatever she said, however much she insisted, they would always be given the best food, and enough, while the others went short.

Nymue looked straight and true at her mother. "Yes, I know."

Lady Vivianne smiled. "And what is this about Gareth Swineson? Let me know everything before I hear it from the gossips."

"I think I like him. No, I *do* like him. And maybe I have looked kindly upon him and smiled at him. But I know that he is not for me … *cannot* be for me. Maybe he has Afera, although I believe him when he says not. But I will not look upon him again." She bit her lip. "I know that you and my father will choose a suitable love for me. Perhaps a man of royal blood from another settlement, or at least the son of a royal thegn." She shrugged. "Gareth Swineson is not for me. I know that, mōđor."

Yet Vivianne heard the quiver of sadness and yearning in her voice and her heart felt heavy. She nodded. "Duty," she whispered, thinking how lucky she and Roland had been, "and the royal line."

A cough across the room reminded Vivianne of Matilda's presence, guarding the door for their privacy. "My lady, remember that you wanted to speak with Gareth Swineson in the mead hall and I believe I hear Sir Godwyne outside, probably wanting to draw your attention to his arrival down from the livestock fields."

"Thank you, Tilda. I will go to the mead hall at once. No, not you, Nymue," she added as her daughter made to stand. "I must speak with him alone."

Nymue bit her lip again and Vivianne noticed the blood red mark it left. "What will you say to him?"

"I will gently dissuade him from sharing glances with you," Vivianne smiled. "And I will seek to discover his true relationship with Afera. Although I think that girl has a vivid imagination and believes something is true just because she wants it to be so. But I must also seek to discourage Afera's alliance with Edyth. I see no good coming from it. And I do not want to have to dismiss Afera from my close service as maid of my chamber if I cannot trust her. At any rate, not yet. I will give her another chance. But only one."

"Mōđor, you are good to give her another chance. I do not think she meant real harm. But maybe she is just jealous because she fears she might lose him."

"My lady." Matilda was almost hopping from one foot to the other in her agitation. "She cannot lose him if she never had him in the first place! Pfft!" Her impatience with Afera was evident and Vivianne and Nymue shared a smile. "But, my lady, your audience …"

"Yes, yes." Vivianne rose and made for the door.

"AND SO, GARETH SWINESON," LADY VIVIANNE concluded. "I think that maybe my maid Afera is a little confused. Perhaps there is some wishful thinking there. You would be wise to be aware of that. But more than anything, please hear what I have just said about my daughter Nymue. She is still at that impressionable age and even a little glance can imply to a young girl something that is not necessarily intended by a young man."

Gareth bowed, although Vivianne saw his frown. "Indeed, my lady, and I would hate to think that I had upset either you or your daughter. Please forgive me if I have offended."

"Of ..." Vivianne's dismissal comment was left hanging in the air as the door to the mead hall was flung open and the door guard entered.

"My lady, I apologise for the interruption, but there is a messenger come from the south! From the battle camp!"

Lady Vivianne rose from her bench, heart thumping, hand pressed to her heart and face drained of blood. "Let him come!"

Gareth stood aside and the messenger entered the hall, a guard on either side holding him up as he staggered. His legs barely had the strength to set his feet on the floor. Vivianne gasped to see his tunic and hose stained with dried blood, the side of his face open with a gaping wound, his head beneath his long wild hair, broken. His boots were torn and his hands shaking uncontrollably, clutching at his ripped jerkin.

Vivianne made to approach the man, but one of the guards held out a restraining hand. "My lady, he is in a grievously bad way. We tried to stop him, but he just wishes to tell you his report personally as is his duty, before his breathing renders it impossible and then he can sink onto his bedding."

She stopped in her tracks and gestured to the man to speak.

"Lady Vivianne, chieftain of the ... dear place of my birth ... Cūning's Mere. I know that I return to my certain death. But I had to stay alive long enough to tell you ... to tell you what has befallen your thegns." He coughed painfully.

"Gareth," Vivianne cried, "Fetch a seat for him, for heavens' sake!" But he already had one ready in his hands. The guards settled the messenger onto the stool but remained on either side, holding him up as gently as they could. Gareth grabbed a goblet of wine and a cloth from the table behind Vivianne and poured a few drops down the man's throat, wet his lips and swabbed the sweating face. But it did little to revive him. Vivianne could see that he was near to death. Yet he responded to Gareth's kind gesture with a faint twitch of his mouth in a parody of a smile.

"Tell me what you can," Vivianne whispered.

"My lady, the warriors from Deorabye never came to join us; we were alone. Yet we rode on towards the Angeln for the honour of our land. But we were led into ambush by a traitor as we rode towards the Angeln. They were giants of men and covered in rough hair like wild bears. But even so your thegns did not hesitate to engage battle. So brave were they that the battle hung in the balance for many days ... the thegns fought on all sides refusing to give up even when they were gravely injured." He drew in a rasping agonising breath. "Then as it looked as if we were making headway and their leader, Icel, was faltering, that one same thegn seemed to signal to the Angeln and another battle cry went up ... and suddenly we were surrounded and it was impossible ... we were routed. I am severely injured, my lady ... I can no longer ..." Another bout of coughing wracked his body.

"I thank you. But the thegns? My lord Sir Roland? What of him?"

"Many dead ... "

"Dead? Is he dead?" She had known it but had not wanted to believe it. Now it was to be confirmed and when the truth was spoken it would be real.

"... Many captured. Sir Roland too ... they said they could bargain with his life ..."

"But he is alive, you say?" She could hardly believe it.

"Alive. I think. When I left. But weak from his wounds. And it has taken me many moons ... to get here through the floods and landslides ... and my sickness. I have had to stop ... I feared I would not make it back to you with the news. So who knows ... whether it is still true?"

"But alive," breathed Vivianne. "Alive when you left. I thank you from the bottom of my heart. Guards, make him comfortable on a bed in the thegns' quarters, get his wounds tended and get the women to prepare herbal draughts. And give him any food or drink that he wants." But she knew that even if he could manage to eat, it would be his last meal on this earth. At least their task was to prepare him comfortably for death.

The messenger began to speak but his rasping voice petered out as he collapsed and the guards who were supporting him heaved him between them towards the door.

"Wait! Who?" Vivianne called after them, "Who was the traitor?"

"Aldwyn," said one of the guards.

CHAPTER 18

LADY VIVIANNE

Cūning's Mere 520 AD

"What am I to do?" cried Vivianne, wringing her hands as she almost fell into the sacred hall of her dear dead parents. "Roland is many moons ride away, a captive of Icel and the Angeln, and the weather will be closing in again soon for winter. How do I bring him home? And the other thegns too. Do I send my remaining men to find them? Through the coming winter?"

She sank down onto the floor before the altar and looked up at the icons as if to beg them for an answer. "We have so many old men left here. How can I send the only strong younger ceorls and geburs that we have? The few thegns? For then we would not have enough to help the settlement to survive the winter. And who do I sacrifice?"

A soft breath of air wafted into the hall and drifted over the altar. She watched it as if she saw her father and mother there. It surrounded her in a close embrace, just like those they had given her in life. They stroked her forehead and lifted her head rail to caress her hair.

"Vivianne. Our little lady Vivianne. Our dearest daughter who now rules the kingdom in our name. You feel alone. But we are still with you. We never left."

Tears were running down her cheeks and she tried to brush them away with the back of her hand. But it felt as though her mother stayed her hand, held it and turned it to kiss the palm and press it to her own face.

"Have strength. You are no longer our little Vivianne. You are the wise and steadfast Chieftain queen and you are as strong as any other, as strong as any man. You need but to know it. In your heart you know what you must do. It will become clear and soon it will lift from your heart to your mind and you will prepare yourself for what must come now."

Vivianne could smell the dried lavender strewn on the floor but through that sweet heady perfume she could also breathe the bergamot scent that always reminded her of her father and of Roland. "Where are you?" she whispered. "Roland, my love, where have they taken you? Are you well? Are they treating you as they should treat a battle leader, a king?"

But she also thought of the other battle thegns and her heart went out to their wives and families, their children and parents. They were hers. They were all hers.

Somehow she had to bring them all home. The messenger had said that Icel and his band of Icelings of the Angeln, might want to bargain with Roland's life. She had to find a way to negotiate with them. What might they need? She had to find something that would be worth to them what Roland's life and that of her thegns was worth to her and to her settlement. Gold? Jewellery?

As she returned to her chamber through the mud that still lingered, now becoming cold and hard, she thought of what little she knew of the Angeln. They were fighters, she had heard of their battles, and Icel and his Icelings seemed by repute to be some of the most efficient, deadly and brave of warriors. They came over the wild stormy seas from the north east to reach this land. Why would they do that? For the spoils of war: the gold, the minerals, the articles the people of these lands made? To carry their spoils back to their own land and become rich for themselves and for trade?

Or maybe they came for the rich soil? If they wanted the rich soil, then they desired it for growing, for grazing, for living in these lands.

Did they want to drive her people of Cūning's Mere away and take their land and their homes, their livestock? Bands of raiders had attacked Wermunds Low, Cerdic the guard had reported a while ago, men from the Angeln pushing in from the eastern coast to raid stocks and crops from the fields under cover of darkness. At the time she had thought only that they wanted food for their camp. But maybe it was something different. Maybe they wanted to settle here.

Instead of returning to her chamber she headed for the mead hall and sent for Godwyne, and after some thought, for Acton and Gareth also. They would also know about the messenger's words by now. All the settlement would know by now.

Gareth was the last to arrive, shaking the field dirt from his cloak at the door before he entered, apologising. They stood before her as she warmed her hands at the fire.

"I thank you for coming so promptly," she began. "I have been giving thought to the messenger's words." She paused and surveyed their grave faces.

"My lady," said Gareth, his voice low and soft. "I am sure that we all feel a great sadness and fear at what has befallen our battle thegns. I speak because I was the only one of the three of us to hear the messenger's report as he drew his last breaths." He looked keenly into her eyes. "I do not have the words to express my sorrow for the loss nor words of comfort at this time. But I am sure that I speak for us all when I say that we will offer ourselves to you for anything you may need." He bowed. The other men murmured their agreement.

For a moment Vivianne was taken aback at his kind and unexpected words. That a swineherd – no, of course, a chief ceorl – should speak so nobly like a thegn touched her heart. She nodded. "I thank you, Gareth Swineson. You are most kind and your words are most welcome." She smiled at him and a little warmth seeped into her fearful heart. She looked from one to the other. Acton was fidgeting awkwardly and Sir Godwyne appeared more crumpled and withered than usual. "I called for you three to discover as much as I could about the warrior Icel and his men. Whatever you know, or have heard tell, or whatever you can find out for me I would be grateful to hear. I need to know what manner of men these are and therefore how I might deal with them."

Godwyne and Acton frowned in puzzlement. "Why, my lady?" asked Godwyne, shrugging his thin shoulders. "They are warriors, they fight battles. They are powerful opponents, as we have heard tell from the messenger's report. They are bad enemies to have. They are merciless. What more do you need to know about them?"

"I can add no more to Godwyne's words," said Acton, shaking his head. "That is all I have ever heard and all anyone has ever known. Unless we engage in battle with them, which we can no longer do ..." He twisted his mouth in anguish.

But Gareth glanced sideways from one to the other, then inclined his head and spoke hesitantly yet his voice was strong. "If I may speak so boldly, I think I understand your thoughts, my lady. I am no battle thegn and understand no strategy of battle engagement. But I know that we cannot go into battle again with them to retrieve our captive thegns. And so we must find another way. If we know our enemy then maybe we can discover another way to defeat them rather than with our blood."

Lady Vivianne smiled. "Indeed, you have my thoughts entirely, Gareth Swineson. I thank you."

Godwyne and Acton looked at Gareth, still puzzled. He did not look at them but nodded at Lady Vivianne and she noticed for the first time how deep and dark his eyes were, how strong his features. He seemed much older and more authoritative than he ever had before. "The messenger said that Icel held Sir Roland perhaps to bargain with his life."

Vivianne raised her eyebrows. "You heard that too? It was not just my imagination?"

Gareth bowed. "Yes, my lady. I heard it."

"Ah," breathed Godwyne and Acton in unison as though had they been present at the messenger's report they too would have thought of this way through despair.

Vivianne kept her eyes on Gareth. "So I would like you all to do all you can to find out anything possible about Icel and his Icelings. Do they want the spoils of war to return riches to their Angeln homeland, or do they want something else? Are they looking to settle here in this land they have journeyed to, are their sights on capturing settlements or are they going to build their own? So would the bargain they want for Sir Roland's life be our gold or our land?"

Gareth smiled as though he liked what she had to say and nodded.

LADY VIVIANNE COULD DO NOTHING UNTIL SHE HAD gathered information about Icel and his people. But facts were hard to come by, and the reports she received, especially those from Acton and Godwyne, were clearly tales and fantasies that were circulating around the villages. All she heard was that the Icelings were cruel warriors, they were ruthless conquerors, they were plunderers, they were rapists. Some said they were wanting to steal riches to take back to their homeland to enrich their own people back there. Some said they were intent on forcing the peoples of the midlands out of their homes so that they could take the settlements over for themselves without the need to build. Some said they would kill all the population, or enslave them all, in order to take over power and make their own strange and cruel kingdoms.

Gareth's reports were a little more moderate and seemed to come from some intelligence gleaned from who-knew-where. He had word that the Angeln, and Icel in particular, wanted the land of the Brythons and the Romans because their own land was exhausted of nutrients for crops and cattle and so they had to seek elsewhere for their living.

She did not know what to believe. And all the time the weather was becoming colder yet again and bitter winds were again howling around the houses and roads of the settlement. The skies were heavy with snow even in the clear icy brightness. The doors of the workshops and the selling shops were shut tight against the chill and if anyone needed to buy or set an order they had to beat on the door for attention. The air was filled with the smoke of fires as the people tried to keep warm. The glimmer of brightness had disappeared, and the returning rain was replaced now with the snap of ice. The children slid and skittered in delight on the smooth slippery tracks while their anxious parents endeavoured to keep the fires going, to feed their thin families with morsels and their lone cow and small cluster of chickens, and to weave warmer clothes for them all.

There was no need for Vivianne to tell the younger children about their father or the disasters of the battle, only that she had heard news and that it would be several moons before he was back with them. To Tristram and Nymue she had carefully explained that the thegns were captured but well, even though she knew that this was not entirely true, and that the Icelings were waiting to speak with them. She decided that she should also tell them that Aldwyn had betrayed them and that this was the reason for their capture.

They were both shocked, but Nymue more so than her brother. She raged through the hall.

"I hate him!" she yelled.

Tristram looked up from the battle plan he was drawing. "And to think you gave him your token!" he mocked.

Nymue swung round to him angrily. "Yes, and how stupid I was! You need not say it, Tristram. But I did not know he was a traitor! How could I?"

"Peace, both of you. None of us were to know what Aldwyn would do. I can only assume that he was bribed with riches or position to do such a thing to his own people. After all, his mother is still amongst us, although I guess that now she will be regarded with suspicion by her neighbours and disgraced." She shook her head and sighed. "Did he have no care for her at all?"

VIVIANNE'S BELLY WAS GROWING ALTHOUGH SHE KNEW that there were another four or five more full moons yet before the child needed to be birthed. Matilda had already found her old fuller robes that she wore through her previous pregnancies, and, with her skill with her bone needle, had set about mending and altering and trimming with new edging. Afera was of less help; she was still ill-tempered and moody, especially in the vicinity of Nymue, and Vivianne was sorely tempted to dismiss her and find a new girl who might be more cooperative. But she held firm in the hopes that she would learn from her dear Tilda's example.

The Icelings and her beloved Roland were never far from her thoughts. She needed council but for some reason which she did not completely understand, she hesitated to send for Godwyne, so she asked Matilda to send for Gareth instead to attend her in her chamber which was warmer than the mead hall.

Matilda looked quizzically at her mistress but sent the guard for Gareth and took the younger children through to the ante chamber to play. Tristram was allowed to stay by the fire with his toy soldiers and his battle plans, and Nymue bent her head further over her tapestry in the corner under the window, her long fair braids falling over her work. Afera she sent out for bread.

"Nymue, you may stay if you wish but it will soon be time for your archery practice in the mead hall with your tutor. If you prefer to go now, you may."

"I ... I will stay."

"Then keep your eyes on your work, if you please." Vivianne noted that her daughter was already dressed for archery in her plain and modest homespun tunic.

"My lady?" Matilda bustled Gareth inside and brought goblets and a jug of hot ale to place on the table. "Will Tristram be allowed a little ale today to beat the cold, my lady?" She winked at him.

"Indeed, he will. And please pour a goblet for Nymue also, Matilda. She will take it in her place at the window as she is busy with her wools. Gareth, take this stool before me by the fire." She heard Matilda's gasp, but chose to ignore it and gestured her to go to the children in the ante chamber.

"My lady, I have just come from the fields. I think I smell of the sty." Vivianne saw that he glanced towards Nymue but quickly looked away again as she studiously stared at her tapestry, eyes intently down, the effort clear on her face.

"No matter, Gareth. I have smelled worse. But I believe I can smell bergamot."

She saw Nymue look up briefly from her work and raise her eyebrows.

Gareth sat awkwardly, his back towards Nymue, but Vivianne smiled at him and offered him a goblet of ale.

"I have sent for you, Gareth, because you know as much of the seasons and the weather as anyone, living as you do in the fields and tending the livestock according to the wind and rain and snow."

"Yes, my lady."

"So I need to know whether it would be safe to send out an emissary to the Icelings? I receive little information other than unreliable tales and gossip and so I must plan to send envoys who can judge the bargaining required." She frowned. "Although I know how dangerous a mission this will be, without the vagaries of the weather."

Gareth hesitated. "I am no thegn or trader or traveller. But if I judge correctly, my lady, and from what I understand about the terrain and the siting of the camp, I believe it would take at least one or two full moons, maybe more, to ride to Icel's camp. Longer if there needed to be baggage carts. The snows will be with us long before then and the going would be tough, if not impossible. In fact, I sense the snows are not far away. And once the winter weather closes in, we will be unable to venture out or travel far from here."

"Your advice is 'no'?"

"My advice would be to wait until the better weather, until the danger of snow is less. And if I might say, my lady, in the meantime, the Icelings will not treat Sir Roland and the thegns any less than well if they wish to bargain with you. It would hardly be in their interest. And they also will not be able to engage in any more battles or distant raids until the better weather. So, for what it is worth, I would say that there is no advantage to sending an emissary yet."

"So you think we should sit tight here?"

"I do, my lady. But perhaps you would be wise to seek the advice of others more experienced than I."

Vivianne inclined her head. "Others may be more experienced, but not, I think, as perceptive as you are, Gareth. That is why I sent for you."

"I thank you, my lady."

"You have finished your ale. I thank you for your words and now you may go back to your work."

Gareth rose but as he reached the door, he turned back to Vivianne. "And, my lady, could I be so bold as to say that if you have need of a volunteer for an emissary and none is readily forthcoming, I will be honoured to offer myself."

"You can ride?"

Gareth smiled. "Yes, of course."

"And use the battle seax and bow if needed to protect yourself?"

"Indeed, my lady." He bowed and left.

CHAPTER 19

LADY VIVIANNE

Cūning's Mere 520 AD

It was wise that Lady Vivianne heeded the words of Gareth Swineson, for the settlement was soon holed in with the snow. It began a few nights after their conversation and fell heavily and unceasing for so long that the roadways were deep and almost impassable other than the narrow channels that the geburs were able to dig through so that the people could walk between the houses and workshops. There was barely enough room for the horses and certainly none for the carts. People were forced to stagger through the snow carrying their loads on their backs or their heads.

Vivianne shivered on the roadside by her hall, pulling her thick fur cloak closer around her body, against the swirling snow that spun and billowed in front of her face. Everywhere was wreathed in white and it was hard to tell where the ground ended and the sky began. Her hall-geburs had dug pathways for her, and themselves, to make their way through to the bakers and the cooking houses, and the ale brewers. She watched them as they laboured to finish the channel to the leather worker's workshop. She could see that there was a whole network of pathways as far as she could make out through the blizzard, so that the villagers were not completely isolated in their homes. She had directed the serfs to ensure that there was a good way through to Gareth's house at the foot of the hills, and knew that he and the field geburs had cleared the snow, as much as they could, up to the livestock fields. Acton had reported to her that the arable fields were under snow, but they were doing what they could to manage the barns and the grain bins, half empty already as they were.

She could see only a few paces in front of her and the snow was falling almost as quickly as it was being cleared. As difficult as it was for the work of the settlement, Vivianne could not help but feel the delight of the children throwing great handfuls of snow at each other and she smiled at the beauty of the thatched buildings swathed in pure white. For once everything looked clean. She turned her face to the leaden sky and let the cold snowflakes fall softly onto her cheeks, knowing that she could return to her chamber and the roaring fire if she was too cold and wet.

Yet her heart bled for her battle thegns so far away and for those killed and injured. And of course for her dear Roland held captive by Icel. Was the Icel camp also holed up with the snows? When would her thegns be back home again? Were they cold or ill or hungry? Who was tending to their needs, like children if they were injured?

Her own children were being kept strictly indoors by the fire by a stern Matilda, after the boys had come in to break their fast, soaking wet and dripping, laughing with fingers blue and mouths too frozen to speak. Launce and even Tristram, despite pretending he was too old for childish games, wanted nothing more than to run outside all day with the other children, pushing each other into the snowdrifts and rolling around on the ground, making patterns on the snow. But Matilda was strict and gave dire warnings of chills and fevers and all manner of illnesses. Nymue was keeping little Nini occupied in the warm, teaching her how to fix an arrow into her bow and how to keep them smooth for better flight.

Vivianne licked a snowflake from her upper lip and shook out her cloak before returning to her hall and its warmth. A vision of Roland filled her mind and she hoped that he was warm and safe, and wished with all her heart that she could see him and wrap her arms around him again. Gēol, as Roland had called it, and she smiled fondly at the memory, would be a thin sparse celebration this year. Christ's Mass would not be the great feasting and merry-making it normally was. Partly because the food stocks were low enough before the snows and now with the coming of the wintry weather were so depleted that she knew that they would be reduced to a poor meal to celebrate the birth of Christ. And partly because of what was on all their minds: they were all only too aware of the absence of the thegns. Her own heart twisted at the thought that Roland, wherever he was, would not be marking the festival at all. The Angeln were, as far as she knew, pagans.

But perhaps they had their own mid-winter festival, she mused, as her own settlement had so long ago before her father brought Christianity to them from Rome. She had a vague memory from her youngest childhood of some of the villagers dressing in strange rather frightening costumes with faces painted, and of holly and mistletoe from the hedgerows hanging from their houses, wreaths of holly on their doors and circlets of greenery on the women's hair. Were there not huge green men running from house to house, or was that her imagination? She wondered how many of her villagers now would still secretly hide the trappings of their pagan ancestors in their little houses. How many would still beg for the coming of the new, the rising again of the sun, by cleaning out their houses and hailing the new year's spirits with incantations and a brush of yew.

Perhaps Roland would be allowed to share in the Angeln's feast. Perhaps Icel would bring him to the fire and feed him with their roasted swine. Or would they keep him and the other thegns imprisoned in some small dark cramped shelter, cold and hungry?

She could not find joy in Christ's birth this year, nor relish the simple feast they would share in the mead hall. She had already spoken with Godwyne about what they could spare for the Christ's Mass meal. There would be only simple roasted swine and a little salted wild deer and boar, a few root vegetables and the poorer rougher rye bread to share around the table. She knew that the cooks would produce a good meal with tasty juices to dip the coarse bread in, and there would still be ale and possibly an amphora of wine. It would not be the same, but it would be as good as she could make it.

All the same, she felt guilty that they had even that much while her beloved Roland might be poorly kept – and maybe even sick or dying of wounds. But she must not imagine the worst. As Gareth had said so wisely, it would not be in Icel's interests to treat him badly if he wished to bargain. She must fix her mind on that.

There would be few gifts for her children. For Launce she had paid the bowman to make him a small sized bow and a quiver of arrows, for Tristram the metal worker made a newly decorated sword. Matilda fashioned a pretty little doll for Nini, made from an old dress of Vivianne's, and for Nymue there was a cloak trimmed with fur, although it was old wool that had been re-dyed. The children gave Vivianne a beautiful gold brooch clasp to hold her mantle and although she was aware that it had been melted down and re-worked, it touched her heart dearly that they had been so thoughtful.

But after the Christ's Mass meal in the mead hall everyone had trudged back home through the snow without any entertainment from a scōp or a glæman for nobody could face poetry or laughter or dancing, least of all Vivianne, and they all crept away to their beds to wonder what the Wolf Moon would bring.

IN FACT, IT BROUGHT THEM THE GREAT THAW. THE SNOWS melted and the roadways were again awash with water. The air became unusually mild and Lady Vivianne wondered at such changeable and unusual weather. It was not too long before she was able to climb up to the livestock and arable fields above the village again without having to wade through thick snow.

The villagers seemed brighter and more hopeful for the coming moons and as she greeted them some of the older ones spoke of a good *æftera gēola* in the old language. She could see through their open doors the swags of holly alongside their crucifixes. But she would not speak of it sternly because she knew that it brought them comfort.

From the hillside, Vivianne looked down upon the settlement. The clusters of houses in the villages were wreathed in smoke from the fires and she was thankful that there were enough branches cut from the forest to keep her people warm and keep the cooking fires going. Even though the air was no longer icy she knew that it would surely not last and the colder weather would surely return to them. It still struck her with wonder that her settlement stretched so far now. She narrowed her eyes and strained to see but she could not make out the borders in the far distance, although she mused that a wisp of smoke far away could be the border guards' camp way to the east. How much the settlement had grown from her parents' days until now, with new comers arriving from other desperate ravaged villages, eager to share the land and resources of Cūning's Mere. And Lady Vivianne and Sir Roland had welcomed them because they knew that these new settlers would share in the work and the growing prosperity and peace of their home. Until now ...

So lost in her dreams was she that she did not hear Gareth until he was right beside her. His voice was soft as though he hesitated to interrupt her thoughts.

"My lady, are you well?"

"Oh, Gareth Swineson!" She swung round and nodded to him. He was leaning on a long hewn branch and also staring out over the settlement. "I am considering what to do now that the snows have gone and better weather may lie ahead."

"The snows have gone for the moment in the thaw," he nodded, "but we are seeing such changeable weather. I fear that it will not be the last of the cold, and certainly until the Lenten Moon it is not even usually unknown for snows to come heavily again, let alone in these unpredictable times."

"So you think that it will still be unsafe to send an emissary to Icel's camp?"

Gareth frowned. "I would say that it may be possible to start out on a journey but to be cut off before that journey's end."

"I see." Vivianne bit her lip.

"You are anxious, my lady, I know. And of course we would never be certain of the weather until well after the Paschal Moon, and even then ..."

"Indeed I am anxious, Gareth. And ... I wonder if we might just take the chance. I do not wish to put my emissaries into danger ... although of course even the journey itself spells danger, let alone the vagaries of the weather. But I cannot wait until after the Paschal Moon. I want them back by Lenten."

Gareth drew in a deep breath and nodded. "Then perhaps taking a chance is all you can do, my lady."

"Yes, yes. But I am afeared to send my working men into danger at all. Yet how long can we go on without our thegns? On either side there are dangers and disasters. Whatever I do ... I must return to the sacred hall and draw strength to consider what I must do for the best. Soon it will be resolved."

"THAT IS MADNESS, MŌÐOR!" NYMUE PACED UP AND down the chamber, hands in the air outlining her exasperation. "How *can* you?"

"It is for the best," said Vivianne firmly.

"But mōðor ...! Matilda, tell her ...!"

Matilda stood like stone, the blood drained from her face, mouth gaping open in horror. She shook her head as if to summon the power of speech. "My lady, how can you?" The baby will be coming before three or four more moons! You cannot ride out!"

"If I need to birth the baby while I am away, so be it. I will take a birthing nurse with me in case of this, one who is experienced as a wet nurse."

Matilda shook her head in disbelief. "Then let me go with you to look after you in your last moons and the baby if he comes ..."

"No, Tilda. I thank you for saying so, for I know how such a journey and such a mission would bring terror to your gentle soul. But I cannot. And I need you here to look after my children so that I will know they are safe. While I am away."

"Then you will kill the baby and yourself," cried Nymue. "And then what will we do?"

Vivianne rested her hand on the small mound of her belly and closed her eyes. "I know that you are afeared for me. But how could I send an envoy on my behalf if I am not prepared to make the journey myself? I have to see for myself of what manner of men the Icelings may be and what might be the nature of their desire for bargaining. I must be the one to negotiate their terms with them."

"But the thegns can do that!"

Vivianne shook her head. "What thegns, my beloved daughter?"

"The ... I do not know! The ceorls then!"

"Which of the ceorls can we send that might not be needed here? And I cannot send ceorls for this business. This is too important a quest."

"But *you* are needed here. Everyone is needed here."

"So we send nobody? We leave our thegns in the hands of the Icelings? I have to bring them home. I have to bring Sir Roland home."

"I ... I ... the baby!"

Matilda knelt down before Vivianne, on the rushes and a waft of dried lavender arose into the air. Vivianne breathed in the sweet scent and it helped to keep her calm.

"My lady, please, I beg of you, do not embark on this ... this madness, for lady Nymue is right, that is what it is. I know that you want Sir Roland back – and the rest of the battle thegns – we all do, but to put yourself and the baby into such danger ... you are our cūning. What would the settlement do if we lost both you and Sir Roland?"

Vivianne straightened her back and pulled herself up to her full height. "My mind is made up. After all, how many cūning battle leaders do the same? That I am a woman makes no difference. So this is what will happen. I am leaving Nymue in my place to rule while I am gone. It will not be for long, I hope and pray. Nymue, you have Ealdorman Godwyne as advisor and counsellor whilst I am away."

Nymue looked stunned. "You trust *me*?"

"Of course I do. You are the first ætheling. And you have shown me in the past few moons that you are as strong and wise as I could hope for. You are ready to prepare for what will eventually be your role anyway. And I am asking Gareth Swineson to be your advisor also."

"What?" Nymue blinked, hands flying up to cover her mouth.

"I expect comely behaviour as befits a cūning and her advisor. You will each know your place. And, mind, he will still be working as our livestock ceorl. But I trust Gareth too and I have come to welcome his wisdom and insight perhaps more than anyone else. He offered to go himself and I nearly accepted that, but we cannot manage without him here. So what do you say?"

Nymue knelt before her mother and Matilda rose

to step aside. She hung her head in thought for a while and presently she said, "I am honoured that you are asking me to hold the settlement for you while you are away. But, oh, mōđor, please I beg you, do not endanger yourself like this. Even if you take guards with you, you will be putting your very life in danger and that of the baby. Please do not go ..." Tears began to roll down her cheeks and she did not brush them away so that they pooled darkly on the pale fabric covering her lap.

Vivianne reached out her hand and touched the top of her daughter's head. "I say again. My mind is made up. I ride out the sunrise after next."

VIVIANNE, FOR ALL HER BRAVADO, HELD A HEAVY HEART within her. She had always been an excellent horse rider, but she had no real idea of the terrain she was facing. Her messengers and fore-scouts had known the way south but not the end of the journey, the exact location of Icel's camp. That, she would need to ascertain when they drew close.

She imagined the journey ahead, its stretches of forest and tracks, its hills and crags. And with a full belly and the discomfort and pains she had been feeling for so long now, she knew that it was probably unwise. But what else could she do? Even if she died on the mission, at least she would leave the settlement in good hands and that the people would know that she had done her best for them. She held her breath steady as she sent for the items she needed to take on her mission.

Her inherited gold lay on her bed ready to be packed in the saddle bags on Sir Roland's second battle horse that she was taking instead of her own lighter steed. There were gold clasps, brooches, finger rings, and bracelets, all newly polished and gleaming. They would be hidden beneath cloths and would not leave her sight for the whole journey. It was not her whole inheritance but a gesture to offer to Icel to start the negotiations.

She had the hall-ceorls pack a rich heavy cloak dyed with precious red and bedecked with blue glass beads as a gift for Icel to demonstrate her good faith, and a ceremonial sword encrusted with jewels and engraved with intertwined *wyrms*, a replica of the Witan sword. For herself she had them pack her regal cloak of red and purple with the embroidered white dragon of her family upon it, and her cūning's gold circlet for her hair.

She sent to the kitchens for earthenware jars of honey and precious wheat bread marked at the top with Icel's name, although she knew it would not be edible by the time she found him. It was a gesture after all and a gift to say this is what we produce, these are our skills. She would take a sample of their honeyed mead and wine. Perhaps they would consider a trading arrangement, although she did not know what the Icelings could offer to Cūning's Mere as trade, unless they had brought exotic items from their homeland or had the skills to make stemmed wine glasses or sturdy storage amphora. Somehow she doubted that.

Vivianne had held a short Witan council with the ealdormen, the chief ceorls and the few elderly thegns left, to announce her plans to the settlement. It was a statement, not a discussion, and the people in the mead hall received the news in near silence. A ripple of unease and bewilderment shivered across the hall. But as she neared the end of her speech, proudly and defiantly holding the Witan sword aloft, she saw that a few raised their seaxes in support. The others looked astonished.

Then, all of a sudden, as the ceorls and thegns began to understand the momentous nature of her intentions, the sound of many a clashing seax arose and the hall erupted into noise as victory roars resounded to the rafters.

Soon all the villagers knew what their cūning queen was prepared to do to bring their thegns home, and they began to arrive at the mead hall with gifts they thought would aid Lady Vivianne's negotiations. It seemed that the journey carts would be full of the offerings they brought, more than they could possibly carry, and indeed she soon had to ask for them to be given out to the most needy of the settlement instead.

But there were some that she knew she must take.

Matilda offered herbal infusions in little storage jars and Edgard the leather tooler brought one of the jerkins with gold rings that he was making for the highest thegns on their return.

In the cold light of a Wolf Moon dawn, she received the 'gōd speeds' from her children and the hall ceorls, and raised her hand in farewell to Nymue and Matilda. Afera was nowhere to be seen but Gareth Swineson stood apart and bowed to her as she rode out. It seemed that all the village was out to see her go, and as she swept by with her baggage train of guards and carts, they raised their hands and their voices to her, and she could hear the echoes of their applause in her heart far far down the road south.

CHAPTER 20

VIV

Derbyshire. Present day

The unexpected applause rang in Viv's ears as she looked around the pews from where she sat just in front of the chancel steps. Rory nodded his thanks to the audience and moved away from the huge screen that barely fitted in the small space by the lectern and turned to sit beside her. She noticed Dr Helen Mortimer in the front pew lean towards Tilly, who was bouncing Ellie on her knee and covering her with kisses. Helen whispered something at which Viv's old friend winked and smiled across at her.

"I think that must have gone well," Viv murmured to Rory. He reached over to press the 'exit' button on the laptop and switch off the PowerPoint.

"Looks like it, thank goodness. I had no idea

whether it would be OK or whether it would go down like a lead balloon. Or worse still invoke angry comment. But as it is, great response. So now I guess more Q and As."

But before they could invite further questions from the floor, the Bishop, who had arrived after all, despite his original doubts, strode forward from the back of the nave, nodding graciously to the audience as he progressed along the aisle to the transept. He had appeared just as they were about to start the meeting and refused the seat at the front with Viv, saying he could view the slides better from the back.

He approached the chancel steps, beaming and nodding his thanks to Rory and Viv. Then he turned to the audience.

"What a marvellous, most interesting presentation, Reverend Rory. How good it is to have such a dynamic priest here at this wonderful church." His eyes swept the church interior and up to the roof trusses as he held his arms aloft. Viv hoped to goodness that he wasn't about to pray earnestly, knowing that not all the folks who had come today were by any means church-goers. "I am sure that we all wish to thank him for his work today – and of course his supportive wife, Mrs Netherbridge ... er DuLac ... er whatever." Viv frowned, not only at his continuous refusal to remember her name, but also at her relegation to a supporting role. Rory turned to her and mouthed his apology. "Of course, I have been entirely approving from the beginning of this whole idea of filming the research into the stone cross and the ancient king ... er Aethelred."

"Aethelbold," whispered Rory.

"Well, hardly even Aethelbold," Viv murmured. "Lady Vivianne we think."

She looked across at Helen and shrugged, wondering if the Bishop had in fact been listening at all to her presentation after Rory's intro about the history of the church itself.

In her bit, Viv hadn't spoken specifically of Lady Vivianne but of a previously undiscovered queen of a kingdom that used to stretch around from Cooney's Mere to this and the neighbouring parish, back in what was often popularly referred to as the 'dark ages'. There had been great excitement amongst the local historians about that and a number of people vying to declare that they had found various artefacts in their gardens which they were convinced were pre-Anglo-Saxon and valuable finds. Viv doubted that but nodded encouragingly.

Several of the audience had begun to ask for a village excavation along the lines of Professor Michael Wood's work at Kibworth some years before and which had been made into a television documentary. Viv rather liked the idea but wasn't sure that the particular villagers enthusing about the possibility weren't more interested in getting themselves on television than discovering the history. But neither of them wanted to quash enthusiasm for the project so they both made encouraging noises, smiled, and promised to look into it. Viv could see Helen cringing.

When the Bishop finally finished his rambling speech, Viv came forward to thank him for his support, and Helen and Tilly for their contributions, and to offer refreshments at the back of the church to anyone who would care to stay for coffee and cake, or indeed a glass of wine, or perhaps to ask any further questions personally to themselves, Helen or Tilly. She pointed out the plans and pictures at the back for people to browse if they wished to learn more, and she reminded them all to complete the feedback cards at the back of the church.

Viv signalled to the helpers in the kitchen area at the back of the church and received the 'thumbs-up' as people began to rise from their seats in search of free refreshment. She breathed a sigh of relief.

"Wow, that was really great!" cried Tilly. "Wasn't it, sweetie-pie?" She caught one of Ellie's hands and held it up to Viv in an approving wave. Ellie bounced and kicked in delight. "I think they were reassured about the filming, weren't they? But you two are so good together, d'you know ... I'm wondering about a presenting duo, a partnership like Richard and Judy, or Eamonn and Ruth ..."

"No, no!" Rory took a step backwards, bumping into the screen and held up his hand in a restraining gesture.

"Oh, Tilly, I don't think so, thanks all the same," Viv grimaced. "This was enough."

"It was certainly interesting to see the reactions," said Helen. "But I'm not entirely sure that they got my stuff about the carbon dating."

"Actually, I think they were really interested in the procedure. They were just maybe a bit overawed to ask many questions," said Viv, taking Ellie from Tilly's arms. "But they seemed fascinated to me."

"I guess I'm used to talking to students who are specialising in archaeology."

"Well," laughed Viv, "this is a quite different kind of crowd. And I think they rose to the occasion."

"Oh good, I'm glad you thought it went well and that we can proceed," Helen said. "I think I'll just go and get some wine. I need it after that. Tilly? Can I bring you something?"

"Bet your bottom dollar you can!"

Rory caught someone's eye and moved off.

"We'll mingle a bit," said Viv. "Do our host thing. I'll get a drink later."

As she moved through the crowd, answering questions as she went, she noticed Michael the curate standing apart deep in conversation with Sadie, of all people. Goodness!

Viv did a double take. Sadie looked quite different: a pretty pale pink dress, three quarter sleeves and high scooped neck, her long blonde hair piled up in a messy bun. She looked really lovely. And was she smiling at their shy curate? She hadn't noticed Sadie at all during the event. She must have been at the back of the nave, or behind a pillar or something. Michael had been on the front pew, near to Tilly and Helen, supporting them. Viv paused in her progress and watched, fascinated, as ... heavens, did Sadie just reach out to touch Michael's arm? Viv's assumptions roared into overdrive. She looked across for Rory, but she couldn't make him out in the crowd.

Then she heard her name shouted out and turned away from Sadie. That voice could only be one person. Her heart sank. A solitary figure stood, red-faced and agitated, at the back near the main church door. Ivy. Most people were politely trying to keep well clear of her but in fact her smell was not so pervasive, and Viv wondered if she had actually had a wash that morning. She was beginning to feel guilty that the woman was alone and started to approach her to offer coffee, when she realised that Ivy was glaring at her angrily and Viv saw an expression of fury and disgust on her face that sent a chill down her spine. Ivy's eyes seemed to be sparking a fire of hatred.

"Ya best beware," she spat at Viv. "What'cha be doin' ain't right. I told ya. The runes are dangerous powerful. Evil. And you're summonin' up them ancient curses on the village. Ya canna mess with the devil's own runes. I don't care what ya Bishop says. Ya shouldna be messin' with the runes, Mrs Rev'rend." She turned and pushed her way through the church door, leaving mouths agape and appalled faces on those near enough to have heard.

Viv gulped. Rory was nowhere to be seen and Tilly was chatting to excited looking villagers near the kitchen sink. She smiled an apology at the horrified faces and shrugged, moving away. She couldn't face any curiosity or explanations. But she stroked Ellie's hair and hugged her more tightly to her chest.

"So, you think it was Ivy who pushed that note through our door?" Rory frowned as he sifted through the feedback cards on the rectory table with Viv later that evening.

"Well, I'm beginning to wonder whether we misjudged Sadie and it was Ivy all the time. But I don't know. How could it have been Ivy? That note and the email were very literate and well-written ..."

"That's rather judgemental, Viv," Rory said, placing another card on the growing 'approval' pile. "I know she talks in the old dialect, but it doesn't mean to say she's illiterate."

"I know that, but somehow it just didn't sound like Ivy. Quoting the Bible in the note and all that."

Rory laughed. "She's quoted the Bible to me on several occasions! Mainly the Old Testament and always to show me where I'm going wrong. I did make the mistake one time of quoting another passage from the Gospels that was contradictory. I don't think she's ever forgiven me." He put the card down and took another swig of the red wine beside him on the table.

"Hmm. Well, maybe we'll never know. Talking of Sadie, did you see her and Michael together after the presentation? They looked rather cosy."

"He looked somewhat embarrassed to me – out of the corner of my eye," Rory grinned. "I thought he was trying to get away from her. In fact, he sidled up to me quite oddly and looked very awkward."

Viv shook her head. "We clearly interpret these things differently," she smiled indulgently at him. "Well, look, we have a huge approval pile. Only a couple of 'not sures'/ 'don't knows' and one scribbled over in thick black ink. Either that's Ivy or someone's child's used it as drawing paper. No name. Can't think even Sadie would do that – pretty childish."

Rory reached over to her and stroked her cheek with his thumb. "I think," his voice low, "that I am the luckiest man in the world. This is all down to you, and it seems to have resolved the issue once and for all. I was talking to Bishop Jonathan before he rushed off and he was effusive about the event and the idea of the filming. He seems to imagine that it was a brilliant piece of outreach and that we're suddenly going to increase our congregation fourfold!"

"As long as it means we can go ahead with the research into the Rune Stone and maybe find out more about what it means – what the runes say and why there's a memorial to Lady Vivianne, or whoever?"

CHAPTER 21

VIV

Derbyshire. Present day

*V*iv's heart filled with pride and her stomach with butterflies as she stood in the middle of the churchyard with Ellie lodged on her hip, watching Rory, so handsome in his black clerical suit and white dog collar, standing by the Rune Stone. A make-up artist was unnecessarily dabbing his nose with powder and the camera man was adjusting his position to get the right angle of the twelfth century window embrasure in shot.

"Good, good," nodded Tilly, standing to one side with her interview sheets on a clipboard. "Let's get this wrapped this time and then you can do my shots looking intelligent and nodding wisely!"

The camera man laughed, and Viv thought what a surprise it was to see Tilly serious, professional and in action at her job. Helen was to be interviewed in her lab that afternoon and Viv was invited to go along to listen.

The day was bright with that warm golden sunshine of early autumn and only a few clouds scudding across a deep blue sky above. A slight breeze rustled the trees behind her. The churchyard looked pretty with the grass newly trimmed and the graves that would be in shot around the Rune Stone bedecked with fresh flowers specially for the occasion: pink carnations, the symbol of a mother's undying love; white freesias, for purity of heart; deep red ranunculus, for charm and trust; and purple iris for hope, courage and journeys.

Viv was pondering on the meanings of the flowers, their symbolism, eyes drawn to a little purple iris at the base of the Stone, as Tilly began her intro to camera. But even as she tried to concentrate, the words seemed to drift around her in a waft of mist, and the Rune Stone shimmered and shifted out of focus.

The air grew thick and still around her, the strange heaviness was almost tangible, and Tilly's voice dimmed. The Rune Stone, the church, the churchyard, receded into the distance. Viv clutched Ellie to her, but she felt insubstantial, wraithlike.

As if at first from far off, slowly a rumbling sound grew in magnitude as if a storm approached but gradually Viv could make out distinct but distant noises, of horses hooves and the wheels of carts jangling over rough tracks, shouts of warning and cries of fear. And the loud beating of her own heart. She was afraid that she might be going to faint and looked wildly around for solidity, but the churchyard was as it should be, tranquil apart from the filming, although somehow faint and distant, the ancient walls and buttresses still standing. She could still hear Tilly's questions to Rory, and the almost imperceptible whirring of the camera. There was a group of parishioners whispering quietly at the scene before them, but they were way over by the gate watching the proceedings with interest.

Her eyes seemed to be drawn inescapably again and again to the perfect shape of the little purple iris that nestled up against the foot of the Rune Stone. One tiny flower that symbolised hope, courage and journeys.

Those words swirled around her, yet what she was feeling was danger, hopelessness and despair. She looked up and saw trees arching above, their branches meeting over her head in a dark canopy. Impossible. She was standing in the open churchyard. The nearest tree was the huge yew several feet away. Yet as she looked down she saw the deep ruts of a well-used drover's track. Either side of her the banks of earth rose high, as if the roadway had been carved out of a hillside. A holloway. She shivered with claustrophobia as the trees overhead and the scooped-out ground beneath closed her in. Horses' hooves clattered beneath her and around her. Cart wheels behind rang out. But nobody spoke; they rode on in silence. It had been like this for days, she felt, although she knew that this tunnel was a protection and that soon they must ride out into open countryside where they would be exposed. Dread filled her heart, and all she could think of was that she had made a grave mistake.

Her horse beneath her seemed to tremble and her whole being cried out that she should turn back, return to the safety of home, of the settlement. How could she have imagined that she could do this, that she could have the strength to travel south like this. Pains gripped her belly as her horse plunged onwards. Her hands gripping the reins shook uncontrollably and she could see that her knuckles were white on the dark leather. This was indeed madness, as Nymue and Matilda had said. They were right. She should never have been so arrogant as to imagine that only she could make this journey, appeal to Icel, and free Sir Roland and her thegns from the Angeln. But yet … who else was there to bring them home?

A shout of warning and a cry of fear, the rumbling and crash of a cart overturning, dragging on the ruts of the holloway. Pulling her horse to a halt she looked around and saw the whole baggage train drawing up, and a cart on its side, contents spilled over the roadway, chests burst open disgorging their cargo. Her guards leapt from their horses and ran to help the serfs gather up what they could from the roadside, righting the chests, shaking out cloaks and robes, and thrusting them back into the safety of the boxes. She closed her eyes as the noise of anxious activity rumbled around her and sighed deeply. Was this accident a sign that the journey was fated? Yet they had travelled several sunrises already, she was too tired to remember how many, setting up camp by the wayside in the dark hours when they could no longer see the track ahead.

The front wheels on the cart had caught in a pothole, a guard told her. But they were not broken or even mis-shaped, thank God, so the cart was righted again, and the contents all recovered and replaced. They had roped it all over more firmly and checked the other carts while they were about it. And all was well, my lady, they said. So now it was safe to continue their journey, but perhaps they should make this their stop for refreshment? She nodded and slipped from her horse, handing the reigns to her attendant, and listening to the chattering of the birds in the arching trees above her head. Their stop had brought them, fortunately, to a cross roads in the holloway where there was room for the company to pull off the roadway on flatter ground, and for the serfs to retrieve the bread, cheese slabs and ale from the carts.

She walked a few paces away from the company, rubbing her stiff legs. A flash of colour caught her eye and she saw, nestled amongst the brown undergrowth of winter, a tiny purple iris. How strange that it was blooming here in this inhospitable landscape, surely it should not be here. Though small, the flower stood proud and erect on its sturdy stem, branching up to its sword shaped leaves and crowned by its elegant little dappled purple petals like blades, with their bright yellow centres. One tiny flower amidst the nettles and brambles and heather.

The symbol of a journey, and of hope and courage. She drew in her breath and suppressed the niggling pains in her belly. She was ready to continue her journey to its end.

The Rune Stone came back into sharp focus and Viv heard Tilly say, "So, Reverend Rory, thank you for joining us for the third programme in the series, but why do you think this fourteen centuries old Cross, or Rune Stone we should say, is relevant to the village today?" Viv saw her wink at Rory conspiratorially from behind the camera as he smiled and followed her cue.

So she hadn't missed anything. Just a strange blip of her mind then. She listened to the interview and marvelled at how well they worked together to clarify the history for a non-specialist audience and grab their interest, her husband and her dear friend. But she held Ellie closer to her and tried to push away the feelings of lurking danger and unease that gripped her heart.

That night, Viv's dreams were vivid. Trees reaching their gaunt branches down to trap her, rough holloways where the deep ruts could catch horses' hooves and tumble them. A strange silence as the miles swept by, occasionally lowered voices as they journeyed on further and further south into a territory that felt hostile and full of danger. And from time to time through her dreams, as she tossed and turned, unable to find a comfortable position, a face, painted and framed with long wild hair, eyes dark and terrifying, and the glint of spears, seaxes raised aloft, came into focus and then dimmed.

She woke with a feeling of dread still pervading her soul, to find Rory gently stroking her face.

"Are you OK, Viv? You were moaning and crying out."

It took a moment for her to adjust to where she was, in her own bedroom, at the rectory, home, safe and secure.

"Just a nightmare. Bad dreams. Go back to sleep. I'm OK."

"What happened at the interview in the churchyard? I know you said it was nothing but that was in front of other people. Was it another ...?"

"Slip, yes. It was the emotions, the feelings as much as anything else. But up to now I've just had a weird sensation. This time it was, for a while, as though I actually slipped into her body – like before when we had to return the chest."

"Lady Vivianne?"

"She's on a journey – that I could make out."

"Like a medieval progress, as a queen?"

"No. It was with a small entourage. And it was a journey that filled her with dread and fear. Her mind seemed to be full of Sir Roland. Something about bringing him home."

Unable to settle now and seeing that the bedside clock showed six she knew that she wouldn't get back to sleep again. Viv sat up and propped herself on her pillow.

"It's all a bit hazy, misty. But I do remember a flower. I – she – saw it beside the roadway. There's one at the base of the Rune Stone too. I hadn't really noticed it before. A little purple iris."

"Don't they signify journeys?"

"Yes, and hope and courage." Viv took a deep breath and stretched her neck on the soft pillow. "I think she was on a quest to find Sir Roland and help him escape from somewhere. There was a name that echoed in my mind ...Oh, what was it? A warrior. A quest. And I think it was all extremely dangerous. It needed all her courage and all her hope. Oh, and there was a face."

"A face? Whose face?"

"I don't know but someone that frightened her, someone quite different from anyone she had ever seen before. There was ... sort of painted facial marks ...oh and spears and seaxes."

"So, perhaps it was the person she had to free Sir Roland from? An enemy. We're talking early sixth century, so an invading tribe, perhaps. Well, we all know that the British settlements were fighting off invaders in the sixth century, the Angles, Saxons and Jutes."

Viv frowned. "She's reaching out to me again, isn't she? Like she did before. There's some danger to her settlement, to Cooneys' Mere and she wants my help for ... I don't know what." She shivered.

"Goodness, Viv." Rory pushed himself up beside her and wrapped his arm around her back. "You seem to be the go-to person for helping people in the past with their terrors!" He kissed her cheek. "Lady Vivianne here in the village when we met. Ana d'Arafet and Anja-Filipa in Madeira. Now back to Lady Vivianne again." He sighed. "I thought she was all sorted now after the last time. But this time it's about the Rune Stone, isn't it?"

"Something happened again at Cooneys Mere, much later on than when she first reached out to me. Maybe twenty or so years later. She was their Chieftain, their queen. But something new was endangering the settlement. And she had to deal with it." Viv suddenly felt a great sadness fill her and she caught the sob in her throat. "Oh, God, Rory, do you think she never made it and the Rune Stone erected to commemorate her bravery in trying, her death in attempting to save her settlement, her kingdom?"

Rory hugged her closer. "Oh Viv. I know how close

it all is to your heart ... how close Lady Vivianne is to you ... because you actually time-slipped into her body before. I guess it must feel almost like it's you out there."

"It does. I know it sounds stupid, but yes, it's me."

"Oh, my love." He kissed her head. "I understand because I was so involved with it all, too, what, two, three years ago when it all kicked off. But now ... how can I help?"

"I don't know. God, Rory, I feel frightened." She frowned and bit her lip. "It's like ... you know that thing about dreams ... that they say lots of people dream of falling? Then they wake up before they hit the ground? It's a quite common phenomenon."

"Yes, I have that dream myself sometimes."

"Well, the thing is ... they say that if you dream the fall right to the end, if you hit the ground ... you've met your own death."

Rory turned her to face him. "What are you saying, Viv?"

"What happens if I time-slip into Lady Vivianne's body and experience her death?" It took a moment for Rory to catch up with Viv's train of thought and when he did, he caught his breath. "Rory, she's in great danger. I can feel it. She wants me with her." Viv felt a memory of pain in her abdomen and rubbed it. Her whole body shuddered with the realisation. "My God, she's pregnant! And she's riding into an impossible situation."

CHAPTER 22

LADY VIVIANNE

521 AD

"My lady!" called Vivianne's nurse as she drew her horse up beside her mistress. "Do you not think that you should rest a little now? You have been riding for hours this day, and the days before. It cannot be good for you or the baby."

Vivianne, deep in her own thoughts of reaching Icel's camp, turned to her nurse and saw her face, dark and twisted with worry. "We must be near now. I think it is not far and we may make it by this nightfall. The directions from the fore-scouts have been good to now. We are not so certain of the last stretch of track."

"My lady, please, I beg of you to stop. The day is drawing on and already the sun is preparing to sink in the west. And we are all exhausted."

Lady Vivianne shook her head and raised her chin up high. "I am not exhausted. We ride on."

The nurse turned back to Vivianne's guard riding behind her. "How far now?" she asked curtly.

Vivianne's face was set on the road before her and the destination ahead that none of them could see. The holloways were far behind them. The land around them was flatter, the hillsides gently rolling, not steep as they were around Cūning's Mere and the vegetation at the roadside more lush, despite the winter. It was unfamiliar open country and she felt exposed and uneasy.

The guard shrugged. "A day perhaps?"

"Then, my lady, it is not so near, and we cannot ride through the night again. Please! For the sake of your unborn child, I beg of you to stop. It cannot matter to that pagan at the Angeln camp. His spies most like as not know that we are on our way."

"My lady," called the guard behind her. "With respect, she is right. And if they know we are approaching and send out fighting men to intercept us, we stand no chance in the coming darkness."

"They will not attack us. They mean to bargain with our thegns' lives," said Vivianne, though her heart was beating faster, and her hands gripped the reins tightly.

"So, my lady, if they do not mean to kill us, but to bargain, then what harms our mission to keep them waiting a day?"

Vivianne sighed. She knew that she was being stubborn. She did not know any more than they did. They were all ignorant of what might pass. Nothing had prepared her for this. "You are right. We must stop for the night and meet the Icelings tomorrow when we are fresh and rested."

The serfs set up their overnight camp by the roadside. But Lady Vivianne could not sleep when night fell and the next sunrise she was not rested. Her head pounded with what was to come. Oh, what had she done? Was she so consumed with her own importance that she imagined that Icel would listen to her pleas? Why should he accept her gifts and proposals for a bargain? She had thought that the Angeln could not be so different from them but what if they were ... what if their needs and wants were not at all as she imagined them to be. All the gifts in her baggage train, they could mean nothing to them. She thought with a growing realisation that the world outside of Cūning's Mere was strange and unknown. What was she riding into, and taking her attendants with her?

And on top of her concerns about the reception they might encounter, whether it would all be in vain, she knew what she had refused to recognise on this whole journey south, that the baby within her was not happy, that he no longer kicked against the wall of her belly, that he was causing her a pain that she recalled so well from all those years ago when it happened before. Was she to lose another child, like the ones she lost after her handfasting to Sir Roland and who were now sleeping in the cold earth at the edge of the settlement? Was she to lose her husband as well, were her children to lose their father, and her settlement their warrior king? And perhaps their queen also.

Her heart was cold, but she made her voice strong and clear. Nobody could know what fears were there deep inside her. When she mounted her horse again with the wintry sun high in the sky, she held her head high, though her hands shook as she stroked her horse's long dark mane.

"Let us proceed," she called out and she breathed in the quietness and tension of her train behind her. "This day we meet with Icel and free our thegns to bring them home. Ride on!"

THE SUN WAS SINKING AGAIN AS THEY RODE INTO THE Icelings' camp. The roads had been worse than she had expected, and the fore-scouts and messengers had ridden out and twice they had come back to Lady Vivianne with conflicting directions for this final part of their journey, so well had the camp been hidden. She surveyed the roughly built temporary shelters but could see beyond them that there were the ruins of stone buildings amidst the overgrown woodlands that encroached upon them. Vivianne signalled a careful and slow approach.

They were stopped by the lookouts just outside the camp and challenged, Icel's men unable to understand that the band was led by a woman, and that she was indeed Lady Vivianne, chieftain and warrior queen of Cūning's Mere. Even though Vivianne spoke firmly through her interpreter, a Saxon serf whose language was not too different from that of the Angeln, their faces were twisted with disbelief. But they spoke amongst themselves while Vivianne stayed straight-backed and head high against their incomprehensible discussion. She heard the name Icel, once of the few words she could understand, repeated over and over.

Then the Icel guards herded Vivianne's attendants and baggage carts into a curral and stood over them with aggressive faces and threatening seaxes held high. Warriors surrounded the curral with shields and spears, although Vivianne showed them that they bore few weapons themselves, only those of defence not attack. She could see that they had taken over a group of old dilapidated Roman houses that the legions had abandoned many years before when they returned to Rome. She had no idea what settlement this had been. She could see no sign of a Brython occupation. It looked as though it had been deserted a long time ago, for Icel to move into for shelter on his advance west and north.

A guard, huge of physique and with long unruly

hair, gestured to Vivianne and her interpreter to approach. But she stayed him with a raised hand and indicated that she must change from her travelling clothes before she approached Icel. He hesitated, then pointed to a small building. It looked as though it had once been a Roman bath-house. She called for her guards to bring her chest and for her nurse to attend her. There in that half-ruined room amidst stone dust and creeping undergrowth, she prepared herself. Her nurse took off Vivianne's dust stained mantle and her stale smelling kirtle, and pulled her purple-red robe over her stained undergarment. She knew that she must appear before Icel with authority and status, otherwise he would not listen to her or bargain with her. This was the man who had fought her thegns, who had injured and killed, and who had taken Sir Roland and others, she knew not how many, captive. She prayed silently to her God, as she had done so many times on their journey and indeed ever since she had heard the news of the disastrous battle. She prayed that the survivors were still safe.

"Fix my royal cloak with the gold clasp," she said, her voice trembling. She dusted down the royal purple cloak, her hands skimming the fine embroidery of her family's white dragon that adorned the front, praying for her mother and father to be with her the next hour and to give her strength.

Out of the simple hemp bag, the nurse lifted the gold jewellery and set the rings on Vivianne's fingers, bracelets on her wrists and the wide gleaming gold torque about her neck. She stood back and admired her queen, as Vivianne tried not to wince at the pains in her abdomen.

But it was as the nurse carefully placed the heavy royal circlet upon her head that Vivianne could not help but gasp at the violent pain that racked her body, and she bent forwards clutching her belly.

"Oh, my lady!" shrieked the nurse, hands flying to her mouth. "Is the babe coming early?"

Vivianne could not speak but fought for her composure. Then when she could breathe freely again, she stood straight and took a deep breath. "No, the baby will not come until I have spoken with Icel and seen my beloved Sir Roland." She drew herself up to her full height and holding her head high, she said, "Come, we are ready."

Her guard and interpreter met them at the entrance, and they proceeded into a larger stone building which clearly served Icel as a hall. Vivianne noticed the decaying Roman frescos, now faint with age, on the walls at the entrance, the once stately pillars, the square of the pool-fountain that once had impressed Roman visitors. A nobleman's hall, now crumbling and infested with weeds.

Icel's door guards fell back a little when they saw her. "They perhaps have never seen a queen before," Vivianne murmured to her guard and he shook his head in bewilderment. Perhaps these Angeln did not have chieftains and royal leaders at all? Perhaps they just had warrior leaders and so her finery confused them.

Vivianne walked slowly towards the large imposing figure she supposed to be Icel, who was seated on a bench with guards on either side, heavily armed with seaxes and spears held aloft and great golden shields in front of them. As she did so, she became aware of a shifting atmosphere. The men fell silent and the air felt close and thick as they stared at her. She determined not to be daunted or afraid. Her footsteps seemed to echo in her head, and their gleaming weapons glinted in the waning light that filtered in from the broken roof above and dazzled her sight. She wanted to squint to see more clearly but she did not wish to appear blinded and weak. Her head was high although her gold circlet weighed heavy and made a pain shoot up her neck. She drew in the muscles of her abdomen, determined to hide the pains that encircled the baby and shot through her.

Icel rose, a huge towering figure above her, amidst the ruins of this hall that seemed to her to signify the fleeting nature of victory, the fragility of existence. And yet she knew that it was possible to reach out through time, to touch immortality.

Now she was close enough and out of the beams of light to see that his face was painted with black and red markings, and his eyes were glaring dark and terrifying as he looked at her. His hair long and wild escaped from the gleaming jewel-encrusted helmet he wore. This was the man who had fought her people, who had killed her thegns, who had taken her husband captive. She fought down a shiver of anger and disgust. Then she thought too that in that battle her thegns had killed Icel's men; they had all fought to the death. Every one of them, whichever side they were fighting for, whichever banner they rode under.

One of the guards stepped forward, beat his spear on the ground thrice and spoke.

"What is he saying?" whispered Vivianne to the interpreter at her side.

"He says, this is Icel, son of Éomēr, of the Angeln people."

She nodded and held her arms wide to show that she held no weapon and as she did so her cloak fell open and she knew that her fecund belly was revealed. But she did not close her cloak to hide it. She looked up defiantly into Icel's eyes. They seemed to open wide as he looked upon her with astonishment. And something else she could not quite place. He stared down at her full belly.

One great bellow left his lips, and his eyes narrowed as his face beneath the paint, paled.

Vivianne turned to her interpreter again. "What does he say?"

He says, "Earth Mother, Nerthus!" the interpreter whispered, fearful eyes never leaving Icel's face.

"What does that mean?" Vivianne asked between

277

gritted teeth. Her knees were trembling, and she feared they might give way and she might crumple onto the ground.

But before the interpreter could reply, Icel pointed with a shaking hand to the white dragon on her cloak and said, in a clear language that she could understand, "Woden also has come to me," and he seemed to Vivianne to grow even taller with his great spiked helmet, as he reached up holding his seax aloft, shouting and wailing what seemed to Vivianne like battle cries. His roaring went on and on as Vivianne dared not move a muscle but stood statue-like before him.

The interpreter spoke, not whispering now, "He thinks you are Nerthus, the earth mother whom the Angeln worship. And he believes that you, Nerthus, have been sent to him from Woden the God of war who they bow down to, and who, with the white dragon on his banner, leads them into the coming battle. As they believe *you* will."

CHAPTER 23

LADY VIVIANNE

521 AD

as that good or was that bad? Did that mean he might worship her or expect her to join battle? His eyes looked angry but maybe they always did. Or maybe this was the look of great shock. Or puzzlement? Either way, she must disenchant him without disrespecting his beliefs. She wished she could grasp his real meaning and understand the import of his words.

"You must tell them that I am not a warrior from Woden, the God of war," said Lady Vivianne to her interpreter who stood nervously now, at her side, his eyes fixed on Icel as though the great man might suddenly leap towards him and drive his seax into his heart. "You must tell him that the white dragon on my cloak is the symbol of my family. I am the Peace-Weaver."

The interpreter spoke hesitantly and jerkily, stumbling over his words and she did not know whether his words and gestures were received kindly for Icel's brow furrowed and his mouth set in a thin hard line, yet it twitched as though he was bewildered at the turn of events, as bewildered as she herself felt.

When the interpreter stopped, Icel shook his head and held out his hand towards Vivianne. She heard the insistent repeated word, "Woden, Woden."

The name rang around Vivianne's head and she began to hear the name Ođinn. Were they one and the same? She knew that Ođinn was an old God of some tribes of pagan Brythons, but some said he was of wisdom and poetry, not war. Yet she remembered seeing a wall painting of him depicted as a warrior on a horse, with a sword and shield aloft and a seax at his waist. Some also said that he gave his name to 'Woden's day' in the middle of a seven-night when they held their markets. She remembered that she had heard tell from eastern traders of Woden being worshipped by the Norse peoples and those Germanic peoples across the sea in the land to the north east. Was their God the same as the one of the pagan Brythons, and if so, how could that be, that across the wide seas people prayed to the same God?

A vision came into her mind: her mother rising from the waters of the Mere. Her mother had come from a pagan Celtic-Brython people and at times prayed to the Goddess of the earth, as well as the Goddess of the lake, although she herself had taken her father's Christian religion. She remembered her mother's rituals at the Mere, the magic that surrounded her, the Lady of the Lake. Vivianne felt her heart twist. But perhaps, somehow, her knowledge might help the words she chose.

The interpreter began again but Icel stopped him with a raised hand and a shake of the head. He nodded towards Vivianne.

She took a deep breath and prepared to speak out loudly and clearly, with more confidence than she felt. But she knew that everything may rest on her words. She must do anything she could to reach this man's heart, though it may be dark with the blood of her thegns. Anything to bring her husband home. Even, if needs be, the manoeuvring of her own true feelings. She must act for her life and the life of Sir Roland and his thegns.

With her hand she brushed the embroidered image of the white dragon on her cloak and then held it still over the dragon's heart and said slowly, "Icel, great warrior of the Iceling tribe of the peoples of the Angeln. You have come over the seas to the land of my peoples. I show to you that this is my family, my moðor and my fæðor, my eald-fæðor, my cyðð and my cynn – my mother, my father, my ancestors, my people – and," she gestured towards his heart, "and maybe this sign is of yours too, this white dragon. Woden and your people." She traced a circle to include Icel and herself, his guards and hers. "Maybe we are one."

Listening carefully as the interpreter spoke, she held out her hands and invited his response. Icel was silent for some time and Vivianne wondered if she had mis-spoken, or if the interpreter had. Perhaps she had made things worse and should have kept her peace. Perhaps he was offended, and she lowered her head waiting for the angry words or the blow across her head.

Neither came but instead she felt a hand touch hers. She opened her eyes and raised her head. Icel stood before her, his hand upon hers as she still rested her palm on the white dragon's heart of her cloak. His eyes were on hers and no longer terrifying but it seemed to her that they were full of awe. He had decided.

He knelt and she heard the sound of his guards kneeling also. Her guard and interpreter hesitated a moment, looking around in consternation, and then they too, as if mindful of its significance and overwhelmed by the magnitude of the moment, nudged each other, and knelt. Only she remained standing.

Icel spoke low and although she did not understand his words, she grasped his meaning. "My lady, mother of my earth and of my God, we share in the same peoples, we *are* one. You are the Peace-Weaver."

Vivianne knew she should say that they did not share in the God Woden, that she was Christian, that she was merely saying that they all were somehow the same underneath, that their beliefs may be different but they ultimately had many similarities. But she could not even begin to explain her thoughts and so she remained silent and simply smiled. Because it seemed somehow appropriate she touched the top of his helmet. He looked up at her and slowly lifted his helmet off, holding it under his arm. He bent his head again and she thought she should lay her hand on his head as she remembered her father doing as a blessing when she was little, and as she did for her own children.

Then, her heart full of the purpose of their long journey and of her fears rising again, she spoke out in the quietness of the hall.

"My husband? Is he captive here? I need to see him."

Icel stood and the moment was broken. But he gave her a little bow and gestured that she should come with him. He turned to his guards and spoke his commands. They scuttled in front and led the way out of the hall and into a building that could once have been a small Roman villa. Broken mosaics were still clinging to the walls at the entrance.

As Vivianne looked around she saw that it was

dilapidated, falling into disrepair, dust and crumbling mortar everywhere. But of course, Icel and his battle troops had not and would not settle here; they were using the old Roman buildings as a camp before moving on northwards. There would be no restoring or repairing. It was a useful temporary shelter from the elements, the place they retreated to after their battle out in the wastelands. They were only occupying it between battles. She wondered if ultimately they wanted to settle in this land, find a better settlement and bring their people over to make their own kingdoms. Or whether they would take their spoils of victory back home across the seas.

Icel's guards led the way across a crumbling vestibule and into a maze of rooms behind. Their way was blocked by his fighting guards in their war dress, but they fell back at his command. They stared at Lady Vivianne and lowered their spears. Icel flung open a door that opened out to a hall that was clearly Sir Roland's prison, for he rose from the filthy floor and turned cautiously round to see who had entered.

Lady Vivianne, no longer caring for niceties and convention, pushed past Icel and ran to her husband, flinging her arms around him and hugging him close, though he smelled bad. She felt his kiss on the top of her head within the ring of her gold circlet. "Oh, how good it is to see that you are alive! I hardly believe it. I have dreamed of this for so long."

"My love," came his muffled voice buried in her

thick bronze-red hair. "I knew – I hoped – you would come."

She released herself from his grasp and stood back to look at him. "Of course I would come. How could you ever doubt it? But you are thin and gaunt of face. Your eyes are dull. Oh, my love, your head is gashed and there are old dried wounds. What have they done to you?" Then she looked down and saw the shackles on his sore red ankles. "Oh, my lord!" She turned to Icel, "Have these irons taken off at once! How dare you! He is a chieftain, a warrior *king*. He is my husband."

"My love, I am a captive from battle. This is what is done. At least I am alive."

But Icel gestured to his guards and they cut the chains and set him free.

"Roland! You mean that this is what we do to our captives of battle?" Vivianne shook her head.

Roland forced a weak smile. "Of course. How else would we ensure that our captives would not run away? Or attack our guards when they come with food?" He shook his legs and bent to rub the circulation back into his ankles, staggering a little, and Vivianne reached out to catch him. "I am sorry, my love. I am dizzy. My legs are not as strong as they should be and I fear I am weak, but I have been allowed some time in the courtyard, and my wounds have been tended. But, my love, how can it be that you command our enemies, Icel and his guards?"

She shrugged. "Not command. But hopefully we

are ready to bargain." She touched his rough homespun tunic with distaste and noticed the blood stains upon it. "Is this what you have been forced to wear? A serf's clothes? Worn and dirty?"

"My dear Vivianne, it is better than a shroud over my corpse, is it not?"

"Yes, yes, of course. I forget my place. But how many thegns are safe, and how many are killed in battle?"

Roland raised his eyebrows at her directness but proceeded to tell her of their losses and their survivors, the absence of the warriors of Deorabye, but their own determination to fight on to save the peace of the settlement. Vivianne nodded with narrowed eyes.

"I am saddened at our losses and we must make their memorials when we return safely home to Cūning's Mere. We will not forget their sacrifice for our settlement." She hung her head a moment in prayer. "But some good will come of this, I am sure. And it surely could have been a great deal worse for us. Where are the rest of my thegns?" Roland gestured towards the rooms off the hall.

She heard Icel speak behind her and turned to him. "Have my thegns released at once." But he shook his head and spoke roughly. Her interpreter whispered that Icel would not release them until the negotiations were settled and they had received their due. Then they would be accompanied away from the camp. She realised that she must be cautious and keep his trust.

Even though he considered her a kin to his God, the trust was a fragile and the battle warrior could so easily return.

She bowed to Icel and nodded her understanding and agreement. "Please to have your serfs wash and dress Sir Roland in his rightful clothes as warrior king, and then we can meet in your hall to discuss the price of his life and that of all my thegns." She looked to her interpreter to ensure that Icel had understood.

THE GIFTS WERE LAID OUT IN ICEL'S HALL IN AN imposing display. The replica of the ceremonial Witan sword, the gold brooches, cloak clasps, rings and circlets for their womenfolk gleamed in the light of the flaming torches set in their sconces on the walls. The stemmed wine glasses caught the light on their crafted facets and the carved wooden bowls and tooled platters bearing silver filigree glowed. The cloak with the rare precious red dye was draped over the bench, and the leather jerkin with the protective rings upon it that Edgard had made was laid alongside. Under the watchful eyes of Icel's guards, Vivianne's serfs and attendants put the finishing touches to the display of offerings: the stale wheat bread loaf with Icel's name upon it to mark his importance, the pots of honey and herbal infusions carefully arranged, the jars of honeyed mead and wine to catch the eye at the front.

Two serfs stood by holding bowls ready to offer Icel and his guards a taste of the victuals.

Icel's face showed no expression as he moved forward with his guards. Sir Roland, who had learned a few words of their Angeln language during his captivity, explained each of the gifts in halting words. Icel pointed at the herbal infusions.

"He wants to know what these are and their uses," said Roland.

Vivianne described the contents of each pot and explained that these were but a few of their potions and that the serfs and geburs who made them were highly skilled and their abilities highly prized in all the lands around their settlement. He seemed particularly interested in those for battle wounds and for sickness. And also for those to treat the sickness after too much ale, Roland said with a smile.

Icel seemed to regard the ringed jerkin for a while, clearly pondering its value to him, before he moved on to view the rest. Then he paused at the honey and honeyed mead. He gestured abruptly to the serf to bring him a sample to taste. He licked his lips and nodded before he spoke.

"He says that honey is rare in his homeland and that honeyed mead is surely a gift from the Gods. He says it is the drink of the Gods across the water, rare and prized at their feastings." Between them the interpreter and Sir Roland caught the gist of Icel's rapid speech.

"Please to tell him that our land is the land of honey and mead," said Vivianne.

Roland frowned. "We do not want him to think that he can invade Cūning's Mere to command all the richness we have here to take it all for themselves. Be cautious."

"Well, if we were expelled from our settlement then we would call our bee swarms to go with us and take our source of yeast also! They would not know how to make the mead as we do, I am quite sure."

Icel laughed, a great roar that rose to the rafters, and Vivianne glanced at Roland. "Does he know more of our language than we think?"

"My lady of Nerthus and Woden," said Icel, his speech a little hesitant and fragmented as he stumbled through the words, but clear enough for them to understand. "I know some of your words. From our battle captives and our trading with your peoples. But I do not show it too early. I see what you want and what you offer first." He laughed again. "No, I do not wish to take your settlement from you. Why would I? You are from my earth mother and from my God." He bowed and then, as though exhausted from the effort, he lapsed into his own language again and between them the interpreter and Sir Roland translated his meaning.

"He says that they will come soon to near Cūning's Mere, but down river and if the land is adequate, they might make their home there. They will trade with us for our skills and we will protect each other. But they will want you to be at their feastings to bless their peoples. You are Nerthus and Woden in a woman's body and they respect and worship you and your kin as their Peace-Weaver."

"But the battles?"

"He says he will not join battle with you or your kin. He says your thegns have fought bravely and well and that he wished they were his. But he will not take them from you. We are free to leave."

Vivianne nodded but Icel said haltingly, "When we finish the herbs and the mead, we will find you for more. We trade."

"Yes, thank you," she smiled. "We trade."

Icel gestured at the gifts and then around the hall. "You give us the gifts. I give you your people." He looked pleased with the transaction.

"As well he might," thought Vivianne but she smiled graciously and when he knelt before her again, she touched his head in blessing, gritting her teeth against her desire to fell him to the floor.

She took Roland's arm and turned, then she paused and looked back. "Icel, where is Sir Aldwyn?"

Icel shrugged, his face closed, and Vivianne knew that she would not get any more from him. Aldwyn may be alive or dead, she had no idea, and she would not be able to report back to his mother Edyth. But she had what she wanted, what she had come on this dangerous journey for. Sir Roland had borne up well during the negotiations and had the clarity of mind to interpret well and to support her, but she knew that he was failing, and she felt the heaviness of his weight bearing upon her. She knew him well enough to know that he was determined to walk tall until he was away from Icel's camp, and she guessed that then he would collapse. She touched his arm to impart her strength into him and he smiled at her, relief dawning behind his eyes.

The tension and stress that she had been feeling slipped away. Roland was alive and they would bring him back to full health at home in Cūning's Mere where they had all the herbal infusions and tinctures to revive him. She thanked God for that, at least.

But it was as they made their way back to the entrance, not far from safety, that she was wracked with a rising agony across her belly and she was forced to bend double, dropping Roland's arm and clutching herself.

At once there was noise and disorder. Through her pain she heard Icel's roar and the urgent shouts of men as she was surrounded. She was aware of people crowding around her and she fell, or was lowered, in her agony she knew not which, to the floor.

Where are you? I need you, Viv! Help me again!

She thought she heard her nurse calling out and crying as she felt the wetness pooling around her skirts and knew that it was blood and that the life within her was draining away into the dirt and dust and crumbling mosaic of the floor.

CHAPTER 24

VIV

Derbyshire. Present day

*V*iv clutched her stomach with the sudden violent pain that wracked her body, and bent double. "God! It can't be ... I'm absolutely *not* pregnant ... it can't be a miscarriage again ... but it's like ... Ana!"

She felt herself slide down the kitchen unit to the floor. In the distance she could hear Ellie crying in the nursery, but she could do nothing. She couldn't move. Her head was pounding, and she saw the zigzags before her eyes – the sign of her recurring migraine, although she had not had one for ages. Everything was spinning and it felt as though terrifying thoughts were bombarding her, memories of that awful time, that time when she lost Ana from within her, way before her due date ...

She'd relived that drugged horror so many times: the flashbacks of ripping and emptiness. Seeing herself as if from outside, a couple of metres above that sweat-damp, bloody hospital bed. Struggling to breathe, struggling to focus, despairing. Resisting the young nurse's gentle kindly-meant proposal to take the tiny swaddled body away to be 'disposed of' by the hospital. Good God, what *was* that wretched nurse thinking? Then later, relief, as the hospital chaplain, taking in the clerical collar on Rory who had been rushed away from evensong by the verger, softly suggesting a proper church burial and hesitantly asking Rory if he would prefer him to officiate. What a lovely sweet man, stilling her frantic heart. Rory nodding in silent gratitude. The chaplain asking the baby's name. *Ana*. A beautiful name, he'd smiled. A real person, though still and pale and lifeless in Viv's arms, asleep forever. The name they'd chosen, from a distant ancestor of Viv's late mother. *Ana*: with one 'n'. She'd wondered at the time where on earth that memory had come from?

Ana, whose tiny body they had buried in the little grave under the spreading cherry tree by the wall in the churchyard. That sad little funeral not so many weeks before they flew off to Madeira for a secondment – and for what they hoped would be a restorative escape.

Now, Viv lay immobile on the cold floor of the rectory hearing her beautiful daughter Ellie crying and yelling for her. And she could do nothing. She tried to move her arms to push herself up, but her brain couldn't connect to her muscles. Her body felt numb, she couldn't even feel the pain in her abdomen now, and her mind felt too confused to collate anything of sense. She wanted to shout for help, but she didn't seem to have any voice. And anyway, she had the fleeting thought that Rory was out, and she was alone with Ellie.

Pain flashed behind her eyes as though her brain was exploding. She was lying on a dirty crumbling mosaic floor and her life blood was pumping out of her. She was falling down, down, unable to stop herself, into an abyss of darkness. She was whispering to Rory: *they say if you dream the fall right to the end, if you hit the ground ... you've met your own death. So what happens if I time-slip into Lady Vivianne's body and experience her death?* Viv tried to lift her head, but her neck muscles failed her and her head fell back and hit the ground. The world went black.

A RUSH OF WIND SWIRLED AROUND HER. DARK SHAPES. Murmurings, movements, and the soft thud of feet on mosaic floor tiles. The brushing of a robe, the creak of leather, the metallic hardness of metal. Cool hands touching her, something stroking her bare flesh, wiping away the stickiness of blood. Cold air shivering her body, the sweet smell of frost on grass and the deep earthy odour of undergrowth and horses. A flash of faces and frightened eyes, for a moment holding hers in a silent plea. Noises swirling around her head, growing louder, reverberating through her consciousness. Then a memory of a dark painted face, gold - a lot of gold - spears and seaxes gleaming in the firelight. Someone calling for her. Lady Vivianne! *If I dream falling ... hit the ground ... if she dies ...*

Then deeper, deeper, falling, her brain splitting, fragmenting, waves of mist and dizziness, she saw herself from above in a strange room of little doors, not high enough for people to walk through, and a wooden floor, hard and smelling like pine trees. She was looking down upon herself, yet she was there in her own head. Blood, too much blood, seeping into the ground. Crowding, jostling figures shrinking back, and one voice above all, a soft gentle voice, almost like music, and hands on her belly and between her legs. A searing pain and then nothing but echoes, emptiness. She tried to lift her head, but her neck muscles failed her and her head fell back and hit the hard earth beneath her. The world went black.

VIV COULD HEAR RORY SAYING SOMETHING ... AT FIRST from a long way away, but gently coming closer to her, his voice clearing away her visions, soothing her thoughts, words becoming more comprehensible. His hand was stroking her face. Dizzy, the world whipping round and round like a carousel, she slowly opened her eyes. The kitchen units above her juddered.

"Oh my God, what on earth happened?" she stuttered, her voice thick and growling. "You must have fainted. Hit your head on the edge of the worktop or on the wooden floor as you went down. You're awfully pale. I thought you were unconscious."

Viv screwed up her eyes, trying to remember something important. "Ellie, she was crying. I can't hear her. Is she OK?"

"She's fine. Gone back to sleep again. From the look of her red sweaty face I'd guess she wore herself out crying. But she's peaceful now." He slipped his arm behind her shoulders and eased her up a little. "Good thing I came back early. Look, can you sit up, can you move?" Viv rubbed her forehead and her eyes. "What's your head like? Migraine?"

She took a moment to remember. "Everything was spinning. Zigzags before my eyes. I thought it was a migraine. But it was very strange. Terrible, actually. I had a dreadful pain in my abdomen, all of a sudden. Like my miscarriage with Ana. But for a moment I really thought I was pregnant and miscarrying..."

"You aren't, are you?" Rory's voice was worried.

"No, no. I was sort of aware that I wasn't, so it couldn't have been true, it couldn't have been another miscarriage. It couldn't have been me. Yet ... it was exactly the same. And I had echoes of what happened then, in the hospital, that young nurse, the chaplain." She frowned. "Except that ... I saw crowds of people round me, a lot of noise and bustling around. And, oh, how odd, I was lying on a mosaic floor, all crumbling and old and ruined. But then I was outside, in the air, a breeze swirling round me ... and I remember the smell of horses."

Rory grimaced. "A slip into Lady Vivianne? Were you both experiencing something at the same time?"

"She was calling me, Rory. She said *Where are you? I need you, Viv! Help me again!* I need to do something. I don't know what. But it's something to do with the Rune Stone."

Viv struggled to sit up. She closed her eyes for a moment and when she opened them again her head was cleared, and the dizziness had gone. She saw everything in high definition. Lady Vivianne's life had fast-tracked across her mind. She saw it all in that split second.

"Is she dead?"

"Who?" Rory felt her forehead for fever.

"Lady Vivianne. Everything went black, for both of us. It was like that saying that your whole life flashes across your head as you die. That's what just happened."

"But what do you mean? You're very much alive!" Rory snorted.

"God, I'm stiff. I need to stand up," she said.

"Are you sure you're OK to stand? Do you think you should be checked out for concussion? It must have been a hard bump. And you seem to be saying some odd things, Viv."

"No, I think I fainted and mainly slipped down the kitchen unit. I did knock my head on the floor at the bottom, but I think the effects were more the memory of Lady Vivianne. It can't have been a migraine or I'd still be getting the after effects. But yes, it's all cleared now, amazingly. I'm fine." She held out her hand to Rory and leaned on him as he pulled her up to standing. "Wow, that's better. I hope I don't have any more of those! Rory, I'm not speaking nonsense. I'm saying – you know they say that in your final throes, your life flashes before your eyes? Well, I honestly think I just had that, but with Lady Vivianne's life."

"Really? That's ... weird."

"I saw everything in a nano second of time. Her marriage, her children, her eldest daughter Nymue, Gareth, Aldwyn, the troubles with the harvest, the departure of Sir Roland to battle."

"I have no idea what you're talking about!"

But Viv was not listening to him. "And I saw Icel ..."

"Icel? I *have* heard of *him*! Wasn't he an Angeln, one of the Germanic tribes from Denmark or Norway or Sweden or somewhere to the northeast-ish? Southern Scandinavia anyway. Didn't they invade Britain around the sixth century and fight and kill their way through southern East Anglia and into the Midlands?"

"Yes, but," she frowned against the crowded memories, "I'm not so sure it was exactly like that."

"Yes, Icel, the Icelings." He tapped quickly on his iPhone Google app. "Yes! Sometimes called the Iclingas, the House of Icel. Son of Éomēr. They joined forces with the Saxons and Jutes at some stage, didn't they, and – hey presto, we get Anglo-Saxon Britain!"

"Um ... as I said, not quite like that. Let me explain ..."

"Wait a minute. Sit down and let me get you a cup of strong tea and you can tell me all about it."

"I'm OK now."

But Rory insisted that Viv sit down and have a cup of tea. As Viv explained all she knew, she stretched her back and took a deep yoga breath and released a long sigh. It was like the release of tension and stress, but not hers, someone else's. Lady Vivianne. She'd heard Lady Vivianne calling her. Finally, she'd heard her voice and now she needed to work out how she could help. But help with what? The loss of her baby maybe? Something else – something at Cūning's Mere?

"Oh," Rory exclaimed, still staring at his iPhone, "I'm on this interesting site about the fourth to sixth century invasions of Britain by the Anglo-Saxons ..."

"My theory is that it was more about migration and social absorption," Viv interrupted. "But go on."

Rory looked up. "OK. Well, anyway, here it says – I

mean it's only a summary, but – it says that Icel's ancestors may have started to come over to Britain as early as the fourth century AD. There's someone called Wermunds ... and Offa, the ancestor of the King Offa who built the famous Dyke in the eighth century ... But the thing is, their descendants took over East Anglia and the Midlands – I was right about that! – and created the kingdom of Mercia. So, they were the kings of Mercia and the line included King Creoda of Mercia ... oh, he founded the royal fortress at Tamworth – interesting ... and ... wait for it ... King Aethelbold who is commemorated at Repton!"

Viv blinked. "Well, the internet is a fine thing! I have my own theories about how it all happened. But nevertheless, that's an interesting timeline. So, Icel is a forebear of Aethelbold. Hmm." She took another sip of her tea. "I'm beginning to see a chain here. But there are some links missing. Gosh, the plot thickens, doesn't it?" She chewed her lip.

At that moment, a wail arose from the nursery as Ellie woke up again.

"She's ready for her feed," murmured Rory as he continued to tap his fingers on his iPhone.

"OK. See you later then, Rory." Viv drained her cup of tea and made for the door.

"Well, *I* can't feed her, can I?" he called after her, but she heard the smile in his voice. "Oh, hang on - are you OK enough now to feed her?"

"It's fine. *I'm* fine," Viv called back, "You can get the

evening meal, then, please, while I'm occupied with Ellie!"

But secretly she was glad of the quiet interlude to try to work out those missing links in the chain. Perhaps she was on the way to discovering the secrets of the Rune Stone.

CHAPTER 25

VIV

Derbyshire. Present day

"*I*'m terribly sorry, sweetie-pie!" Tilly shrieked down the phone and Viv held the receiver away from her ear for fear of being deafened. "I'm afraid that gorgeous hunky priest of yours is going to have to do it all over again!"

"What?"

"The filming, honeybun! Oh, my days, this has never ever happened to me before. You must believe me."

"So what on earth has happened then, Tilly?" Viv was juggling with the phone extension in her study as she worked on her new paper on the dating of the Anglo-Saxon epic poem Beowulf. Now that she had been looking further into the evidence of the early kings of Mercia, the birth line of Icel and the House of Iclingas, she had become absorbed by the theory that the poem could have been written for Offa II to glorify the Mercian royal house, through Offa I and Éomēr, the father of Icel whom she'd now discovered. They both appeared to be referenced in the poem. But she was struggling with the linguistic forms in the poem that suggested it was written in an earlier eighth century dialect than perhaps would have been used in Offa II's time. Her mind was only half on what Tilly was saying. "Sorry, Tilly, what was that?"

"Sweetie-pie, you've got your head in that book again! I'm telling you that we've got to do the filming at the Rune Stone all over again."

"Yes, I got that bit. But why?" Viv reluctantly tore her eyes away from the text and swivelled herself away from the laptop.

"Because you'll never believe it ... but there's a shadow."

"Oh. But I thought that the camera man had been incredibly careful about the light and the sun."

"I know! It's like a ... well, you'll have to see it for yourself. I'll send it over. We really can't broadcast it as it is. We'll just have to do another take. In the meantime, can you let your man out to play again this afternoon? Is he priesting or can he find another half hour for me?"

"I'll ask him when he gets home for lunch, but as far as I know there's nothing in the diary for this afternoon. In fact, he was hoping for a good couple of hours on his sermon for Sunday."

"I'm so sorry."

"Don't worry about it, Tilly. These things happen."

"I'll check very very carefully this time, I promise. I mean, I did check on the monitor before, but I didn't see anything at all untoward. It all looked great. A real mystery. I simply cannot understand it." Viv heard a click. "Right. I've sent it over to you. Have a look. It's weird. See you later in the churchyard." Tilly made an exaggerated comic ghostly noise as she hung up.

Viv opened her emails and the link that Tilly had sent. She clicked on it and on the 'open/view the film'. The footage was clear, and Viv was becoming absorbed in the interview. A few minutes in, there was a strange movement behind Rory and the Rune Stone, something that hadn't been there before. She clicked the frame on freeze and peered more closely at her screen. There was certainly what looked like a shadow, maybe a figure, but it was faint and blurred. She could see why Tilly didn't want it kept because it did look odd, and she was always the perfectionist when it came to her work. Viv knew she would have been the same if it was hers.

She clicked through the next few frames, but the shape disappeared and there was nothing on the rest of the footage. Viv backtracked to the frame where the 'interference' began and enlarged it, but the zoom only made it more hazy and the edges seemed to merge into the church wall behind the Rune Stone. She returned to the original sizing and fiddled with her settings to try to make it clearer.

It was hard to make out, but it looked to Viv as though it was the figure of a woman in a long robe holding her hands up in supplication. It – she – moved into view behind – or was it in front? – of the Rune Stone as Rory was about to speak. She shuddered.

She remembered that she had drifted into a vision of Lady Vivianne at just about that moment in the filming. She hadn't seen that shadow behind the Rune Stone, but she had experienced the journey through the holloway and the cart overturning. She had felt Lady Vivianne's fear and also her determination to find her husband and bring him and her thegns back home. And then of course she had experienced that fainting episode in the kitchen when she thought she was lying in pain on a mosaic floor, bleeding and in despair, and when she heard that plea *"Where are you? I need you! Help me again!"*

She was there, wasn't she, through time, into the present, into the churchyard? She was there, by the Rune Stone, calling to Viv for help across the centuries. She'd been there all the time.

As her eyes became more accustomed to the dim shadow of the figure, Viv thought she saw her move her raised hand towards the eastern part of the churchyard. She was holding something in her hand but Viv, try as she might, squinting hard, couldn't make out what it was.

THE SECOND TAKE THAT AFTERNOON WAS EVEN BETTER than the first, Viv thought. Somehow it felt more polished. She was looking out carefully for any sign of a shadow but there was nothing that she could see. Neither did she feel any connection with Lady Vivianne for the whole session.

Tilly drew the session to a close. "Great! That's a wrap. Ooh, I love saying that! Excellent stuff. Thanks, Rory. Thanks, team. I'll just whizz that back to check there's no shadow or movement behind this time, and then I think we're done."

Rory was walking over towards her when she became aware of a figure under a tree over by the gate. The breeze was in the other direction, coming from the east, so she hadn't detected the smell until Ivy moved out from the tree's shadow and approached her.

"Ey up, Mrs Rev'rend, Mr Rev'rend."

Viv was glad that Rory's step didn't falter; he came to her side and put his arm around her shoulders. Viv glanced down at Ellie, chortling in her baby carrier that lay on the grass at her feet. She was aware that Tilly and the crew had stopped looking at the playback and were staring at Ivy. There was something aggressive about her stance. Viv looked over to Tilly and shook her head. Tilly's team resumed their scan of the footage and gave her the thumbs up.

"All OK this end, but we'll see more clearly when we get back to the studio," Tilly called over. "Fingers crossed, but it's looking good." Her team packed up and began to take their equipment over to their van. Tilly came across to Viv and Rory. "Goodness," she said looking at Ivy.

"Are you all right, Ivy?" Viv asked, determined not to hold a grudge. Ivy planted her feet firmly, legs apart, at the side of a large stone angel with bowed head and hands clasped in prayer. Thankfully, she was at a distance. But Ivy seemed to have forgotten the fury at Viv at the end of the meeting in the church, although she clearly hadn't forgotten the message.

"Ah'm areet. But I see you're still summonin' up them ancient curses on the village! You're still messin' with the devil's runes. An' filmin' it for all to see. Ya shouldna be messin' with the runes, Mr Rev'rend."

Viv felt Rory squeeze her shoulder and take a deep breath to speak, but suddenly Tilly, who had been hovering nearby and listening in, said, "Hey, er ... Ivy is it?" Ivy nodded but screwed her eyes up suspiciously. "Wow, you know, this is really interesting! Ancient curses and the devil's runes, you say? D'you know I'm wondering, Ivy, if you'd care to take part in this film and tell your side of the story? How'd you feel about that?"

Viv glanced over to Tilly and grimaced, but Rory

said, "Actually, you know, that might not be a bad idea." She caught Tilly's wink and grasped what she was trying to do.

Tilly called her crew back and said, "What d'you know! Here's another intriguing addition to the film, chaps. A lady who's sceptical about the research into the Rune Stone and I think has some ideas on the more ... let's say, magical side of the runes. Maybe stuff on ancient curses and such like."

"OK, Tilly. Just as you like," said the camera man pulling his gear back. "Won't take a moment to set up again."

The make-up girl began to open up her case. "No," said Tilly. "I think we'll take her as she is. More effective for the things she's going to say."

Goodness, thought Viv, she's going to look like the local witch.

"Stay where you are, Ivy, by that angel," called Tilly. "Let's get that into the picture. Atmosphere."

Rory turned to Viv with a puzzled expression, but Viv shrugged and whispered, "She knows what she's doing."

Ivy stood as still and rigid as the stone headstones around her and looked terrified. "Oooh, I dunno ..."

"It's fine, Ivy." Tilly checked that the camera was ready again and got the thumbs up. "You have something to add to the film. It'll give it a ... an edge. We'll just film your ideas about the runes just now and then we'll tidy it all up and cut it in to the footage later in the studio. It'll be great. You OK with that?"

Ivy nodded slowly as though she was realising her advantage.

"Um," the camera man frowned. "You want it warts and all? Spoken just like that?"

"Yeah, sure, why not? OK, are we set up and ready to go? I'll use the handheld extension mike, not the clip-on."

On Tilly's signal, Ivy began her diatribe about the runes, just as she had spoken to Viv and Rory before. They watched, both fascinated to hear objectively how strange her accusations were, yet at the same time troubled by them.

"An' then them folks came, diggin' up the east side of the church before we could make the new graveyard, an' they found a baby's burial. All alone an' by itself there." Ivy nodded. "An' it were lyin' there ..."

"Sorry, Ivy," Tilly interrupted, "Who were these people, and what was lying there?" She moved the mike on its long handle a little nearer to Ivy.

"The folks that were diggin' for old remains. Archaeologist people, ya know. Had to do it 'cos I told 'em there's ancient stuff down there, ya canna dig it up. Found all sorts, they did. Took it all to the museum," Ivy smirked conspiratorially, "well, nearly all. I saw a bit of metal when they were packing up and I had it for a keepsake. Well, why not?" she added, her face clouding over with anger. "They wouldna' miss it. Why should they take it all? It belongs to us, who've lived all us lives in the village, me mum and gran' folks before 'em. Why should some hoity-toity university folks take our stuff?"

"What was the bit of metal that you kept, Ivy, the keepsake?"

"Oh," Ivy shrugged. "Just a shiny thing, like a lump a' metal with a hole at the top. I polished it up a bit an' it shone like gold."

Viv gasped and whispered under her breath. "The missing bracteate! Oh, Ivy, what have you done!" She turned to Rory. "She's talking about the 2003 dig before they could create the new churchyard extension. The bracteate was recorded in the report, but it was later missing from the museum's inventory."

Tilly's eyes widened. "Thank you very much, Ivy. That was really interesting to hear your personal take on the mysteries of the Rune Stone. What d'you know? Ancient magical signs or historical memorial to an important personage?" She signalled to cut. "Well. We'll add a bit about that from Viv later. But tell me now - what's a bracteate?"

"It's a pendant often worn on a leather thong round the neck in the early Anglo-Saxon period," said Viv. "Often from Scandinavia, or the original Germanic lands. But it was more usually found in adult female burials. And especially those of high-ranking people. Its disappearance has been bothering me for a while. So that's where it got to."

"Ooh," grinned Tilly, "This is getting *really* good!"

"Hmm. Not sure how to handle this."

"A theft!" Tilly whispered, winking at Rory, "From church property!"

Rory dropped his arm from around Viv's shoulders and grimaced, speaking low. "This one's for me, I think. I'll have a word with her and then if there's trouble I'll have to resort to the Bishop. Yes, it is church land it was found on. Not sure it's exactly church property. It may well be treasure trove. But I guess it certainly needs to go to the museum with the other finds."

Viv grabbed his arm as he began to move away toward Ivy who was standing by the angel looking pleased with herself and not at all bothered by the concern on everyone's faces. "Wait a minute! Please – I'd really like to see this bracteate, if that's what it is, and perhaps we need Helen to date it? To think ... it might have belonged to Lady Vivianne! Although ... where did it come from? And how did it come to be in a baby's grave? Or ... oh dear, was this originally part of Lady Vivianne's grave?"

CHAPTER 26

LADY VIVIANNE

521 AD

"Oh, no, no!" wailed the nurse, furiously crossing herself. "Both gone, and it was a son as well. I am so sorry, Sir Roland. Oh Lord above, help us in this time of need. My heart is broken. I came to love her like family. This is a grievous loss to us all. Her people will never recover from this. Oh my God." She sobbed with despair but she desperately busied herself wiping clean the still little form lying between Lady Vivianne's bloodied legs. She could not stop the tears falling in her grief but she gently wrapped him up. "Dear God, what should we do?"

Sir Roland's voice was full of his own tears, and it broke as he spoke slowly and grimly. "I cannot bear it. She was my sun and my moon, my life. I do not know what I shall do without her now. Or what our settlement will do without her wise guiding hand. Oh Lord God, help me. Help us all." He gulped and drew in his breath to collect himself. "Of course, I will take them both back home and bury them together." The inhaling of his breath was audible. "A Christian burial as she would have wanted, in the right way. To think, she came here on this perilous journey in order to bring me and the thegns home. And now she herself has to be brought home." The shock had clearly made his body feel numb and he visibly struggled to kneel beside his beloved wife's head. He tenderly reached out to push aside the circlet and veil, and to stroke her forehead. "I have never seen anyone so white. Even on the battlefield. She is almost blue. My love," he whispered, "how do I ride with you like this and how do I bury you, when it should be me? And our children ..." He could no longer hold back a sob nor stop his tears from falling, and her cheeks glistened wet with them.

"Sir Roland!" A hand was shaking his shoulder and the nurse knelt beside him on the grassy courtyard. "Look! Is that a stirring of her breast?"

Lady Vivianne heard their voices through the fog of her brain. She knew that she must move to show them that she was alive. But all she could do was take a deep breath.

She knew that the baby was lost. She had felt it all along, but she had a mission to enact and that had always been at the top of her mind, and she had crushed the fear deep within her.

"My love!" She heard Roland's voice, trembling, faint, then growing stronger. "Are you really breathing?"

He turned away, "She's alive!" he bellowed and Vivianne sensed the scurrying of crowds around her, pushing themselves through to see for themselves.

"Alive?" A voice she recognised. Icel. She could not see him but knew that he was kneeling across from Roland. "She has come back from the world of the dead. A miracle.

"Indeed," whispered the nurse. "She showed no sign of life. It *is* a miracle, sir." She crossed herself again, more urgently than before. "I have never seen that before."

"Please," murmured Vivianne, "Please give me air... for I can hardly ... draw breath."

"This is truly Nerthus, the earth mother," Icel intoned. "She has lost her baby, but she fights for life like Woden, our God of fighting."

Vivianne sensed that Icel was rising to his feet and as his bulk moved away, she felt the air and struggled to draw it into her chest. She looked up and saw that Roland was no longer trying to hold back the flood of his tears and they coursed down his face. He did not push them away but let them fall.

"Have you really come back to us? My love, I thought we had lost you."

"Ah," Vivianne whispered, her breath rasping and thick. "You do not ... rid yourself of me ... so easily!" She struggled to smile, and Roland bent to kiss her and stop her efforts.

"Quiet now," he said, "let us find a chamber for you to rest and recover." Reluctantly he rose from her and turned to Icel. "Where can we take her to tend her and restore her?"

Vivianne felt strong arms lift her up and gently move her into a chamber. It smelt of decay but at least there was a bed, of sorts, a straw mattress at least and her nurse strew herbs around her head as she lay.

"Roland," she croaked, "You must have your wounds tended and chamomile to drink or maybe a draught of ..."

She did not finish her words because the darkness came upon her and this time it was a welcome release from her pain and loss. As she drifted away, she heard Icel say again, "This is truly Nerthus sent to us from Woden."

LADY VIVIANNE HAD NO IDEA HOW LONG SHE SLEPT AND how long her serfs, and Icel's, tended her. She was faintly aware that her nurse soothed her body with sweet smelling herbs and her mind with tinctures. She mourned her lost baby and cried for him in the darkness.

In time she felt strong enough to rise and walk by herself. Always Sir Roland was there beside her, seeming much stronger now, wounds bound and his flesh no longer stinking but smelling sweetly of herbal ointments. He had eaten properly of Icel's bounty and was dressed in his own freshly cleaned robes, and together they began to make it into Icel's hall and speak with him of their mutual requirements. Eventually, it was agreed that they were ready to travel back to Cūning's Mere.

"I will send with you warriors from my guard to accompany you safely home," he said, checking through the interpreter. "And to see where we might build a settlement if we move further north."

Icel turned to his guard and took something from his hand. "Here, I have for you this sign of our good faith and of my respect for you, Nerthus. It is inscribed with your symbol of fecundity. And we pray that there will be many more to come."

But Vivianne glanced at Roland at her side and she knew that there would be no more children. He had told her that he would not put her through that ever again and she herself did not want it either. They had four children survive out of seven babies and that was enough. Indeed, two were already near to adulthood and the other two healthy and growing, and that was better than most women. In the past dark days, she had thanked God for her fortune as well as grieving for her loss. She knew that she would never bear any more.

Icel carefully hung a gold pendant around her neck, the leather thong soft against her skin. She could see that it was decorated with signs, the old runes of Nerthus, and encrusted with jewels. He bowed to her.

But now it was time to make the journey back home.

AS SHE RODE BACK IN WELCOME SUNSHINE THROUGH THE village, acknowledging the bows and applause she received from the villagers at the wayside, she saw Nymue waiting for them outside the mead hall. She looked so much older than when Vivianne left and she marvelled at her tall elegant daughter dressed in a purple robe and a red mantle to mark the occasion, a small gold circlet on her burnished hair.

Matilda stood behind her with Tristram, Launce and Nini, the little girl sucking her thumb shyly. Of course, they would be disconcerted that their parents had been away so long in frightening circumstances. Vivianne knew that she would never forget her lost son, but her heart felt full to see her children looking so grown up and healthy. She held out her arms to them and the younger ones rushed into her embrace, Tristram holding back a little at first, clearly trying to be restrained and then running to her.

She hugged them tightly then looked up to Matilda. "Where is Afera?"

"She has gone to live in Edyth's house, my lady. She would not attend to the lady Nymue." Matilda frowned, not making any effort to hide her disgust.

"I see. That is probably for the best. But she is well?"

Matilda nodded with a grimace. "I have found another maid to take her place. She is tending the lady Nymue at present in your absence, but I have another I am training for you too."

Vivianne nodded her thanks and hugged her children even more closely.

"Oh, how good it is to see you all again," she said, fighting back her tears.

Nymue bowed her head to Vivianne and Roland, but nobody could fail to see her glance sideways at Gareth Swineson who stood at her side.

"My daughter, is all well here in the settlement?" said Vivianne. "We have worried so much about you all."

"All is well. But we know about your troubles from the messenger who heralded your arrival and gave us news. We are truly sorry to hear of the loss. It is a loss to us all, our bereavement and our grief."

Vivianne tried to smile her thanks. "We will bury him at sunset so that he can see the sun going down for the last time before the earth takes him."

Sir Roland dismounted and helped Vivianne from

her mount. She felt the familiarity of her home soil beneath her feet and sighed.

"We will lay him to rest in the grave with our daughter Ana, lost so many years ago. They will be together. And there they will be near to the sacred hall, so that they can hear our parents' voices soothing their souls."

Nymue nodded and bowed her head, then she ran forward to hug both her mother and her father, and Vivianne could tell from her face that she could feel how thin and bony her father had become despite the noble aspect he was determined to show the people.

"Well, after we have buried our tiny brother and are feeling stronger, we must hold a feast for your homecoming," Nymue said. Vivianne could hear the catch in her voice as if she was hiding something. She turned to Roland with raised eyebrows.

"How does the settlement really fare? We need to know the truth even if it is bad," Roland asked with a frown.

Vivianne looked around her at the villagers who stood outside their houses and workshops, despite the cold, and whose faces she could see were smiling and healthy.

Nymue turned to look at Gareth and waited for his response.

"As well as can be expected, my lady," Gareth said, his voice strong and clear. "We have come through bad times, as you knew from before your journey, but we are managing. Our rations have meant that everyone has had some share of the food, nobody has starved, nobody has gone totally without, although there has been hunger and sickness. We have – no, Lady Nymue has – led the way and shown how we must all look after each other."

Vivianne and Roland looked at their eldest daughter, their eyes and hearts filled with pride. Vivianne reached out to catch Nymue's hand and said, "I knew it! I knew that you would grow into your role. But you have clearly surpassed anything we could have dreamt. You have looked after our settlement well. I thank you, daughter." She turned to Gareth, "Both of you. You have done well. Gareth Swineson, you will be properly thanked and honoured for this."

Gareth bowed to her. "I did my duty, my lady, as you requested, that is all. Now, I must go back up to the fields, but I shall come back down for the burial."

He turned to smile at Nymue and took his leave. Vivianne glanced at Roland who shrugged, then at Matilda who grinned.

Vivianne became aware that the villagers over on the road had fallen silent. She looked up to see the warriors of Icel's guard who had ridden the whole way at the rear of their band. They approached slowly and cautiously. She stepped out into the road and raised her hand. The Icelings drew to a halt before her and bowed their heads. The interpreter moved beside Vivianne and spoke with the warriors.

"They say that their duty is done. They have seen you safely home to your own people. Now they must go back to Icel."

"Wait," said Vivianne. "I thank you and for your kindness you must take rest and refreshment before your journey home." She called Gareth back. "Gareth Swineson, please to find Ealdorman Godwyne to arrange bed and food for these our guests. They must feast like chieftains with as much as we can share, such as we have."

The Icelings nodded their thanks and their spokesman said, through the interpreter, "We can report back to Icel that your land is fine, your soil as productive as any we have at home, and your people good. We hope to make our home not too far away and there we will share and trade with you as our treaty demands."

THE SUN WAS SINKING ON THE WESTERN HORIZON AS THE sad little group led the villagers out past the sacred hall to the old grave and Vivianne remembered that last time and the way her heart had broken. Sir Roland carried the tiny, cold and swaddled form gently in his arms and as they stopped before the open chasm beneath the mound, he kissed the top of his son's head, smelling the oils and unguents he had been bathed in. He wrapped the burial shroud more firmly around the little body and lowered him into the dark chamber of earth, back into the wooden bed he had lain in on the silent journey back from the Icelings.

He bowed his head a while, then moved aside as Vivianne and Nymue stepped forward with the goods that were to be placed in the grave with him for his final journey: little pottery jars of honey and mead and herbal infusions, a gold brooch, and a glass goblet, adding to the grave goods that had lain there for years with the first baby they had lost.

Vivianne unwound the leather thong from her neck and ran her finger tenderly over the markings on the bejewelled gold pendant: the old runes and symbols of Nerthus set around the edge and the image of the Goddess to honour her. The gift of respect and friendship from Icel and his people. But she felt that it should go with her lost baby for the memory of the miscarriage and her near death was too heart breaking for her to continue to wear it round her neck for the rest of her life.

She bent and placed the bracteate in the burial chamber along with the other precious grave goods. As she straightened up, Roland slipped his arm around her shoulders.

CHAPTER 27

VIV

Derbyshire. Present day

Rory slipped his arm around Viv's shoulders again and squeezed her gently. She knew that he felt the tension across her back.

"I need to see the bracteate – the pendant, Ivy." Viv said. "Please could you let me come with you to the cottage to see it?"

Ivy frowned and puffed. "Dunno about that, Mrs Rev'rend."

"Please, it would mean such a lot to me. You see, I think it's really important to this investigation. To my research."

Ivy raised her eyebrows. "Important, eh? Precious? Worth something, eh?"

Viv paused and considered. "Well, I can't say until I see it."

"Hmm. I'll 'ave ter go an' find it then," said Ivy, her eyes narrowed. "Dunno where it is."

Viv looked at Rory, wishing she didn't feel so suspicious. Was Ivy going to hide the bracteate and claim she couldn't find it so that she could sell it? But then, why hadn't she done that already if that was on her mind.

"But you wouldn't be able to sell it, Ivy, anyway, if that's what you're thinking. It's a known artefact."

"Ey, I might be thinkin' that. Or I might not."

Rory stroked Viv's arm. "Ivy, let me come with you to the cottage to find it. In case you have any difficulty."

Ivy grunted but made off down the path. Rory gave Viv a reassuring smile and strode after the hobbling old lady. "Back in a minute."

"You don't think ...?" Tilly started. "Oh my, this is too good to be true."

In fact, Ivy and Rory were back very quickly. Clearly, she knew precisely where she'd kept the bracteate. Rory returned to Viv's side and gave her a wry smile. "Well, that was an experience!" he wrinkled up his nose and grimaced.

Ivy held out a filthy bit of cloth and carefully unwrapped its contents. Viv peered at it, a tarnished golden disc about two inches in diameter in Ivy's outstretched palm, dirt encrusting its surface.

"Watcha think?"

"Could I just hold it a moment, Ivy?"

Reluctantly Ivy slipped the pendant into Viv's

hand. Viv stared at it, then she took a face wipe from the bag on Ellie's carrier, and gently wiped away the dirt. Underneath the grime of ages, the gold began to shine through, and she saw the markings, knowing them to be runic symbols, circling the engraving of a woman. She did not want to rub too hard at the surface in case she unknowingly caused any damage. There were tiny stones around the edge that could have been jewels, although it was hard to tell what they were. But already she could see that, meticulously cleaned, it would be a fantastic artefact. She was holding in her hand something that she was sure was a fifth or sixth century bracteate. And the thought of the physical connection to Lady Vivianne made her shiver. Goose pimples prickled her skin.

She thought she heard Rory say something, but it was growing fainter as though from far off. Everything seemed to dim and fade into the distance. The birdsong she could hear only a few minutes ago drifted away, and there was no longer the sound of car engines roaring over on the A38. The trees around her in the churchyard rustled as a breeze arose, and she felt something waft across her hand, a gentle touch, fingers tender and soft. She did not look up but knew that the churchyard was swathed in mist.

Noises arose from the mist, slowly but with purpose as if they were reaching out to her. Horses' hooves thudding on dried mud and clattering on stones. The rattle of cart wheels. Looking back to see that the precious cargo was safe. Looking back even further, to people crowding around her, murmuring, wailing so that she could hardly breathe. A huge figure leaning over her, worry etched into his weather-beaten features. Wild hair, paint on his cheeks. Then standing before him, a large dominating figure in the hall, raising his hands to her, then pressing his palms together in respect. Holding something out to her, gold and glinting in the light of the sconces.

She felt herself drift and move away from herself, as though she saw herself from outside her body, in a dream. A woman, stately, regal in fact, standing before her, deep red robe and wide gold circlet like a crown upon her head, upon her thick bronze-gold hair. She tilted her head to indicate the metal in Viv's hand. *Please help me.*

Viv looked down at the artefact lying on her palm. "What do you want me to do?"

The figure turned towards the east and stared into the distance. *It must go back home, back to where it belongs.*

"I will do it."

"Viv! Sweetie-pie! Are you OK?" Tilly's voice shrieked through the mist. Viv shook her head back into the present and reality. The figure had gone, and the churchyard was as it should be.

Yet only Rory, breathing loudly beside her, felt real. "Did you see her?" she whispered, and Rory nodded, tugging at his clerical collar.

She turned in Tilly's direction. "I'm fine, Tilly. Just had a little moment, you know?"

Tilly nodded but looked at Viv strangely. Then her eyes brightened as though she too had seen and understood. "I was just wondering. You know, Ivy was the one to ... er, *find* the pendant by the burial place. And I'm thinking," she raised an eyebrow at Ivy. "Would you, if Viv agrees, be filmed returning the bracteate to the grave site?"

Ivy cocked her head to one side.

"It's a very important thing to do," Viv added, pulling herself back to reality, "for the village, the parish. And I think it should be a long-time resident who is the one to perform the ceremony."

She looked questioningly at Ivy, who stood there belligerently, feet planted apart on the grass. "What do you say, Ivy?"

"Great idea," murmured Rory in Viv's ear. "And we can always dig it up afterwards and send it to the museum."

"Well, I was thinking more of sending the film to the museum, let them decide what's best. And a photo of the bracteate in close-up to the curators and to Helen Mortimer." The real reason for caution was that she knew she couldn't risk delaying matters by getting Helen to assess the artefact first before they could persuade Ivy to let it go. Anyway, there was no physical burial site now that anyone could see, no actual grave to place it in, so it would just perhaps be a ceremony.

Yet after her previous experiences she wasn't even sure that the physical burying was even relevant. Lady Vivianne wanted it returned through the centuries "back home" and "to where it belongs". She'd made a promise and she must fulfil it without delay.

Ivy furrowed her brow. "I dunno." She turned to Tilly. "Would I 'ave to say anythin' on the film?"

"Not if you don't want to," said Tilly. "Would you rather just be filmed laying the bracteate to rest?"

Ivy nodded. "D'you wanna do it now, 'cos I'll 'ave to get ready?"

They waited some time for Ivy to return and had almost given up. The camera man started to pack, wanting to get off home. Viv took a photo of the bracteate on her iPhone. It had a good camera so she hoped that it would be clear enough for Helen to be able to undertake a preliminary assessment. Then Ivy appeared again.

Viv couldn't believe the transformation. The old woman had clearly washed, and she smelled of sweet lavender. She wore a faded but clean dress. In fact, it was more like a robe than a modern dress, and it swept the ground as she ambled towards them. Her long grey hair which was normally scraped carelessly back was piled up on her crown and covered with a thin voile like a veil, and around it was a silver circlet. Over her arm she held a cloak and she stopped in her tracks to drape it around her shoulders like a mantle. Viv held her breath.

"Goodness, Ivy, you look spectacular," she managed to say.

"This is fantastic," breathed Tilly and even the camera man looked impressed. "This will really enhance the film. Where did you manage to get this fabulous medieval costume?"

"Ey, ah used ter do them re-enactment things, yer know? In the old days." Ivy stroked her robe. "Made this 'un meself."

How sad, thought Viv, that she should have turned into such a miserable dirty antisocial old woman. Perhaps this was something they could work on to help her. She'd never thought of Ivy as having a life, an interest, especially the early medieval world, an interest that she herself shared. But she blamed herself, she should have found out before now. She really should have made that effort to get to know such a thing. She'd just taken Ivy at face value.

"So where is the location of this burial site?" asked Tilly, signalling to the camera man.

Rory picked up Ellie's carrier and Viv led the way into the newer eastern part of the churchyard. She remembered where she had found the position of the burial from the 2003 excavation map.

"But there's nothing here!" said Tilly, poking around at the graves and brass flower holders.

"No, there's nothing to see. But I'm sure it was somewhere around here."

A wisp of cold air wafted around her and she

shivered. A drift of mist swirled and formed itself between two headstones and stilled.

"Here. It's here."

Viv felt Rory shudder beside her and heard him whisper the words of the Lord's Prayer as he had done on that previous occasion when Lady Vivianne had called to them for help.

She turned to Ivy and handed her the bracteate, laying it carefully on her upturned palm. In the distance she heard the soft whirring of the camera. But all else around her sank into a deep silence. She was aware of Ivy bending down and felt compelled to kneel beside her. Viv took a deep breath and she called silently to Lady Vivianne to receive the gold pendant and keep it safe once again within the burial site. She closed her eyes and felt Rory's hand on her shoulder, warm and comforting, and heard his murmured prayers.

The mist wafted across behind her eyes and the earth shifted, the ground beneath her knees trembling. She thought she heard a voice sighing. And she was aware of a ripple in the air, a rising of the wind, a murmur of time, of worlds. In her mind she saw tears and a faint light rising from the earth, becoming more intense as it approached her. But she did not feel afraid. She felt instead that it enfolded her in warmth and gratitude.

She did not see it but she knew that, beside her, Ivy held out the bracteate to the earth and that it sank down through the soil and came to rest amongst the hidden forgotten bones that had lain there for so many centuries and had become absorbed into the earth. A long receiving sigh reverberated through the earth beneath Viv's knees and although it was not her who held out the bracteate, she felt the warmth of the gold and saw its glow as it slipped away to where it truly belonged.

Rory whispered a blessing and Viv stood. She heard Tilly whisper, "My God, what just happened there?" A silence except for the gentle whirring of the camera.

She touched Ivy's shoulder as she still knelt there. "Ivy, it's done."

"Aye, it's done, Mrs Rev'rend." Ivy struggled to stand as though her body was so frail she could hardly feel it any more. "I saw her take it, y'know. That lady."

"Yes, I know," Viv whispered, "so did I."

"Yer saw it? I didna think you rector ladies saw that sort o' thing. So yer believe it, all those ancient stories? All that aboot some lady o' the lake and Cooney's Mere and people that lived 'ere in them olden days? Yer believe it?"

"Oh yes, I do believe it, Ivy."

"Well, ya's better that ah thought, then."

"I've found out a lot about it all, and maybe I could talk to you about it some time, Ivy?"

"As yer like." Ivy paused and gripped the skirts of her robe tightly in her hands. "But them runes o' the cross. I dunno." Somehow Ivy's voice was softer. "They smack o' evil and magic ter me."

"But there were runes on the pendant, and you didn't think those were evil, did you, Ivy? You kept it safe and respected it."

"Yeah. But that be diff'rent."

"Not so different, actually. Just old ways of writing. It's just that they look mysterious. And they're about things that folks used to believe in. The runes on the cross are about the lady we both just saw."

"But there be a curse, I jess know it!" Ivy insisted and a flicker of aggression rose again. "Me mam used ter tell me the story of the curse."

Viv sighed. "To be honest you might be right, that there *is* something engraved on it that people might have thought was a curse. But we think it's warning not a curse. To warn people not to damage or harm the cross in any way. But my associate at the university is looking into it and we'll know more shortly. It's not easy to read the runes and of course, Ivy, it's as much about interpretation as anything."

She became aware of the camera whirring and realised that Tilly was still filming.

"Hey, Tilly, are you filming this?"

"We kept rolling 'cos it's really interesting but we can delete if you'd prefer. We'll replay through the whole thing and you can put the mockers on anything you want. Your choice 'cos this last bit's a bit personal, isn't it?"

"I'm probably OK with it, although I would like a veto when we see it through. It depends on Ivy, too. We'll watch it together."

"Of course."

"I'll be interested to see what you got on the bracteate."

"What *did* happen then?" Tilly narrowed her eyes. "Was it some kind of trick? One minute it was there in Ivy's hand and the next it was gone. Like some magic trick! Really weird!"

"More things in heaven and earth ... and all that," murmured Rory. "Are you OK, Ivy?" He held out his arm to her. "Do you want me to walk you back to the cottage?"

"If yer will, Mr Rev'rend. I do feel a bit wobbly." She turned to Viv. "But thank you, Mrs Rev'rend. And ah'm sorry fer the trouble ah've caused."

"It's OK, Ivy. No harm done. And all's well now, isn't it?"

Rory turned to Viv and smiled with such love that Viv trembled, and her heart was full.

CHAPTER 28

LADY VIVIANNE

Cūning's Mere 521 AD

I t was the time of the Paschal Moon, but the sky was dark and brooding. Two full moons had passed since her return from the Icelings and Lady Vivianne stood at the site they had cleared for this momentous occasion, not far west of the sacred hall and the burial mound. Sir Roland was, as ever since his return from captivity, close by her side, and now having regained his health and strength, stood tall and strong with his arm around her waist.

Icel stood beside her and Sir Roland, watching with pride the shrouded stone monument he made for her, his Nerthus. The interpreter explained that the runes upon it told of Lady Vivianne's honour and worth after the field of battle had fallen silent. It told of the respect in which they held her, for her skills at negotiation and most of all for her bravery. She was to them a true warrior and one worthy of becoming an honorary member of their tribe, the Icelings.

Vivianne had welcomed Icel and his warriors with mixed feelings. Of course they reminded her of her heart-breaking miscarriage, the loss of her baby son, wrenched from her body before his time. She could not shake away the knowledge that they had killed so many of her thegns and wounded her beloved husband. Yet at the same time she knew in her heart that Sir Roland and her thegns would have done exactly the same to them. It was turn of the gaming dice that had determined the battle's conclusion. And she knew too that her battle thegns had killed many of Icel's men in their turn. This is what war was about. It seemed to her at times that it was all a game to them. Would men never learn?

But she thought about why they had gone to battle with the Icelings in the first place. To stop them rampaging northwards to threaten their settlement and that of their friends in settlements nearby. And maybe that might have happened. But she had managed to secure their peace without bloodshed, with only words, and she knew that it was a much more lasting peace than would have been won through battle.

And then she remembered how she herself had spoken in the Witan – so long ago now it seemed – when she had raised the Witan sword in the council and agreed that Sir Roland and the thegns should ride south to stop the Icelings from advancing northwards. She thought she was protecting her boundaries, of course she was, and this was all she had known from childhood – protection of your own.

Yet she was glad that the Icelings valued negotiation as much as war, and that Icel had honoured *her* part with this great stone monument. The runes named her, not only as Nerthus and as Woden but also as the woman she knew herself to be, the cūning of this kingdom, Vivianne.

Icel gestured to his guard to remove the cloth that covered the Stone so that all could see its glory.

The figure on the painted stone beneath the carved runes showed a magnificent queen in red and purple robes with a golden circlet, just as she had appeared to Icel that day in his hall. The gold of the jewellery gleamed and stood out beautifully as they were picked out in gold leaf. The pigments were rich and wonderful in Vivianne's eyes; she had never seen anything like it before, not on a stone monument. She drew in her breath as the great Stone was raised and she could see it in all its glory. And she heard Roland gasp beside her.

"My love," he whispered, "It is indeed you, our queen. You saved us and what a fitting tribute to your bravery and courage this is indeed. This will stand here forever. And in future ages people will look upon it and wonder – who is this warrior queen, so heroic and valiant? And they will see, it is Lady Vivianne." He smiled at her with admiration and love and her heart was full.

She turned around and saw behind her that Matilda and the children stood, Launce and Nini fidgeting, wondering what all the fuss was about, and Young Tristram looking proud with his puffed-out chest in his new leather jerkin with its gold rings. She saw that Nymue regal in her own red and purple, like herself, stood elegant and stately, and that Gareth Swineson smiled at her a little way off, tall and dignified as any thegn.

As the group of Icelings and her own ceorls finally raised the great Stone to its full height and fixed the base firmly in the ground, the sun moved out from behind the clouds and shone upon it, the gold gleaming, and everyone gasped at its beauty. Even Launce and little Nini clapped their hands together in awe at the sight.

THE MEAD HALL ECHOED WITH THE NOISE OF FEASTING and merriment. Icel, at first hesitant over the unfamiliar food, overcame his doubts and took from the platters of wild boar and deer that were offered to him, and Lady Vivianne could see that he was savouring them with enjoyment. He signalled for the serfs to fill his goblet yet again with the honeyed mead

JULIA IBBOTSON

he seemed to favour over the ale or even over the wine.

Vivianne's eyes swept the hall, seeing with relief her thegns mixing with the Iceling warriors on the benches. Icel had chosen his most favoured warriors to attend this day while the others were busy building their own settlement a day's ride away. They had made a good peace treaty and a promise of trade and mutual support, although Vivianne knew that they must work hard to keep it that way. It would not take much to break those fragile bonds. But she was hopeful.

She also saw Nymue smiling confidently from the top table over towards Gareth on the side bench as though they shared some secret understanding, and she frowned. But before she could intervene, Icel's scōp stepped forward. He had asked if the scōp could attend to entertain them in appreciation of Vivianne's hospitality and she had agreed, although she doubted that they would understand a word.

The scōp bowed low to Lady Vivianne, Sir Roland, and their older children beside them and she gestured to him that he could begin. Her eyebrows raised as she realised that the poet spoke in her own language as well as that of the Angeln and that she could begin to understand many more of the words of the Icelings than she had anticipated. The poems and stories were of the Angeln homelands, tales of legendary warriors and kings, and a beautifully rhythmic epic poem of a long-ago hero who fought dragons and monsters to protect his king and his homeland. Before long she was captivated. So lost was she in the music of the words that she did not at first realise that her ealdorman Godwyne had left his place at table and was talking to someone at the door the far end of the mead hall. Just as she noticed him, he turned and hurriedly approached her.

The hall quieted as everyone looked around anxiously, aware of a change of atmosphere, and the scōp stopped mid flow.

"What on earth is it, Godwyne?" Vivianne demanded as she saw her old adviser's worried face. She rose from her bench, hands gripping the edge of the trestle table.

"The Stone!" he gasped, barely able to catch his breath. "They have ...they have wrecked it!"

"What! What on earth do you mean, Godwyne?"

Sir Roland beside her put down his goblet and also rose. He laid his hand upon hers and she could feel his strength and reassurance emanating from his palm into her skin.

"Please come to see, my lady," Godwyne managed to say, clutching his chest in dismay.

Lady Vivianne signalled to the thegns in the hall to stay seated, for the serfs to refill their glasses and for the scōp to continue. She beckoned those on the high table to follow her and Sir Roland as they hurried outside.

They made their way out through the darkness,

two serfs holding flaming torches to light the way. The moon veiled its eyes with drifting clouds. They hurried past the sacred hall to the great Stone and saw the ceorls ringed around it. Scuffling noises and muffled cries drew her eyes to a group to the side, where guards were holding two writhing figures. It was too dark and the guards too broad for Vivianne to see who it was they held.

"Look!" the guard beside Godwyne exclaimed. "Here! They have ruined your precious memorial, my lady! Oh, what will Icel think of us now?"

Vivianne stepped forward to peer at the Stone and one of the serfs held his flaming torch high so that she could better see in the darkness. Someone had attempted to erase the runes with a sharp blade and scratch at the painted image of Lady Vivianne. She gasped with horror. How could someone have been so disrespectful?

"Who has done this?" roared Icel at her side. His hand went straight to his sword at his waist. "What man has dared to deface our work?"

Vivianne turned to him and placed her hand on his sword hand to deter him. "Wait. Let us see what this is all about. Why was this done?"

She turned to the guards restraining their captives. The men thrust forward two figures and as the serfs held aloft their torches, she could see that it was Edyth, mother of Aldwyn, and her own maid of the chamber Afera. She drew in her unsteady breath.

"Why? Afera, why would you do such a thing? We have looked after you well in our hall, our home, trusted you with our family, with our lives. And you have sought to erase this mark of respect. Why would you do such a thing?"

Afera did not hang her head in shame but held it high in defiance. She looked at Edyth and said, "It was Edyth's idea. Because of Aldwyn ..."

"She disrespected my son and broke her promises," shrieked Edyth, struggling to free her arms from the guard's restraining hands and butting her head towards Nymue.

Vivianne heard Nymue's gasp behind her and a low soft murmur from Gareth.

"Edyth, we have spoken of this already. We thought that we had quashed this lie and resolved your anger. Why do you now return to the argument and why damage this stone?"

"Where is he? Why has he not returned here like the others, why has he not come back to me? What have you done with my son?" Edyth screamed.

"He is gone," said Icel, as his interpreter whispered in his ear. "He ran away from us after his treachery to Sir Roland. Like a thief in the night, he ran. We do not know where he is."

"No, you lie! My son is Sir Aldwyn and he would never do that!" Edyth tugged at her restraints.

"Woman!" shouted Icel, his patience clearly wearing thin. "He may have helped us to win our misguided battle with the good thegns of Cūning's Mere, may Woden forgive us. But he was a traitor to our Goddess Nerthus here and her people. And if we found him, I assure you that we would tear him limb from limb!" He raised his sword in Edyth's direction.

Vivianne held up her hands, "No, no, Icel. Do not speak like this. We live in peace here and we forgive where it is God's will. This woman is wretched, and she has lost her son in dreadful circumstances, whatever he has done to bring this on. I will not have dispute and anger and violence in my settlement."

Icel lowered his sword and brought his hand to his heart. "You are too good, Nerthus."

"And Afera," Vivianne said, turning back to her maid, "Why would you follow Edyth's idea? Why would you do this to us?"

Afera tossed her head. "Because *she* cast Aldwyn aside and took my Gareth!"

"But Afera, again – we have spoken of this and you are holding on to a dream. I understand a young girl's dream. But you cannot force a man to love you. As I understand it, he gave you no promises or tokens of love. I know that it can feel like the end of the world if your heart is set on one man. But if his heart is elsewhere ..."

"Then I hate him! And I hate you and Nymue and ... and all of you ...!"

"Afera, do not say such things. You will regret them by the next full moon." Vivianne shook her head sadly and she felt Nymue and Gareth gasp behind her.

"No, I will never regret them."

"And *I* will never forgive you for the loss of my son!"

Vivianne shook her head. "Then what should we do? In my heart I do not want to bring you before the Witan council as is our custom with wrong doers. I know that you are both heart broken, each for her own reasons. I would not see you imprisoned in the lockup and give you time to brood even more on your sufferings..."

"We have already decided," interrupted Edyth bitterly, "when we brought out our knives tonight to the Stone, that we would leave the settlement."

"We have nothing to stay for," added Afera with a toss of her head.

"Perhaps wait," said Vivianne slowly and sadly. "Wait for this night in Edyth's house and then we will talk after sunrise when you are calmer, and you have had time to reflect."

But she knew that they would not still be there on the morn and that when she sent for them the next day they would be gone.

She ran her hand over the spoiled runes and the damaged painting. "How do we repair this?"

"My lady," said Gareth soft and low. "If you do not mind my forthright words, let me suggest that the Stone is left as it is, to show us all what damage anger and hate can do. And perhaps a further inscription could stand as a warning lest any other harm be brought to this memorial?"

Vivianne turned to see Nymue touch his arm and Gareth to smile down at her.

"A warning," Icel echoed, bowing to Vivanne. "Yes, so be it. I will do this. Guards will stand here through the night, if you permit, Nerthus, and at the sunrise my stone mason will add to the inscription." He puffed out his chest at his boasting. "And the warning will be there forever, better than before!"

CHAPTER 29

VIV

Derbyshire. Present day

"*I*vy seemed quite invigorated when I delivered her back at her cottage," said Rory with satisfaction, appearing from the French doors out onto the terrace of the rectory garden. He handed Viv a fresh coffee. "Like a different person, quite animated and positive."

"Mmm, I thought I smelled coffee brewing." Viv took the mug from him and perched it on top of a pile of papers next to her laptop on the garden table. She stretched, her face to the sun, revelling in the glorious golden light that only early autumn can produce. "Thank you, just what I need right now. So, what's the cottage like inside?" She turned and bent to pick Ellie up from her playpen beside her on the terrace and reached for the book that her daughter had been trying to eat. She began to turn the pages, showing Ellie the large colourful pictures of household items. "Look, Ellie, a red chair. A blue table. Gosh. Never seen a blue table before, have you, Ellie?" Her daughter wriggled and kicked her legs out.

"Oh, I didn't go inside." Rory rested his hand on Viv's shoulder and cast his eyes to the far end of the garden where the old rectory land met the churchyard. Viv looked up and followed his line of sight across the slope of the lawns to the great spreading trees, horse chestnut, copper beech and the English oaks that had been there since ancient times. She wondered what he was thinking as he stared. "Goodness, no, I just hovered at the door to see she was OK. She seemed mentally alert but physically drained." He kissed Viv on the top of her head, then Ellie, who reached up, leaning back giggling, to pat his face where there was the shadow of stubble across his chin. "She looked quite amazing sitting there in her armchair in her medieval costume. I got the impression that she enjoyed the attention of it all, the filming and so on. It may be the making of her. Hopefully she won't be so disgruntled from now on."

"It was all ... well, *weird*, wasn't it? I mean not the reaching out across the centuries itself – we've done that before, haven't we? – but the fact that the filming was going on and there were other people watching. Tilly and the camera man and the makeup girl and so on. I wonder what exactly they saw?"

"Tilly said she only saw that the bracteate was there in Ivy's hand one minute then seemed to disappear. I think they all thought that Ivy had done a bit of a 'sleight of hand' jobbo. I guess they expect the bracteate to come up at auction at some point in the near future!"

"While you were walking Ivy home, like a true gentleman I must say, I looked at the footage on the camera, the last bit anyway. And honestly, it was nothing like my take on what happened. It sort of seemed ... well, *ordinary* really. The camera shot cut from Ivy's hand with the bracteate in her palm, right at the crucial moment, and panned out to the churchyard as though the camera man saw something else further away, then tracked back to Ivy. But by that time her hand was empty."

She shook her head and Ellie reached to grab her mouth. Viv caught the little fingers and nuzzled them, much to Ellie's delight. She kicked out her legs and flung out her arms, roaring with laughter. Viv smiled indulgently.

"Isn't it amazing how such small things can give so much pleasure to a small child?" she said, turning to Rory. "And there we are, mulling over something as momentous as time-slip. When you think about it, it's mind boggling."

"Or quite simple. I wonder what little Ellie would think about it? Probably take it all for granted!"

"Well, we'll never ..." She was interrupted by her

mobile ringing. She passed Ellie and her book to Rory, glanced at the caller name and pressed the green button. "Hi, Helen. How's things?"

"Viv, I think I've found out as much as I can, certainly at this stage, until we get a break-through on analysing equipment." Helen was never one for passing the time of day with pleasantries and small talk.

"OK, good. What have you found?"

"So ... not anything much more than we knew before, not anything earth shattering, I'm afraid. But I thought I'd update you as I've just done an interview with Tilly here in the lab, and I wanted you to know everything Tilly knows."

"Thank you. Appreciated." Viv could also do curt and to the point.

"So ... I'll go through the processes of analysis in a moment but just to summarise what I found ... as I thought, there are some runes at the end of the inscription above the figure like an additional message, a warning. They appear to have been carved at much the same time as the rest, sixth century looks more than likely, but they're a little different as though they were carved by a different hand. The runic carver's work is almost like a signature, a personal style, like a painter. The message is basically that the memorial is to someone you interpreted as 'Vivianne' when you were at the lab. But there is a chieftain sign as though this person was important, someone of ruling status. There is also a reference to Nerthus ..."

"Ah, the earth mother ..."

"Yes, that's right. Often associated with Germanic tribes around the fifth through to the eighth, ninth centuries, maybe a longer span in some places. Angles or Saxons? Nerthus was worshipped as a bringer of peace and stability. And that seems to be what is being glorified here on the Rune Stone. It mentions honour and skill in this respect. But there's something odd too. There are runes that refer to battle fields and warrior status and bravery. And even more strange, she is equated with Woden – you know, the God of ..."

"The God of war, yes. Are these two concepts incompatible, though?"

"Well, yes. It's most unusual. A revered and almost worshipped figure on a rune stone would not be both Nerthus and Woden. It doesn't make sense."

"I see." But it made perfect sense to Viv, although she couldn't explain because she would have to reveal too much, and she wasn't sure that Helen would appreciate or accept the source of Viv's understanding. Better to leave it as a mystery.

"And there's another thing. The photo of the bracteate that you sent over shows runes depicting Nerthus too. You said it was found not far from your Rune Stone? I would say, without seeing it in the flesh so to speak, that this is also around the sixth century, so clearly there's a connection. We're guessing that this is the bracteate that the 2003 dig discovered but which never made it to the museum? I could do with seeing it properly, Viv, to make any definitive assessment and to clarify some of the runes on it that are indistinct."

"Ah." Viv bit her lip. "Um, well, I don't have it."

"You don't have it? So ... can you get it from whoever has it?"

"Frankly ... no." How could she retrieve it when it had returned to the sixth century with Lady Vivianne and the burial of her son, disappeared into the earth again. "Er, it was never actually in anyone's possession. I guess it was always at the burial site."

"Oh? I wonder what happened with the 2003 dig, then? So, anyway ... the photo you sent me was actually a photo of a photo, not of the real thing? How did you get the photo you emailed me, then?"

"Oh, something in an old cottage ..."

"Ah, a house clearance? Well, that's a shame. I thought we'd found the missing artefact. But, well, we win some, we lose some, that's the way my line of business goes. Anyway, there's more I discovered about the Rune Stone. So... the painted figure looks like sixth century, in keeping with the runes. But the carved figure on top was worked a couple of centuries later. As I said before, this looks like a depiction of a warrior queen. Putting all the evidence together and trying to make sense of it all, I would say that something happened – who knows what? – in the eight century in this kingdom, something that turned the people's attention – or that of the contemporary king of the time – to want to reclaim the painted figure on the Stone and endow it with a clearer warrior status. So he had the carving done on top. Maybe the painting was too faint or weather damaged to look significant enough. And to reinforce his point, he carved the likeness of Aethelbold, warrior king of Mercia at the time, but gave it a female shape to reflect the original queen painted beneath. Whereas the Repton Aethelbold is decidedly masculine, this carving is feminine, but yet it depicts a warrior. It is quite likely that the eighth century king was also flattering Aethelbold who would of course have been the high king, as it were, of the whole region of Mercia that stretched right across the Midlands."

"Could the king who had the carving made be a descendant of the queen Vivianne on the Rune Stone?" Or indeed, Viv thought, of Icel as they had discovered Aethelbold himself was. Maybe it was Aethelbold himself who had commissioned the carving of the queen Vivianne? They would never know for sure.

"I would say more than likely. Certainly someone who revered this queen and wanted to retain and renew the Rune Stone that honoured her bravery and skill. So someone who knew her legend. But as to the actual occasion or event that prompted it, we shall probably never know. Undoubtedly she was a powerful woman."

"That's fantastic, Helen. Thank you so much for all your work on this."

"That's OK. It was interesting. Food for thought. And Tilly's company gave us a very generous donation. Always welcome."

Viv wound up the conversation and clicked the phone off. She felt bad about misleading Helen, especially after she had been so helpful about investigating the Rune Stone. But how could she ever tell her what actually happened to the bracteate? It would have to remain a mystery – the missing artefact.

"Interesting?" asked Rory, settled comfortably on the steamer chair with Ellie on his lap reading the picture book together. "Did Helen tell you anything new?"

"Well, not really. Mainly what we already knew from my connections to the sixth century and Lady Vivianne. But it's good to have it confirmed as true history. Set in stone, as it were! Literally. But, oh, I forgot to tell you that Tilly rang earlier to ask if we would like to arrange a preview showing of the film for the village before it goes public? In the church as we did for your presentation?"

"That's an excellent idea. We can arrange that, can't we?"

"Is that a rhetorical question? And do you mean 'me' rather than 'we'?" Viv smiled across at Rory.

"Fair enough. But could you also finish that leaflet on the Rune Stone to go with the existing one on the church's history that I updated, so that we could let people have a copy at the screening?"

Viv nodded towards her laptop on the garden table beside her. "Yes, it's nearly done. I'll just incorporate the info from Helen so that it's more authoritative."

"What a very efficient wife I have!"

"Efficient? That's not very sexy!"

"Ah well, that too …" he grinned over Ellie's head.

CHAPTER 30

VIV

Derbyshire. Present day

"*I*t's fantastic! I'm so pleased with this – and our producer is too!" Tilly beams. "He was so pleased in fact, that we had an amazing night together - wooh!" She winks at Viv.

"Ri-i-ight," says Viv, "But please, Tilly, spare me the details."

"OK, sweetie-pie. But, honestly, he is so …"

"No!" Viv holds up her hand. "Enough. And people are arriving."

She adjusts the screen, not an easy task with Ellie balanced on her hip, and Tilly signals that she has the laptop ready to go.

Viv watches as the villagers walk into the church and begin to fill the pews, buzzing with excitement. She is glad that all this seems to have really caught their imagination. She sees Michael the curate stride up the nave towards her with Sadie in tow – and goodness, are they actually holding hands? Again, as at Rory's presentation, she looks so pretty in a draping below-the-knee dress that manages to look both modest and figure-flattering. And again, her blonde hair is fixed in an up-do that makes her look elegant and sophisticated. Not at all tarty. Viv marvels at the transformation. Hmm, she glances at Michael who grins shyly – what a good man can do! Possible candidate for curate's wife, she wonders. Well, at least she no longer has her claws in Rory. And, goodness, Sadie even smiles sweetly at her. Viv wonders whether she has in fact been involved in those unpleasant events which they are trying to forget – and what on earth she had been doing that day hiding behind the Rune Stone talking to Ivy. Maybe she was just gathering fuel for potential trouble-making. And now hopefully all that is over. Perhaps Rory can find out from Michael.

And there *is* Rory, at the church door greeting folks as they arrive, shaking hands, bending down to the children, smiling and welcoming.

"What a lovely daddy you have," she whispers to Ellie. "Oops, and here's Ivy herself. Wow."

Ivy is dressed in her re-enactment robes just as she is in the film they are about to see, head rail with the silver circlet balanced a little precariously on her scraped up hair. One or two people turn to look at her in surprise as Rory accompanies her to a pew in the middle of the nave, and Ivy actually smiles and laughs at something he says. Unbelievable!

She sees that Ivy is beckoning her over and she hoists Ellie up and moves towards her.

"Ey up, Mrs Rev'rend," Ivy greets her loudly and people look over at them. "Ah'm wonderin' what it's goin' ta show, eh? This filming lark." She looks animated and seeming without any anxiety about what, indeed, it might show. On the other hand, Viv is still nervous, even though Tilly has reassured her that she's done a thorough editing job. "Ah never thought ah'd get ta be a film star!"

Viv looks towards the church door and sees that even more villagers are arriving. She hopes it will be interesting and perhaps a bonding experience for them, that they will identify more with the village history and its ancient church.

"Don'cha think, Mrs Rev'rend, eh?" Ivy continues and Viv realises that she's missed something urgent that Ivy's said to her. "You'll come wi' me, then? To the re-enactment next week?" Viv smiles and nods, no idea what she's committing herself to. "Only I think we're two of a kind, Mrs Rev'rend. We both see things, don' we?"

Viv looks at Ivy's eyes. They are bright and deep, and she can see something there, something centuries old. "Indeed we do, Ivy."

She begins to move away, but Ivy grabs her arm.

"You know that grave digger, Ray, were me gran'dad? There wus al'as a mystery about the old Cross, but now I know about it. Wish ah could tell 'im." She taps the side of her nose. "But 'e wus full o' stories about the graveyard. Ya know there's another mystery ... about when they dug up the plague tomb ..."

But Rory signals to her across the nave. They are ready. The church is full to standing room at the rear. Viv hurries back to her seat, nodding to Michael and Sadie as she passes. They both smile a little shyly and Michael blushes.

Rory comes to the front to sit beside Viv and waits for the nod from Tilly to begin his short introduction.

Viv can't wait. "Darling, what's the story?" she whispers and flicks her head towards Michael and Sadie who are sitting a few pews back, heads together now.

Rory smiles fondly. "Well, from what I understand, she's somewhat needy. But Michael doesn't mind that, he quite likes being the 'strong man' for once, I think. She was in a bit of a vulnerable state from a previous relationship. Had a mental aberration, I guess. Went a bit doolally with us. Then tried to get Ivy to write that note. Played on her superstitions, hyping up her fears of the runes and ancient curses. Played a blinder, really."

"God, did Michael tell you all this? Or did she confess?"

"Oh, Michael explained it all. Didn't want Sadie

embarrassed by having to confront her stupidity with us. I'm guessing she feels more than a little ridiculous, and apparently really regrets it all now, but doesn't know how to back out and retrieve the situation. And now they appear to be an item, I think he didn't want a problem about him, them, having dinner with us."

"Well, OK, it's water under the bridge, to coin a cliché. Moments of madness, we all have them, don't we? And of course we'll welcome Sadie along with Michael."

Rory slips his arm around her and Ellie. "Doesn't matter any more, does it? Do you forgive her?"

"Of course. I guess I misjudged Sadie too. I think she just wanted – needed – attention."

She turns and catches Sadie's eye and smiles. Sadie hesitantly smiles back. All is well.

The film preview is brilliant, Viv thinks, and she wonders at her oh-so amazing friend, Tilly. The interviews with Rory at the church and Helen at the lab hold the audience's attention and the sequences of re-enactment are so absorbing that Viv hardly notices when Ellie falls asleep on her lap with loud snores, clutching at Viv's top and pulling it down rather too low for decency.

She is anxious to see how Tilly has covered the contribution from Ivy and the scene at the ancient burial site with the bracteate. She is thankful that Helen wasn't interested in coming to the preview, only asking to see the footage of the lab scenes. Viv knows that she would have struggled to think of a valid rationale for there being a physical bracteate to cover her lie, even though Tilly has tactfully deleted all the part where Ivy talked about it.

But somehow it all merges in seamlessly and Ivy's re-enactment costume makes it all appear to be part of the role play. The close-up of the bracteate in Ivy's palm looks as 'ordinary' as Viv thought when she saw it on the camera play-back screen at the time. No footage of its disappearance from Ivy's hand back into the earth. There is nothing revealing, only the slightly mysterious atmosphere that Tilly wanted to create and that is accepted as such by the audience. Nothing more than folks see all the time on television and take for granted. Nothing anyone would question. Nothing to see here.

But probably Viv is the only person in the church to notice a wisp of a shadow at the edge of the screen reaching out to the bracteate in Ivy's hand and then slowly dissipating ...

IF YOU ENJOYED *THE RUNE STONE* CHECK OUT JULIA **Ibbotson's other books at http:// Author.to/JuliaIbbotsonauthor and her website at https:// juliaibbotsonauthor.com to read the latest news about her writing life and her books, as well as life in Anglo-Saxon times, and a few recipes thrown in.**

. . .

SHE WOULD LOVE TO HEAR FROM YOU! YOU CAN ALSO sign up for her newsletter from the website if you would like.

IF YOU ENJOYED THE BOOK, PLEASE CONSIDER WRITING A brief review on Amazon. She'd be really grateful. Many thanks!

AFTERWORD

Author's notes: historical background

Firstly I would like to acknowledge the debt of gratitude I owe to my tutor in my first degree course at the University of Keele back in the day, Professor Barbara Raw, Emeritus Professor of Anglo-Saxon, who sadly passed away in 2018 shortly after I published my first early medieval time-slip novel **A Shape on the Air**, the first of the trilogy. From her I learned the language, literature and history of the early Anglo-Saxons and she enthused me with a love for it. She was passionate about this period and was a gifted scholar and teacher. I will never forget her sessions in the language labs learning to *speak* Anglo-Saxon (Old English) and walking around campus talking to fellow students in this beautiful language. I guess we were, understandably, thought crazy! But some of her passion rubbed off onto me. Eternal gratitude, Barbara.

In learning to speak the language of the Anglo-Saxons and to study their writings, and also in investigating earlier Brython and Celtic communities, I also learned to understand the everyday mundane life of the time. I have long been interested in domestic history: the way people lived. So, in the first and last novels of my Dr DuLac trilogy (**A Shape on the Air** and **The Rune Stone**) I wanted to depict another side to the so-called "Dark Ages" (a misleading term I hate!): the daily life of post-Roman pre-Anglo-Saxon communities. Many novels set in this period, and indeed in the later 7th to 9th centuries, have focused on battles, war-making, brutality. Many seem to support the myth of universal barbarism and savagery of the time. As I tried to show in **A Shape on the Air**, this was also a period of continuing culture, craftsmanship, sensibilities.

As an academic and specialist in early medieval language, literature and history, I have long held a belief in the continuation of a certain measure of cultural and social stability, not a sudden tumble of society into chaos following the retreat of the Roman legions from our shores and then an equally sudden creation of a new culture with the coming of the Anglo-Saxons. Traditional belief has it that the indigenous Brython/Celtic communities of the 5th – 7th centuries were a savage people and that the coming of equally brutal war-mongering invaders, the Germanic Angles, Saxons and Jutes from the continent, led to a period of unrelenting ferocity that became known as "the Dark Ages". Therefore, it was a delight to discover the work of researchers such as Professor Susan Oosthuizen (The Emergence of the English 2019 Arc Humanities Press) whose theories reflected my own: that the Anglo-Saxon society emerged gradually through immigration and often assimilation, rather than through sudden traumatic and brutal battle and suppression. Archaeological evidence is now pointing to the probable neighbourly existence of these diverse communities and the more gradual assimilation and change that eventually forged an identifiable English nation with mainly Anglo-Saxon culture at its core but with a Brython/Celtic interweaving.

Please note that I use the word 'Brython' rather than 'Briton' or 'British'(following Jean Manco's example, The Origins of the Anglo-Saxons 2019) to identify the descendants of the Romano-British and Celtic peoples to distinguish them from the 'British', as in the people of the UK.

This is not to say that there weren't battles for supremacy of a geographical region, that new kingdoms were not formed through victory in war. Of course, we have evidence of many battles leading to changes in power across different regions. Britain was composed of many kingdoms, and kingdoms fought to take over other kingdoms and thus wield greater power over a larger region. But our theories of this time of great change are beginning to recognise the way that stable everyday life and the quest for peace were also significant. Hence, Lady Vivianne as "peace-weaver", although her husband is a fighting warrior. Her elevation to respected status over other kingdoms, and especially that of the Icelings, is to all intents and purposes that of honorary "warrior", a status almost always used for men who were normally the fighters, but this is as a result of her peace-making abilities.

The term "peace-weaver" was often used for women who brought peace between two kingdoms through marriage, but it was also used for women who were more active on their own account in the forging of peace between kingdoms, as Vivianne is depicted as undertaking in this novel. These leaders could be strategists, not necessarily fighters joining battle; they could be mainly working for the defence of their kingdom: active peace-makers. These were leaders whose warrior status was conferred not by fighting but by directing. Annie Whitehead (in Women of Power, 2020) refers to a saying about Æthelflaed, the 10th century Lady of the Mercians and daughter of King Alfred, who strategized battles to take Derby, Leicester, York, that she was a "man in valour, a woman in name". So, to all intents and purposes we can take Lady Vivianne as one who, like Æthelflaed, is a brave and courageous ruler; she is a true "cūning" and "peace-weaver".

A quick word here on the use of the Anglo-Saxon term "cūning" (king). It is a generic term for a ruler and is not gender-based. A woman who ruled was not called a queen, a "cwene", as that meant the wife of a king. Lady Vivianne is called "cūning" in her own right and her land is a kingdom.

So, a final word on the term the "Dark Ages". Jean Manco comments that the term is not used by historians because it has become unjustifiably synonymous with a 'barbaric age'. There is growing evidence that these early medieval societies retained their beliefs, pagan alongside emerging Christianity, their superstitions and scepticism, their appreciation of craft and beauty, and thus preserved and developed the richness of their diverse culture from their own and many other influences. It was "dark" only because we lack the more extensive evidence and written records we have of the earlier Roman and the later Anglo-Saxon societies. People have therefore, understandably, made assumptions that this period was uncivilised, chaotic and therefore unrecorded. I do not subscribe to this view and evidence is now redressing this imbalance. As Jean Manco maintains (2019): "it would be truer to say that in the Anglo-Saxon period [meaning 5th to 11th centuries] we see the emergence of a modern state from the wreckage of an antique empire [ie the Roman]." She adds that this emergence took time because it grew from essentially rural communities who gathered under local leaders (as in The Rune Stone), small kingdoms until these were eventually unified under King Alfred.

The history depicted in this novel is as near as I can get to what we currently know of the time. For example, (1) archaeological evidence suggests that there were indeed unusual weather events in the mid-sixth century which affected crops. The main issue here is that these were probably caused by dust storms from volcanic activity in Scandinavia a little after the period of my novel, but I have brought those events forward for the purposes of my story. (2) we have evidence of Christian burials and of Christian and pagan artefacts existing side by side in this period. (3) we also know about the Angeln encroachments of this time from southern Scandinavia to what is now known as East Anglia. We know that these peoples moved westward and that their line eventually established the kingdom of Mercia, and that in the eighth century Aethelbold of this line became king of the region that stretched across the middle of Britain. There is certainly a Repton Stone depicting Aethelbold. But I have also filled in some of the gaps: I have taken liberties with certain known figures such as Icel of the Iclingas. I have no idea what he was like, but then neither does anyone else. So I have used a writer's licence and created the figure I would like him to have been, for the purpose of my story. So we do know something of these early societies and there is now increasing evidence that women played a greater part than previously thought (see Annie Whitehead's Women of Power in Anglo-Saxon England 2020). As

Kathleen Herbert (Peace-Weavers and Shield-Maidens 2012) calls them, they are the 'Peace-Weavers' and the 'Shield-Maidens' who kept their societies together and enabled the growth of communities into, eventually, the kingdom of England.

Dr Julia Ibbotson

2021

Further reading on this historical period (not an extensive list):

Blair, John (2018) *Building Anglo-Saxon England* (Princeton UP; Princeton)

Breay, C & Story, J (2018) *Anglo-Saxon Kingdoms: Art, Word, War* (British Library; London)

Carver, Martin (2019) *Formative Britain: an archaeology of Britain 5th to 11th century AD* (Routledge; London)

Crabtree, P (2018) *Early Medieval Britain: rebirth of towns in the post-Roman West* (Cambridge UP; Cambridge

Crawford, Sally (2017) *Anglo-Saxon England* (Shire, Oxford)

Fleming, R (2011) *Britain after Rome: 400 to 1070 AD* (Penguin; London)

Herbert, K (2013) *Peace-Weavers and Shield-Maidens* (Anglo-Saxon Books; London)

Higham, NJ &Ryan, MJ (2015) *The Anglo-Saxon World* (Yale UP; Yale, London)

Manco, J (2019) *The Origins of the Anglo-Saxons* (Thames & Hudson; London)

Oosthuizen, Susan (2019) *The Emergence of the English* (Arc Humanities Press; Leeds)

Raw, Barbara C. (1978) The Art and Background of Anglo-Saxon Poetry (Edward Arnold; London)

Whitehead, Annie (2020) *Women of Power in Anglo-Saxon England* (Pen & Sword History, London)

Wood, Michael (2015) *In Search of the Dark Ages* (BBC Books; London)

Zaluckyj, Sarah (2013) *Mercia: the Anglo-Saxon kingdom of Central England* (Logaston Press; Hereford)

Printed in Great Britain
by Amazon

17473116R00217